MW01025450

THE
SEVENTH
LEVEL

THE
SEVENTH
LEVEL

A Sexual Progress

WILLIAM NICHOLSON

𝔰𝔇

STEIN AND DAY/*Publishers*/New York

"Me and Bobby McGee" by Kris Kristofferson used with permission of Combine Music Corporation

First published in 1979
Copyright © 1979 by William Nicholson
All rights reserved
Designed by Ed Kaplin
Printed in the United States of America
Stein and Day/*Publishers*/Scarborough House,
Briarcliff Manor, N.Y. 10510

Nicholson, William.
    The seventh level.

    I. Title.
PZ4.N6275Se 1979   [PR6064.I235]   823'.9'14   79–65114
ISBN 0–8128–2683–3

For A.R.

Prelude

1

I was awakened from a shallow sleep by the whine of a motor-cycle in the street below. A dream slithered out of reach, leaving me sweating on the hard bed. I stretched for my watch, not knowing what time of the night it was, and as my hand stumbled over the bedside table my body delivered the first of a series of warnings: it was a brief tremor, an involuntary muscular vibration at the base of the ribcage. Surprised, I lay still, but it was not repeated. I explored the brown air, the hum of the hotel, the street sounds, and found nothing out of the ordinary. Yet my body had flinched.

It was one in the morning. In six hours I would have a precon-ference breakfast meeting with an Australian agronomist. I hated not sleeping, hated having to fight first my exhaustion and then the panic-fear that I was too exhausted to sleep; but my body was behaving like a cooped-up dog. My legs shuffled, minor muscles twitched in my face and neck. I appeared to be in a state of overexcitement. After a few more minutes of restlessness I got out of bed, as I usually do when faced with insomnia, and dressed to go out for a walk. As far as I was aware I had no other intention than this: a brisk walk around the city streets to pacify my fretful body, and then back to bed.

I stepped out of the lobby of the Hotel Nazionale into the Piazza Montecitorio. Apart from two policemen outside the Parliament building I seemed to have the square to myself. Lights were on in the *Il Tempo* building beyond the obelisk, where the presses were rolling out the morning editions. I crossed the Corso in front of the illuminated façade of the Palazzo Chigi and made my way up the Via del Tritone, heading toward the Hotel Eden, where I was to have breakfast in the morning. Most of the delegates to the conference were staying at the Eden.

I walked fast, my hands binding each other behind my back, my arms locked to my sides. I had my body on a tight leash. Yet as I passed a dark entry where a night cleaner rasped a broom over paving stones, it came again, the shuddering in the abdomen: premonitory: like the vibrations made by electric trains before they start to move.

I climbed the cobbled hill of the Via Francesco Crispi, pulling the warm night air into my lungs with strenuous breaths. I wanted to be panting, I wanted to feel my body laboring. A moon sat low on the roofs and parapets, where grass grew out of the ancient walls. I passed under the pink cliff of the Eden. A car came creeping out of the low-level park opposite, trapping me with its headlights. As the beams released me back into the night I felt it again: something is going to happen.

At the far end of the Via Ludovisi I could see the Via Veneto, a bright stripe of expensive shops. I walked toward the lights, no longer hurrying. Between the shuttered shops were recessed doorways, some open, revealing flights of shadowy stairs. I continued down Ludovisi as far as the steps of the Savoy, but instead of crossing into the Via Veneto I turned about and retraced my path. In one doorway leaned the silhouette of a man. I had not seen him as I had passed by, yet I returned that he might speak to me; which he did.

"Hoa," he said softly, jerking his head. "You want girl?"

°

This night walk took place in early November 1974, at the time of the United Nations World Food Conference. Looking

4

back, I confirm both that I had no destination in walking the streets, and that I knew what I would find. In darkness, in a city not my own, accountable to no one, I allowed my body to take me where it wanted, like a man dragged by a silent dog. So it is here in Rome that I locate my first step, clumsy, timid, uncompleted as it was, on the road to the seventh level.

°

I stood motionless under a streetlight on the Via Ludovisi, seeing the man's hand beckoning me, as if he were drawing me in on a thread. Behind him in the dim hallway was a sign: Club Blue Angel. I was no longer shaking. I did not know what I was going to do. I waited, tense and detached, to find out.

"You want girl?" he said again.

I shook my head.

"You don't want girl?"

I nodded. But as I remained standing there, staring into the doorway, he came out and approached me.

"Just looking?" he said. "You want just looking?"

Again I shook my head.

"You like drink? Beer?"

I nodded.

"You drink beer. And just looking."

He took hold of the cloth of my jacket and tugged me delicately toward the doorway. I spoke for the first time.

"Not enough money," I said.

"Money, money." He released me to lift both hands in a gesture of disregard. "Don't matter money. Okay money."

In fact I had just over 90,000 lire in my wallet. And he knew, it was his trade to know, that a reasonably well-dressed foreigner like me had money.

I followed him, after an indecisive pause. I followed him because he was pulling at my coat. I followed him because he had the initiative: his *why not* was more resilent that my *why*.

The stairs led down into a dark basement, in which glowed pools of amber light. My guide swore at some invisible assistant, and a tape began to play, very softly, in midverse: the Carpenters. Near the foot of the stairs was a bar with a shiny black surface and Martini mats. In the gloom I could make out several tables, half-partitioned from each other for intimate conversation, at one of which sat three girls playing cards. I seemed to be the only customer in the club.

My guide spoke in rapid Italian to the bartender, who produced the promised beer. With a kindly nod of his head the bartender indicated that I might sit on one of the bar stools. My guide went over to the girls and sat down with them, no doubt to warn them about my hesitant behavior in the street.

I took several nervous swallows of beer, glanced over at the table, and met the eyes of one of the girls looking curiously back at me. I turned away, blushing with shame. I began to drink my beer more quickly, checking my watch as I did so, wanting to imply private intentions, a plan unfolding, something other to be done. Unable to speak Italian, I spoke by gesture to them, saying: I am not the kind of man who has to pay for girls.

After all, the only sin left is solitude. The fornicators, the adulterers, the cocksuckers, the buggerers, the fingerfuckers, the orgiasts, the whippers and the whipped, in confessing their vice make public their companions. They can name the deeds with pride because implicit in the act is the achievement: *I too have been desired.* The shame remains only for the wankers and the sugar daddies.

These were the thoughts I shared with my peers before my journey began. The attempt is to recount the journey without hindsight; to which end I must make it understood how I too, certainly on a bar stool in the Club Blue Angel in Rome, submitted to such unseen implacable judgment, a victim of victims: condemned men forced to dig each others' graves.

Meanwhile my self-appointed procurer had been busy arranging the turning point of my life. I hope this book is translated into Italian. I hope he reads it. I like to think he would take a fatherly pride in how I have turned out.

He led her to me from the group playing cards: a girl in a green dress, with a mischievous pointed face and short brown hair. I was surprised at how ordinary she was, how contemporary. The stereotype of the whore must be in need of modernization. I had imagined lacquered layers of hairpiece, make-up like Edam wax, hoisted tits. This girl could have been a student or a secretary. She took my hand, and it seemed impolite not to go

6

with her. She led me to a far table, and suddenly we were alone.

All this time it was my sincere belief that I had meant none of this to happen. Moment by moment I was on the point of leaving; my very presence in this dark basement was an accident, a mistake. In order to affirm this to myself, even as I sat there I was constructing in my head the anecdote of the experience, to tell to the others in the office, or to Jeannie: *Little old fellow pulled me off the street. Subterranean club full of unemployed prostitutes. Not particularly sordid, just sad. . . .* My lies ran so deep in those days I could be forgiven for believing the lower strata were truth.

Her name, she told me, was Patti, and what was mine? I had always imagined I would give a false name to a whore, but I heard myself answering without hesitation: William. She looked at me intently, making no effort to charm me, and asked, what did I do? Again, out came the real answer: I was a journalist. I even mentioned the F.A.O. Conference, which can have meant little to her. Because she held my eyes so seriously I experienced the oddest impulse: I wanted to be honest with her. I wanted to be sincere.

She slipped one arm around me and drew herself close on the padded bench. I knew well enough why she did this, and yet I was grateful. It made me like her. I found her limited English endearing.

"How long stay Roma? Where you stay?"

I told her the name of my hotel. She nodded approvingly: not the best hotel, but expense account level. Her hand around my waist crept inside my jacket, and her body pressed warm against mine.

"You have wife? In America?"

"In England."

"England, ah. London."

"Yes."

"Is far."

"Yes."

She gave me a squeeze as if to say: but I am near. Again I felt a childish gratitude. I wished she spoke better English, so that I could tell her about Jeannie.

"My wife . . .," I began; but then stopped. I had been about to say, *My wife does not understand me.* I looked down in confusion.

"Your wife not like the make love?"

I stared at her in silent respect. Was it so obvious?

"Not much," I said.

"I like." And because in my embarrassment I had looked down, she touched one finger to my cheek to direct my attention back to her. She was smiling in the most friendly fashion.

"You like drink? Champagne?"

She stroked my cheek lightly once more, her touch neither coy nor playful: promissory.

"I have little money, Patti."

"Ah, my man. You have money."

I wondered who had taught her to say that: *my man.* Issuing from her near lips the archaic phrase regained its meaning: I was *her* man, and I was her *man* . And the little sigh with which she preceded it, *Ah, my man,* carried echoes of loss, resignation, forgiveness, as if she was the eternally betrayed woman, and I the warrior-seducer.

"How much money must I pay?"

"William," she said, feeling the name slowly, experimentally. "So? William?"

"That's right." I liked hearing her say my name.

"What like, William?"

"How much money, Patti?"

She replied with a swift movement of one hand, and with two words in Italian. In so small a space, a caress and a question, was confined a revolution.

She gazed with the eyes of a friend, spoke with the lips of a lover, thought with the mind of a hustler, reached out a hand. Lightly, precisely, her fingers brushed that ridge of my trousers within which lay my folded penis.

"*Volevi questo?*" she said. Is this what you want?

Had she not touched me, had the words alone conveyed the question, I would have answered as in my imaginings of such a scene I had always answered: *Yes . . . but.* The *but* referred to the many difficulties in the way of simple sexual gratification: guilt, money, shame, erection, uncertainty, corpulence, intimacy, disease, stains. I gave my assent to lechery, my belief in principle, while in practice an invert St. Augustine I prayed: *Lord make me lecherous, but not yet.* Of this self-truth I only became aware in this luminous moment.

For she did touch me. I was awakened from the deep sleep of my own fairy tale not by a prince's kiss, but by a touch on the crotch. I had no experience of, no weapons against, an unambiguous sexual advance.

"Volevi questo?"

I was never conscious of making a decision. The true question was her touch, the true answer was the immediate violent yielding of my body. I believed it then to be no more than a biological mechanism, the generation of desire; but it was a far more potent magic. I wanted to feel her want to feel me. In the passing touch of her fingers I felt for the first time as benign the impact of an alien will.

She nuzzled her brown lips to my ear, kissed and spoke as if it were a secret: "Champagne?"

I trembled with her nearness. I released toward her foxy face, toward her strong will, all the little hidden passions I had not known were shelved inside me, waiting for an object: my treasure hoard of longings. I held her hand.

The bartender approached, in his grasp a napkinned bottle. I did not want to drink champagne. I wanted nothing except to be touched as Patti had touched me. I was no more ambitious than that.

"No, no champagne."

Patti worked my hand in hers.

"For me. I like the champagne."

I shook my head. The champagne was irrelevant, neither she nor I wanted it. Only her job required her to persuade me to drink it. The management of the club made their money on the champagne.

"Una bottiglia? William?"

"For how much, Patti?"

"Mica tanto. Non importa."

I wonder now that I resisted. Certainly it was no moral scruple. It would have made me very happy to have sat with her for the night drinking overpriced champagne and feeling her touch alight on me now and again in modest payment. But I did not want to be shamed before her; it was my image in her eyes that I was protecting. So fragile then was my self-esteem I did not dare to play the client, the john.

She had turned away from me, to punish me.

"Not here, Patti," I said. I would drink with her, buy her champagne if she wished it, but not here. "Come out with me."

For a few moments she did not respond. I sensed the calculation, the balance of effort and reward. Then she looked back at me, put one finger to her lips, indicated the bar where the others sat paying us no heed, and took my hand.

"Come here," she said in a low voice. Her fingernail tapped the glass of my wristwatch, over the four.

"Four o'clock?"

"*Si*. Here." She jerked her face upward, pointing with her nose. "Outside."

"Is that when you finish work?"

"You come."

She did not want to continue the conversation, frightened that the others would become suspicious.

"Okay, William?" She offered me her sweet smile.

"Okay, Patti."

"Now you must pay. The *birra*."

The beer cost one thousand lire. I had intended to ask Patti how much she would be charging me, but she slipped away while I was by the bar.

○

I did not attempt to sleep. I was bewildered by the emotions Patti had aroused in me: lust, devotion, tenderness, gratitude. Above all, gratitude. It seemed not to matter that I would be buying her attentions. I lay on my hotel bed as I had done only an hour before, but now it was as if I had been fitted out with a new body, capable of new sensations, no longer restless but alert, prickly, sharp-edged. I was experiencing for the first time sexual expectation as a delight in itself. Much of the pleasure in any physical act is accumulated in anticipation over the hours or minutes which precede it: the sweet pang of hunger before a meal, the soft suck of the bedclothes before sleep; but one can only be free to enjoy the period of anticipation if satisfaction is

10

certain. Up to this point I had never in my life been certain of sex. Not even with Jeannie. Especially not with Jeannie.

It was the happiest night I had spent for years.

At half-past three I retraced my steps through the streets to the Club Blue Angel. I was early and had to wait. I stood on the corner, twenty yards from the doorway, nervously watching a small group of men clustered around a car. Perhaps they too were waiting for the girls from the club. The night air had grown colder, and I shivered. As the minute hand on my watch crawled past the hour I became less certain about the details of our arrangement. Perhaps Patti was waiting for me inside the club. Perhaps she was waiting for me to go past the doorway. With my hands stuffed into my pockets and my eyes lowered I sidled down the Via Ludovisi, but only the men by the car looked up as I went by.

After another twenty minutes I had begun to doubt my memory altogether. The night had unfolded in such an unfamiliar fashion that it was just possible I had dreamed my visit to the club. My eyes stung with lack of sleep. Then there was the sound of doors slamming, and voices, and the girls started to trickle into the street. Patti was the last one to emerge. She did not look about her. For some minutes she stood by the parked car talking with one of the men. When she moved away, it was to go down the street away from me. I heard the faint clink of car keys in her hand. Her car was parked under a streetlight. I heard the key scratching in the lock as I hurried near.

"Patti?"

For a moment her face was blank in the lamplight, then she remembered. Slowly, wearily, she shook her head. She looked much older now; I could see that she was wearing far more make-up than had been visible in the club, green eye shadow, the color of her dress.

"I've come back," I said.

She opened the car door and got in. The window cranked down. The engine jerked into life.

"I sorry," she said.

Her English was not up to explanations. She must have had a heavy night.

"It doesn't matter," I said.

11

I walked fast, fast across Rome, far beyond the Piazza Colonna, down the Corso Vittorio Emanuele to the Tiber. I was no longer tired. I was not even disappointed. I knew that something had happened to me that I needed time and space to absorb.

2

Jeannie was out when I got back. I dumped my bag on the stairs, kicked off my shoes, and padded about the house turning on lights. Weary from the flight, I sat for a while in front of the television watching "Kojak" and drinking instant coffee. I poured myself a heaped bowl of cornflakes, which I never would have done if Jeannie had been there. The doorbell rang a little after ten. It was Louise Rosenthal.

"Hello, William," she said. "Just got back?"

"More or less."

My first thought was that she had come to see Jeannie. Then, since she did not look over my shoulder as if to say, where is she?, I supposed she wanted to borrow some milk, or some butter, as neighbors do.

"How was Rome?"

"Rome was fine."

She followed me into the kitchen, where the television was shrieking. Her eye fell on my half-consumed bowl of cornflakes.

"Haven't you got anything to eat in the house?"

"Louise, I've just had a week of global famine statistics. Corn-flakes is fine."

She looked at me in an odd way, as if she thought I might be ill. I did not mind Louise looking at me. Her calm brown eyes were comforting, full of acceptance. I had once told Joseph, her husband, that Louise was a "weary madonna," which he had repeated to her. She had indignantly rejected its several contained images: maternalism, sanctity, passionlessness, middle age.

"Mind if I smoke?"

She took out a pack of Gitanes. It made me uneasy to see her light the cigarette. She knew as well as I did how Jeannie hated the lingering smell.

"How are the boys?" I asked.

"Oh, monstrous. You know."

"Something's the matter, isn't it?"

She nodded.

"Joseph?"

"Joseph? When have you ever known anything be the matter with Joseph?"

"What, then?"

Then I guessed, in that way you do before the thought has found the words that name it.

"While you were away Jeannie and I had a long talk."

She drew carefully on her cigarette and stared at the kitchen tiles. I wanted to be occupied.

"Cup of tea?"

"Yes please."

I refilled the electric kettle and hooked two tea bags out of their glass jar. That jar with its ground-glass stopper was typical of Jeannie, she liked everything around her to be of good quality. I would have left the tea bags in their cardboard box. I kept my back to Louise, scrubbed already clean mugs in a busy stream of water, to make it easier for her.

"She's left," I said.

"Yes."

"And you're to break it to me, and look after me if I take it badly."

14

"Yes."

"Kind of you."

I did not want to sound mean to Louise. I was grateful for her consideration. Only I resented Jeannie's consideration. That was my first reaction: not loss, or rejection, or loneliness, but a tight little pulse of anger that she should presume to pity me.

"She couldn't bear to hurt you," Louise said.

"Well isn't that just too fucking bad," I said.

"I'm sorry, William."

"It's okay. We'll have a cup of tea."

The business of squeezing the tea bags and clinking the teaspoon around and around was good; it reassured us both. Louise must have been nervous, not knowing how I was going to take it.

"Do you want to know more?" she asked me.

"What else did she tell you to tell me?"

"Anything you wanted to know."

"When did she leave?"

"On Thursday."

"Thursday? The house has been empty since Thursday?"

"I've been coming in."

"You've got a key?"

She took it out of a pocket of her jeans and left it on the table. It was Jeannie's key.

"Where is she now?"

"I don't know. I really don't, William. She deliberately didn't tell me."

"What does she think I'm going to do? Beat her up?"

"She thinks a clean break is best."

"Best for who?"

"She wanted me to tell you that she could only do it because she really believes you're better off without her."

"She's a cunt." Now I did want to beat her up. "Don't tell me she's doing it for my own good, Louise. It makes me want to kill her."

Jeannie had always been a great one for unselfishness.

"Don't think I give a shit," I said. The foul language was unusual for me. It came instinctively, as a means of degrading Jeannie. "I don't give a shit where the frigid little cunt has

15

gone." I met Louise's mild eyes and became ashamed. "You don't need to look so sympathetic."

"It's good to get the anger out."

I felt light-headed, so I laid my head on my crossed arms on the kitchen table. I felt light-bodied too, as if I had been hollowed out.

"Do you know what, Louise?"

"What?"

"I have to do fifteen hundred words on world starvation by noon tomorrow."

There was no answer to that.

"Is she with another man?"

"I don't know."

"So she is. Is she supposed to be in love, or what?"

"Does it matter?"

"Not much."

When Louise had satisfied herself that I was not going to break down, or attempt suicide, or damage the joint property, she returned to her house next door. My thanks were genuine. I also said: "Don't think I'm under the illusion that my wife leaving me is either original or interesting."

Once I was alone again I examined the house carefully for signs of Jeannie's defection, but everything was in place. It was late now, so I turned out the lights and made my way to the bathroom. Jeannie's giant sponge lay in the bath-tub rack, her toothbrush hung in the holder by the mirror, and her hairbrush was on the shelf, still tangled with strands of her fine sandy hair. Behind the door trailed her ancient candlewick bathrobe, half obscuring the scales on which she stood, morning and night, and sighed and groaned. She seemed to have taken nothing with her. In the bedroom a glass of water stood on her side of the bed, and a bottle of Valium, and the book she had been reading, the second volume of Bell's *Virginia Woolf*. Her clean clothes hung in the cupboard. Her dirty clothes lay in the tall wicker laundry basket, waiting to be washed.

I began to feel peculiar. I emptied the laundry basket onto the floor and picked up one by one the pairs of pants, the bras, the blouses; also my pants, my socks, my shirts; all tumbled together. It seemed to me then that she could not have gone after all, that she was in the house somewhere, and after staring irritably across the room for a while I called her name out loud. *Jeannie.*

Silence. Silence. Silence. Silence.

During this silence everything changed before my eyes. The semblance of familiarity fell away from the objects around me in the bedroom, and I began to see that they were all dead. Jeannie had stolen away their life. These were skins, husks, corpses. The house was an abandoned house. No one lived here any more.

I picked up the phone extension and rang Louise.

"Come on over," she said at once, in her usual calm voice. "Come and have a nightcap."

Louise was opening her front door as I stepped out into Abinger Road. She came up the short path to meet me and put her warm arms around me and I began to shake and then to weep, uttering pitiful thin whining sounds like an animal in pain.

There was a bed made up for me in the little self-contained flat at the top of the house. It had been made up all evening. Louise mixed me a hot toddy with a real lemon and put me to bed as if I were an invalid. She sat by me and talked in a steady gentle flow about the boys, and the plans to build Joseph a studio at the end of the garden, and how bored she was with publishers' manuscripts, until I was calm enough to sleep.

o

Jeannie and I had been married five years. The details of my marriage breakdown, and of the depression that followed, are of some significance to this record because they prepared me, as an athlete strips down for a race, for my journey through the seven levels.

I stayed in the Rosenthals' top-floor apartment the following night; and the night after that. I never asked if I might move in, with an entire house empty next door; but little by little, move in I did. I thought of the house next door as "Jeannie's house," and did not like to enter it. I did not think to wonder at the convenience of the Rosenthals' flat being free. I learned later that Jeannie had been planning to leave me for months, and had asked Louise not to advertise it when the last tenant had left. Only very slowly did I piece together the enormity of Jeannie's plan "not to hurt me."

Why had Jeannie left me? To start with I directed all my

energy toward this one question, as if the answer, once discovered, would bring her back. But deep down I did not believe she would ever come back; deep down I knew she had left me because of sex. It was not that I had been impotent, or that I had ejaculated prematurely; in the last few months we had made love with a novel regularity; yet it had not been right. I knew that it had not been right because I had continued to want to masturbate, and had done so, secretly and alone.

Like all sexually inexperienced people, I attributed to sex semimagical powers. When Louise admitted to me that Jeannie had left me for another man, an actor called Donald, my stomach filled with a cold dread. "I assumed there was a man around somewhere," I said, "but why does he have to be called Donald?" But I knew, and my stomach knew, that Donald gave Jeannie orgasms. Jeannie had left me for orgasms, and so she was hardly to blame; for to my innocent moral perceptions, female orgasms were a force beyond human control.

Thereafter I sank into the lukewarm embrace of depression. The symptoms are familiar: a failure of the appetites, an enfeeblement of the will, as if all experience falls on the ear like an overplayed tune, once delightful, now grown wearisome and dull. In my case, such apathy was professional suicide. Looking back, it is clear to me that I wanted to lose my job; and I recall feeling a perverse elation when at last informed that my contract was not to be renewed.

I know now that I allowed my depression to become so self-destructive because I sensed instinctively that it was my only means of self-preservation. Jeannie had stage-managed her departure so as to leave me little room for rebellion; therefore I had to defy her in order to recreate some self-respect. Mutual friends, thinking to comfort me, would telephone in order to say, "Jeannie is so worried about you"; or "If there's anything Jeannie can do to make it easier for you, she wants you to know she'll do it"; or "The last thing Jeannie wants to do is hurt you." Under these circumstances there was nothing left for me to do but to demonstrate that I was as badly hurt as it was possible to be. I did not want her pity. Nor did I want her back, not now that she had been with Donald Duck. I wanted her to feel dreadful, and despise herself, and not be able to sleep at night; like me.

When I heard about the contract I was glad, because it would hurt Jeannie. She would no longer be able to say to all our friends, "I did it for his own good."

It is no coincidence that I lost my wife and my job at the same time. The bricks of which we construct our lives are all keyed into each other: remove one, and the rest totter. So too it is no coincidence that I turned for comfort to the only kind of women with whom I felt safe, and sought to consummate in London the desires awakened in Rome.

3

Soho was in the midst of a garbage collectors' strike, and the sidewalks were piled high with refuse. I had no idea where to go, except that the darker, less populated streets seemed to me to be the most promising. These were also the favored dumping ground for the uncollected garbage. I zigzagged the alleys off Wardour Street north of Leicester Square, stepping high over the swollen black plastic bags, keeping on the far side of the road from the barkers outside the striptease clubs.

In preparation for my night expedition I had bathed, put on clean underclothes, and removed my wallet from my inside jacket pocket. I carried forty pounds in five-pound notes in my left trouser pocket. As I walked I patted the bulge with my left hand. It was my power.

Not having fun can become a comfortable habit. Before the incident in Rome I had watched the race for ecstasy, the many races, but had never thought to enter. From my place in the grandstand I had picked out the winners, and offered them my ritual envy. Later I had overheard from nearby rooms the haunting noises, the creaks, the licks, the laughter, of other people's joy; but I was complacent in the fiction that those thin doors were locked to me. Abnegation and envy team well.

Even now as I walked the Soho streets I confined my ambitions to the smallest possible space; telling myself that what I sought, what I was for the first time willing to pay for, was little more than assisted masturbation. I did not attempt to explore, because I did not then understand, how complex had been my response to Italian Patti in the Club Blue Angel.

I passed many doors on which the bells were labeled with a girl's name, or simply with the word "Model," but I could not bring myself to ring. I lacked the self-confidence to make such a loud demand. Also I wanted to be able to see the girl before declaring any interest in her. This was a problem. Since the Street Offenses Act of 1959, prostitutes have not been allowed to display themselves in public on the streets of London.

I loitered down Peter Street, and loitered back, proclaiming my errand by my busy eyes and my aimless feet. A dwarfish man wearing a trilby hat saw me go by and saw me return and finally approached me. He muttered a word in what I took to be a foreign language. Only after he had repeated it twice did I understand him to be saying "Business?"

"Oh. Business," I said.

"Nice girl," he told me. "Certainly. Nice girl."

"How much?"

"Ten."

This was so much less than I had expected to pay that I became interested. If necessary I was willing to lose ten pounds with a good grace. "What if I don't like her?" I asked him.

"You like her," he said. "Nice girl. Come, I show you."

I was once told that all the pimps in Soho are Chinese, West Indian, or Maltese. My man was neither black nor yellow, so I decided he was a Maltese. I was glad he was so small, it made me feel more in control. As I followed him across Dean Street into Meard Street I asked him again, "But what if I don't like the girl?"

"Then you go. No problem."

He disappeared through an open red door, beside the office of a cab company. Inside this office, looking out through the plate glass of what had once been a shop window, sat five black men in a circle. They made me feel nervous.

My Maltese called impatiently from the top of the first flight of stairs, where there was a small landing. Two cream-painted doors opened onto this landing. One was unmarked, the other bore a card reading "Anne." The Maltese pressed a bell, which chimed *ding*-dong. At once a female voice within called out, *"Five minutes!"* This was succeeded by a peal of laughter. The Maltese nodded at me encouragingly and said, "Very nice girl." We stood for some minutes on the landing, listening to the exclamations coming through the door: "You do the cha-cha-cha? Show me how you do the cha-cha-cha. You like that? Course you like that."

"Oh, very nice girl," said the tiny Maltese.

The door opened at last to release a man in Hush Puppies, which was all I saw of him, because I looked down as he passed. I hoped the next in line would extend the same consideration to me. From the room within came a hissing sound, and then Anne herself appeared, a young, plump and cheerful-looking woman wearing maroon velvet hot pants. "Hello," she said to me. "Hello," I said. "It'll be ten pounds with a rubber on and no tits." "Do you have the rubber?" "Oh yes, dear."

So it was decided.

She prodded open the second door with the toe of one boot and herded me into a small anteroom. Here a middle-aged lady in a fur coat sat watching a Marlon Brando film on a little Japanese television.

"Can I have the money now please," said Anne.

I felt out two five-pound notes in my pocket and handed them over.

"And something for the maid."

I had nothing but five-pound notes.

"Get four ones," Anne said to the lady in the fur coat.

"You're a mind reader," I said.

"Oh yes. I'm a mind reader."

She relieved me of the third five-pound note.

"Tell you what," she said, "why don't you give us all of it? You can have the lot for this."

I did not know what "the lot" was, but my note had vanished, so I said, "Okay."

"Go on, spoil yourself." The bell rang *ding*-dong. *"Five minutes!"* she shouted, and went through into the second room, closing the door behind her.

The maid and I made conversation.

"Terrible cold, isn't it?" she said. "The cold does for your blood. Your blood gets tired. It's to be expected."

"At least you can keep warm here," I said.

She was sitting forward in her chair so that she leaned over a two-bar electric heater.

"Would I be here otherwise?" she said.

On the wall behind the television was a fairground poster, of the kind that is printed to order. *This year's Miss Universe is,* it read, and in capitals below: ANNE KOSLOWSKI.

"Seems to be plenty of business about," I said.

"Oh yes," said the maid with some pride. "She's a popular girl, there's no denying. Very well liked. It's because she's always laughing, you see. It's the laughing."

Then Anne summoned me into the bedroom.

"Take your clothes off," she said, and went out onto the landing to be displayed to the next customer.

The walls of the bedroom were decorated with pages from pornographic magazines, pinned in a symmetrical pattern on either side of the bed. Laughter vibrated against the landing door. I laid my clothes over a chair and sat stripped on the edge of the bed. The pink nylon quilt cover was cold to my buttocks.

Anne began removing her hot pants even as she closed the landing door behind her, and was naked from navel to boots by the time she reached the bed. She had laid herself down in the semi-reclining posture in which she proposed to receive me when she recalled my forfeited four pounds. "Nearly cheated you," she exclaimed, bounding upright so that she could remove her top. Her breasts loomed whitely before me.

"Actually this is the first time I've done this," I said.

23

"Fucking Jesus. You a virgin then?"

"No, oh no. It's just that I've never before . . . like this . . ."

"It isn't any different, dear."

As if to make the point clear, she seized my limp penis in one hand and proceeded to shake it about, as if it were a dead mouse. I did not dare tell her it was used to gentler treatment, and that she would only frighten it. "Come on, come on," she said to it; and in a little while, more bruised than aroused, it swelled out from between my legs, and laughing cheerily, she trapped it in a condom.

"Now in you go, darling. That's the ticket."

She tucked my lolling penis firmly into the pocket between her thighs. It folded on entry, but there was room enough for it to lie there doubled. The warmth slowly revived it.

"Well hello there," she said, feeling it straighten out. "Fuck me, eh? Fuck me."

I stroked her shoulder tentatively with one finger, but she did not like it. The caress was overintimate. I was lying fully on top of her, body to body, yet we were not touching each other; not as I longed to be touched.

I tried looking past her head to the ladies with their legs apart on the wall, but I knew there was no hope. My penis refused to regard what was going on as a sexual engagement.

"You don't need to worry," I said. "If I know I'm not going to come, I won't keep you."

"Nice pussy," she complained.

"A very nice pussy," I said. "And you're a very nice girl. I hear you are very popular."

"Who told you that?"

"The lady outside."

"Who?"

"Your maid."

"Oh. Her."

She laughed, but her heart was not in it. She churned her hips. I waited politely for her to subside.

"No," I said, "no, I don't believe I'm going to come after all."

"Well, if you're not, you're not. We could be here all night."

"Of course. You've done all you could."

We absolved each other of all further obligations, no doubt with equal relief.

"You can give me a hand with the covers, dear."

Together we straightened out the bed. It was our one moment of cooperative activity. I dressed. She produced a can of pine air-freshener and squirted it into the void over the bed.

The little Maltese was outside delivering his next protégé. He followed me out into Meard Street asking for a tip, but I strode away from him faster than he could keep up.

Once back in Abinger Road I shut myself in my room and turned on the radio. I listened with reverent attention to "Today in Parliament," "A Book At Bedtime," and "The Financial World Tonight." I was reassembling around me the respectable and ordered world.

•

This tawdry episode did not, as might be supposed, disillusion me with paid sex. Within my head certainly there sounded the faint tinkling shatter of a treasured image: not every whore is desirable after all. But its effect was to make me take my impulse seriously, as I had not done before. I was not ashamed of myself for commercializing sex; I was angry with myself for cheapening it. The fiasco in Meard Street reaffirmed my faith in the laws of supply and demand: for higher quality, I must pay a higher price.

My fascination with prostitutes at this time was fed by my depression. Jeannie's action, and her assumption of righteousness, had left me in a curious moral vacuum. I knew how it would hurt and disgust Jeannie to learn what I was proposing to do, and I dearly wanted to hurt and disgust her. Lying in my attic bed at night I would conduct imaginary conversations with her: "How are things working out for you, William?" she would say. "Oh, not too bad," I would reply. "What are you doing these days?" "Fucking, mainly." "What?" "Fucking. Sexual intercourse." She would not know what to say to that. "Prostitutes," I would add. "Prostitutes?" "That's it. Fucking prostitutes. That's mainly what I'm doing these days." "Is it my fault, William? Is it because of what I've done to you?" "Well I have to admit, Jeannie, you always were pretty tight with your cunt."

25

The satisfaction of such daydreams lay not only in insulting my wife, but in confusing her. I did not want her to be able to predict my responses, or to suppose that she had control of my happiness. Since over our years together I had grown to accept her image of me, my aggression toward Jeannie launched me unawares into the process of self-discovery. It was as if I had been dipped in caustic soda, and layers that I had never thought to be paint were beginning to blister and flake away. The startling textures revealed beneath showed my character to be coarser than I had supposed. I found I was shedding not only conventional morality (sex sanctioned by marriage), but also liberal morality (sex sanctioned by love). Why, I now asked myself, had I spent my adult life cranking myself into love in order to get sex? It was like converting to Roman Catholicism in order to visit Chartres Cathedral.

Anger, self-hatred, empty days; and then the catalyzing agent, money. By the end of 1974 our house was sold, and the proceeds divided equally between Jeannie and myself. Because we had bought before the property boom of 1971, we were able to sell for three times what we had paid. My share of the financial venture called marriage amounted to nearly £12,000.

I have always been by temperament a planner, a year-at-a-glance calendar man. I take pleasure in lists, charts, and diaries because they speak of my life yet to be lived, and experience had then led me to believe that the prospect of pleasure outpleases the pleasure itself. From habit, boredom, perversity, and fear of finalities, I began to construct a plan around my newly discovered desire. It became what schoolchildren and journalists call a project.

I had nothing to do all day. Conditions were perfect for the breeding of an obsession. I told myself that my project was an occupation designed to pass the time before I resumed my interrupted life; but I suspect that even then I knew it was to become my life itself.

The project was divinely simple. I had already desecrated my sexual integrity, had lost a second virginity. Now the mechanisms of self-restraint were uncoupled and I could roll free. With due solemnity, therefore, I made myself a vow. I vowed to devote my unspent future and my hoarded past to the pursuit of perfect sex: satisfaction and not my money back, the fuck-than-which-there-can-be-no-greater, transcendental copulation.

It was this vow which led me to Arlette in Brussels; and it was Arlette who first told me of the seven levels.

4

Self-indulgence is a taste that needs to be acquired. I flew first class to Brussels and took a taxi from Zaventem into town. By midday I was phoning the château from a room in the Amigo.

A male voice answered in French, but switched readily to English. As before, when I had telephoned from London, I gave my name and the name of the intermediary who had provided the contact. "Mr. Elliott? Yes, yes..." The line went blank. I guessed he had cupped a hand over the receiver while he checked my name. Then: "Where are you now, Mr. Elliott?" "At the Amigo." "Mr. Akaçan will not be free for one hour. A car will come for you in one hour. This is satisfactory?" "Yes," I said, "I'll be in the lobby."

I drank a Stella in the Grand' Place while I was waiting. High above the Maison Brasseurs, Charles of Lorraine, gold on his prancing horse, thrust his baton into a dull sky. From where I sat I could see two lace shops, their English names traced in neon, Lacy Charm, Fairies' Fingers. On the whole, Brussels does not make one think of sex.

I had brought to my project the systematic research methods

of Fleet Street journalism. Discreet inquiries about high-class brothels had yielded several addresses, but when I asked "Which is the best?," I was met with smiles and shrugs and, "Whose word are you going to take on that?" As a result I shifted my emphasis and asked, "Which is the most expensive?" It surprised me to learn that the organization that commanded the highest prices should turn out to be in Brussels. But Brussels is the home of the Common Market, and NATO, and ITT Europe; and in the words of one of my informants, is a town which "stinks with tax-free incomes."

The organization in question was known by the name of its founder, Madame Arlette. This lady, I was told, was greatly respected. The long-standing repute of the château, the house from which she operated, rested on Madame Arlette's talent for selection, and on her skill in training. It was this last item, the training, which caught my attention. I was willing, even eager, to pay high prices, but at the same time I sought some assurance that what I was paying for was special. One of my sources, a professional call girl in London, was scathing on this matter of training: "The only training you need is how to get the vaseline in without the john noticing." But even she testified to the château's reputation.

Since the series of recent shocks which had left me with no wife, no home, and no job, I had come to feel as if I were starting my life all over again; as if I were recently born, and naked, and helpless. Perhaps even on that gray day, as I sat patiently in the Grand' Place, I hoped to find in Madame Arlette the mother, the protectress, for whom I longed. Certainly my motives were not as innocent, not as hedonistic, as I allowed myself to believe.

The driver was waiting for me on my return to the hotel, his white Peugeot 504 illegally parked outside in the Rue de l'Etuve. I sat in the back, and he did not speak.

We cruised up the Louizalaan past the brown-glass ITT building, and turned into the Bois de la Cambre. It was a cold winter day and the park was deserted but for two horseback riders seesawing solemnly along the graveled way. We emerged from the park following the signs to Waterloo, and so entered the forest by the arrow-straight Drêve de Lorraine.

The concrete sections of the road ticked by beneath the wheels. Through the ranks of slender beeches flashing by on either side I caught occasional glimpses of great houses protected by high walls. Then my driver began to brake. Ahead to the right lay a bright space where the trees had been cut back. As we approached I saw tall iron railings set at an angle from the road, and tall gates standing open. The wheels slewed into gravel. We rounded a lodge, and there at the end of an immense lawn stood a red-brick colonnaded mansion. It was huge and ugly, its steep roof pulled low over its second-floor windows and pocked by the gables of a third floor. Its vulgar scale entirely satisfied me.

We swept in a great arc around the lawn, past statues and ornamental urns, to the crescent steps. When the Peugeot's engine cut, the only sound came from the cars whining up the Drêve de Lorraine to Waterloo.

I was shown into a long light room and asked to wait. Two curving windows opened onto a terrace; below the terrace, a lawn or meadow running down to a small lake. I paced anxiously, planning what I would say; and looking around me, tried to anticipate the tone in whicn the interview would be conducted.

It was not as I had imagined. An eighteenth-century pastoral painting hung over an elegant fireplace. There were Dresden figurines on the mantleshelf. The inlaid marquetry surface of a low table bore a recent *Paris Match,* a *National Geographic,* a volume of Montaigne's *Essays,* and an illustrated book of wildflowers. In a tall amber-tinted mirror I caught sight of myself, cautiously respectable in suit and tie, transparently ill at ease.

I was obliged to wait for some time; but I did not mind. I have never minded waiting. It is what happens when the waiting ends that I have found to be unsatisfactory: years of Christmases failing to live up to the illustrations in *Pickwick Papers;* years of cakes emerging like pencil sketches of the four-color glory on the package. "Please don't have feet of clay," I prayed silently, addressing my approaching adventure, the gift of a new God. "Manifest yourself in whatever form you want, but spare me the feet of clay."

I opened my eyes (for even parody prayers are uttered blind) to see a figure passing along the terrace beyond the tall windows: a young woman in a man's jacket, her fists pushed down in the pockets, walking slowly, scuffing the stones with her canvas shoes. She came to a halt right in front of the window in which I stood, and sensing that I was watching her, turned to look at me through the glass. She was so striking I actually tensed under the impact of her eyes, as if she had thrown something toward me. For a moment longer her eyes reached for me, curious but unsmiling; then she bowed her head again and walked on.

I watched her out of sight. It would have pleased me to believe that she was the answer to my prayer, except that she was too exactly the vision I had been praying for. Also, she had made no sound. It seemed more likely that I had dreamed her, that she was a fantasy projection, a product of psycho-optic wish fulfillment.

Then the door opened and a man entered. He was stocky, as tall as I, but he gave the impression of being smaller because he had no neck. He wore a cardigan with leather buttons, and check trousers.

"Forgive me for keeping you," he said. His voice was hoarse and throaty.

We shook hands. He crossed the room to a cupboard within which were glasses and bottles and a small refrigerator. My stomach was agitating with nerves, so I asked for a whiskey. He had a beer.

This man's name was Bulent Akaçan, and he was by origin a Turk. I did not like him from the first. His breathing was irritatingly audible, a series of low groans, and when he talked his mouth hardly moved, as if his square black mustache were too heavy for his upper lip.

From the way he was looking at me I could see that he had doubts about my financial standing.

"I am obliged to you for making the journey from London," he said. "We so very much prefer to do business face to face."

"I too," I said.

"Do you travel much, Mr. Elliott?"

"From time to time."

"I only ask because one of the strengths of our organization is that we have connections in many countries. The members find this useful. Do you know much about our organization, Mr. Elliott?"

"I know next to nothing?"

"Ah." He breathed at me. "I hope you will not be disappointed."

"I would be glad to learn about it."

"Maybe so." He drank his beer straight from the can, beading his mustache with the froth. "You know of course that there is an initial payment to be made?"

"How much?"

"It is by way of being a registration fee. Five thousand dollars American."

I concealed my shock as best I could.

"Why so much?"

He shrugged. "It is a wall. To keep people out."

"And what are the later charges?"

"That depends. Perhaps one thousand American for each occasion."

He watched me as he named these figures.

"Expensive," I said.

"They say, do they not, that the best costs more?"

"In what way the best?"

"Ouf! Mr. Elliott, what can I say? That is a matter of experience."

"I was told that there is special training."

He rocked one fat hand in the air before him, as if the issue remained undecided. "Some of the girls are advised by Madame Arlette, it is true."

"I should like to meet Madame Arlette."

"Madame Arlette is no longer responsible for the running of the organization."

"Even so."

He bowed his head. There were many questions I meant to ask about the organization, but the Turk's unenthusiastic manner inhibited me. He did not volunteer more information, for reasons he shortly made clear.

"I must ask you, Mr. Elliott, if you are seriously interested."

32

"Yes," I said. "I am."

I had been doing some hasty sums in my head, and had concluded that I could afford the charges. I was more impressed with the high cost of the services than I was with either the château or Mr. Akaçan.

At the Turk's request I made out a check. He took it, thanked me, and excused himself for a moment. I guessed that he had some means of verifying my credit rating.

This large payment was to me a landmark. I could not turn back now.

When Mr. Akaçan reappeared he was as charmless as he had been from the first, but he was more forthcoming. His researches must have proved positive, because he now took me seriously.

"We find that members like to use the organization in different ways, Mr. Elliot. I think we should be able to accommodate you." He pronounced "accommodate" as if it was a sequence of single-syllable words.

"Here in the château?"

"Ah no, sir. Not here. Since 1948, the law has not permitted such an arrangement."

I was disappointed to learn that there were no exotic pleasure chambers at the heart of the château.

"Then what is this building for?"

"Various business matters," he said.

I never did learn what else went on in that monstrous Victorian mansion. Arlette herself assured me even she did not know.

The Turk now produced and handed over a typed sheet of paper. It was a list of cities, mainly in Europe and the United States.

"We can be of use to you in any of these places. The list is being expanded, slowly. We will notify you from time to time. As you will observe, only the one telephone number is necessary, which is of course here at the château. If you call this number, and give your name, also a place and a time, also whatever other details you may be pleased to specify, we will make the arrangements."

"I see. And who do I pay?"

"You will be mailed a bill quarterly."

33

He took down the Rosenthals' London address. I did not tell him that my funds would be exhausted before many quarters had gone by.

"What is the usual system?" I asked. "Do I go to them, or do they come to me?"

"As it pleases you."

"Do you have some means of selecting in advance? Photographs, perhaps?"

"Mr. Elliott, I can assure you that any arrangement we make for you will be entirely satisfactory. Should it not be so, you have only to inform me, and there will be no charge."

Since our business seemed to be at an end, I mentioned again that I would like to meet Madame Arlette.

"Why exactly do you want to meet her, I wonder?" said Mr. Akaçan.

"No particular reason," I said. "Does she not like visitors?"

"I will see." He dialed two digits on a phone, and while it was ringing cupped his hand over the mouthpiece and said to me, "It is only fair to warn you that Arlette is no longer what she once was. She has her own little ideas, her own little eccentricities— *Ah bonjour, madame. . . .*" He spoke in rapid guttural French, and nodded and grunted as he listened to the reply.

"So," he said to me as he replaced the receiver, "there is no problem. She says if you want to come, come."

I now learned that Madame Arlette did not live in the château at all, but in a small lodge on the grounds. Mr. Akaçan took me out onto the graveled sweep and indicated a path running off to the side along a dense yew hedge. He did not offer to accompany me.

"The lodge is at the end of this path," he said. "You cannot mistake it. Until we meet again, Mr. Elliott."

We shook hands and parted.

The hedge gave way to an untrimmed screen of holly bushes, through which the path tunneled. On the far side it seemed as if I had left the château grounds and entered the forest proper; but through the silver beech trunks I made out a small brick building, with smoke rising from a chimney. The path led to its door, . which was ajar.

I was on the point of knocking on this door when a black-and-white collie shot barking around the corner of the house. A distant voice called, presumably to the dog, "Benjamin! Benjamin." The dog made several abrupt darts at me, more to smell than to bite, and trotted back out of sight.

Behind the house I found a walled garden, laid out for growing vegetables. In one corner, by the high red-brick wall, a tiny old lady was slowly turning the soil with a garden fork. The collie now stood protectively by her side. She wore a pair of muddy overalls, and Wellington boots.

"Madame Arlette?" I said.

She stopped digging and leaned on the fork. I picked my way over the soft furrows, trying not to tread on anything growing. The collie scowled at me. The old lady held out her hand. It was strong and bony. As she clasped my hand she searched my face, as if to memorize it, narrowing her eyes in her concentration. In return I studied her: a worn and weathered face, but her eyes were alert. Even then, so early, I felt her power. She lived in the open, not shut away like most people, but out in the open, in her own face.

The more I looked at her, the more convinced I became that I had met her before; indeed, that I knew her well already. The illusion was caused by a simple association. Commonly only those we know and trust intimately allow us full face-contact, so that when we encounter it in a stranger, we presume the relatedness which has always before permitted it.

"I am not as you expected," she said.

"No."

"Why did you want to see me?"

As before when Mr. Akaçan had asked this question, there seemed to be no adequate answer. Curiosity, perhaps; and some assurance that the women I would be dealing with possessed special skills. But the reality of Madame Arlette threw me into confusion. Her untidy gray hair, her wrinkly features, her penetrating eyes, reduced my sexual ambitions to the level of a schoolboy's daydreams.

"Bulent told me your name," she said. "Tell me again."

"William Elliott."

"So, William Elliott, there is something . . ."

She reached out a hand again and clasped my arm, as if she sought to read me through physical contact. "Bulent is satisfied with you?"

"Yes, madame."

"There is something here," she said. "Something not right."

"What sort of thing, madame?"

"I don't know. It does not matter."

She offered me the hospitality of her house. The door opened directly into a dark kitchen, where a coal fire glowed in an old-fashioned range. Various sounds greeted us as we entered: the splat-splat of a tap dripping into a deep stone sink, the hum of an iron kettle on the hotplate of the range, and a curious bubbling sound, which turned out to come from a parrot by the window sill. This parrot also exclaimed "Benjamin! Benjamin!" with a soft *j*, in the French manner.

It took me a moment to realize that there was someone already in the kitchen. She was sitting cross-legged in a wooden rocking chair by the range, holding cradled in both her hands before her a large cup from which steam was rising. Her face in profile was partially concealed by thick tangled brown hair. Even before she looked up at me I had recognized her, as the girl from the terrace.

We were introduced. Her name was Aurora Miller. She seemed not surprised to see me again. For my part, I was thankful for the protective gloom of the kitchen. It was inconceivable that Miss Miller would not know why I had come to the château. Not sure of her own status, I was silently embarrassed.

Madame Arlette offered me coffee or pernod. I accepted pernod. She herself drank coffee, which was already brewed in a stout clay jug standing on one corner of the range. She watched Benjamin snuffling at my ankles.

"No," she said shortly, "no, you are not right. There can be no doubt. Do you see it, Aurora?"

"I don't see it." She spoke with an American accent.

"All my life, Mr. Elliott, I have been meeting men, strangers. Some very wealthy men, some very powerful men. I think you would be surprised. That is how I know you are not right."

"Am I not wealthy enough?"

"Tcha! Bulent is capable of seeing to that. But there is something . . . You will be so kind as to tell me a little about yourself. Your money, where does it come from?"

"Does it matter, madame?"

"Perhaps not. But I am interested in you. I will tell you honestly, Mr. Elliott, you do not have the air of a rich man. You conduct yourself as if you do not deserve attention."

She never took her eyes off me. I began to feel that she could see what I was thinking. Miss Miller rocked steadily back and forth, and drank from her cup in silence.

"So what do we have here, Benjamin?" The old lady placed one hand on the collie, who was now lying at her feet. Her voice was soft and dry and relentless. "A young Englishman, with a fine smile. But he jumps when he is spoken to. He is determined and he is timid. He holds his body very stiff. He does not say much. But he has asked specially to see me. What can he be? Either he is not what he says, or he is not what he seems. He investigates. He is an investigator. Not a policeman, I think. Perhaps he is a newspaperman. Ah! He jumps again." It was true. I had not been able to restrain my reaction in time. Arlette nodded her head in satisfaction. "So he has come to write about us. But I do not think that is a very good idea."

She reached out for a telephone which stood near her on a drain board.

"You did not think to tell Bulent, of course?"

"Please, madame. I have not come to write about you."

"But you will explain?"

"Yes."

She folded her arms before her. The American girl stopped her rocking.

"I have no secrets," I said. "But I am not very proud of what I'm doing."

"Why should you be ashamed? You know who I am. You know my business."

"Yes . . ." I glanced toward the beautiful and uncommunicative Miss Miller.

"Ah. *La belle Aurore*. Have no fear, Mr. Elliott, she is on much the same business as yourself."

I found this hard to believe, but there was nothing I could do about it. As the early winter dusk gathered outside the lodge kitchen, I told Madame Arlette as best as I could what had brought me to this point in my life: the breakup of my marriage, the episode in Rome, the collapse of my job. Incoherent as I was, it was a release to put into words my virgin belief: how I had found myself with no future, and how I had been afraid that this unawaited time would arrive and go by, and I would have no past. How I had looked for a future and had found sex.

"This money that you propose to spend, it is all you have?"

"Yes."

"You have no other income?"

"No. Not at present."

"It will soon be spent. What then?"

"I don't know. That will be afterwards. I don't mind what happens then."

"Do you hear him?" There was a new note in the old lady's voice. "I knew it as soon as I saw him. I said it inside myself: here is one for me."

She left her chair to light a kerosene lamp. The house appeared to have no supply of electricity. The bulbous pearled-glass chimney cast a golden glow all about it, from a shelf high in one corner. The parrot, who had been sleeping, awoke and began to chatter.

From a tall dresser beside the door Arlette fetched a bottle of cognac and poured us out a small glass each.

"One day you will thank me, Mr. Elliott," she said, "for making you tell me the truth."

"I thank you now," I said. "I feel better for it."

"Then drink your cognac and tell me a little more. It is possible I can help you, far more than you realize. But you will have to put yourself in my hands, as Aurora has done."

"What do you want to know?"

"How long were you married?"

"Five years, just about."

"And were you faithful to your wife?"

"Yes."

"And before your marriage, you had many girl friends?"

"Some."

38

"How many?"

"That I slept with?"

"Yes."

"Three." But there was no point in holding back now. "Two. Two that I was with for a while, and one disastrous one-night stand."

"You are not very experienced for a man of your age."

"No." It was my greatest shame; yet as Arlette spoke it, it became no more than one fact about me, one among many. Like most people, I operated two simultaneous identities, one within the other, like clothes: the outer self chill and crisp, the inner self warm and smelly. Arlette had undertaken the slow process of integration. She was letting me know that she could smell me, but that she liked my smell.

"I think I can give you what you are looking for," she said.

"Which is what?"

"Why do you think you asked to see me? Idle curiosity? No. I think you have heard that I am a teacher."

"Yes, I have."

"Still you want to see me. Interesting, I think."

"She means you're looking for a teacher," said Miss Miller.

I considered this in some surprise.

"Now, Aurora, my dear girl," said Madame Arlette, "I want you to finish your cognac and to drive Mr. Elliott back to his hotel. And you, sir, if you can spare the time, I would ask you to spend one more night in Brussels, and to come and see me again tomorrow morning. I have something of importance to say to you, but it is bad to go too fast. We will let the night go by."

"All right," I said.

I had no idea what it was all about, but I trusted her. In so short a time, she had inspired in me a sensation of total confidence. If she wanted me to go, I would go; if she wanted me to come back, I would come back.

Miss Miller and I left the lodge garden by a narrow iron gate, which opened onto the main road. A Fiat 127 was parked on the bridle path. As we drove down the dark avenue toward central Brussels I questioned her about Madame Arlette, but learned little.

"I take it Madame Arlette is your teacher, then?"

"Yes."

"What does she teach you?"

"The levels."

"What levels?"

"Arlette will tell you. When she thinks it is right."

Each time she spoke I permitted myself to look at her. She had an extraordinary face; it was a blend of two faces, a slender almost delicate brow, nose, and chin, combined with strong wide eyes and a strong wide mouth. The lips in particular, prominent, even slightly protruding, were at odds with the slightness of her features. I have never met anyone else, man or woman, who combined to such a degree a pale and frangible beauty, untouched, you would say, by wind or sun or any unrestrained force, and that quality called "cool": an unshakable inner control.

Her age was impossible to assess. Like many skinny people, she has gone on looking the same for years. In 1974 when I first met her she was in fact twenty-eight years old.

"Does Madame Arlette do this for everybody?" I asked her.

"Oh no."

"So why me?"

"She thinks you'll be a good learner."

"But why?"

"Because you're so inexperienced, I guess."

I fell silent at that.

"Come on," she said, "have faith, huh? You're lucky. You have it all to come."

Outside the hotel she turned to me to make arrangements for the next day, but at the same time she smiled at me so completely, with so little reserve, that I was overwhelmed with the desire to touch her. It was not a simple wish for contact, but a compulsion of the sort one senses is destructive, like the urge to leap from tall buildings, or to finger the flames of candles. I raised one hand, and without hesitation she took it and held it.

"So what time do you want to be picked up in the morning, William Elliott?"

I was pleased she had remembered my name.

"Whenever you like, Aurora Miller."

"At least we know who we are," she said with a laugh. "Let's say ten, okay?"

Alone in my room at the Amigo I made extensive notes on hotel writing paper about this, my first visit to the château. I wanted both to record and make sense of what was happening to me. These notes became the beginning of an intermittent journal, which has proved invaluable to me in recalling how I thought before I began to understand what was happening to me. For example, on those first sheets of paper I see that I wrote about Aurora: "Madame Arlette's companion—American, very beautiful—the great question—is she or is she not for sale?"

5

The next morning Aurora delivered me faithfully to Arlette, but then left us alone. Arlette was sitting in her kitchen, wearing pajamas and a tweed overcoat. The parrot, whose name I now learned was Papa, strutted about on her left shoulder, occasionally nibbling at her ear lobe. Despite the coals flickering in the range, the lodge was chilly. The forest outside was still deep in a morning mist.

The night had wrought a change in Arlette's approach to me. On my entry, she beckoned me down to her level, and taking my face in both bony hands, kissed me on the brow. Her lips were dry and scratchy. She no longer called me "Mr. Elliott."

She offered me coffee from the inexhaustible jug. I sat close to the range, in the rocking chair Aurora had occupied the previous day. The collie entered, leaving the outer door open to the cold air. Arlette called sharply: "Benjamin! Fermez-la!" and to my amusement the dog did indeed prod the door shut with one paw.

"Now William," she said. "I have something for you."

It was the check I had made out for Mr. Akaçan.

"I have told Bulent that in your case there is to be no registration fee. You cannot afford it." She chuckled. "Bulent does not approve."

"I'm very willing to pay," I said.

"Yes, yes. But what I have to give you will cost far more, and will take far longer."

"How much more?" I asked, a little alarmed. "How much longer?"

"Perhaps all you have. Perhaps forever."

My heart began to beat rapidly, as if her words had stirred some secret well of emotion.

"And what do you have to give me?"

"We shall come to that."

She rose from her chair, without regard for the parrot, who screeched and flapped his wings to keep balance.

"First," she said to me, "I want you to know a little more about Arlette."

She took me into an adjoining room, which but for a bathroom was the only other room in the lodge. It was part bedroom, part study: a litter of papers, books, and garments. Melted candles protruded from sills and shelves, surrounded by hard puddles of wax. Two rubber hot-water bottles lay on the end of the narrow bed, waiting to be renewed for the night to come.

"Do you not have electricity, madame?"

"What do I want electricity for?" She was opening and closing drawers in a wooden cabinet. "Too much light, too much heat. The body becomes lazy. Why do you suppose I am so healthy, now that I am in my seventieth year?"

She found the drawer she wanted and pulled it out completely. It contained loose photographs. We sat together on the bed with the drawer between us, and using the photographs as an erratic visual aid, she told me the story of her life.

"Now here is the first, you see. This one was taken in 1909, when I was three years old. My father was *sous-chef* then, at the Hotel Normandie in Paris. He was killed on the Somme in 1916. This is the only picture I have of him. Such a fine mustache! You see how my mother holds me, for the photographer, so that I will keep still. Then I have nothing to show you until this one. This is from 1922, when I was seventeen. Here I am, do you see."

It was a group photograph, three men and two girls, posed in languid decadence. The girls lay across the men, supported by the men's arms. Arlette was enchantingly pretty, her mouth and eyes boldly outlined by the make-up of the period.

"You were lovely, madame."

"Of course. ... When I was thirteen years old, in the bad times after the war, my mother gave me to a man for the price of one month's rent. She told me nothing. When I was returned the next morning, she asked me nothing. The man was a confectioner, he made bonbons. I remember because he gave me a drum of bonbons to take home. By this time"—she laid a finger on the Parisian group—"I was receiving more than bonbons for my favors."

The next picture she showed me was from 1924. In it she stood beside a short stout man who wore a coat with a fur collar. Arlette looked intimidatingly sophisticated. She was only nineteen.

"Now here is my protector. He was very rich. He bought me an apartment on the Rue St. Honoré, an apartment in my own name, where he came to visit me. I will not tell you his name. Here is the building. Elegant, you see. This is where I lived until the fall of Paris in 1940. My protector shot himself in 1929. Had he not done so, who knows? But so it was; and I, I had many friends. This is how these things come about: little by little. I help one friend here, another friend there, and soon, all of society. And this when I am not yet thirty!"

She shuffled the photographs, seeking to present them in order.

"Penang. Before the Japanese, of course. And here, Denpasar. And this is Schuman. I did not return to Paris until 1946."

"Who is Schuman?" In the overexposed snap he was an indistinct figure in a wide-brimmed hat.

"My husband."

"I did not know you had been married."

"I am still married," she said. "We traveled, Schuman and I, and everywhere we went, we studied. Now here is the new house, in Rue Seguier, by the Pont Neuf. I conducted my business in this house until the château was purchased in 1959. My interest had become, shall I say, experimental? With Schuman I

44

had learned many new things. This house was my living, but it was also my laboratory."

"Is your husband still alive, madame?"

"Oh yes."

I hesitated to ask more, and she did not volunteer further information on the subject.

"We have been at the château for fifteen years now. On the day we moved here I said: no more administration. My work has been to make perfect all that I have learned, and then to pass it on to others. I tell you about my life so that you will understand how I come to know what I know." The parrot leaned forward to nibble at her lips. "*Et tu,* Papa, tchk-tchk-tchk," she said, kissing his blue-gray beak.

Carefully the old lady replaced the photographs in the drawer, and the drawer in the cabinet. The pictures, and her story, left me feeling melancholy. I was glad to return to the kitchen and to take up once more my place before the glowing fire.

"So now, young man, to you." She raised both hands like a conductor holding the orchestra in readiness for the first chord, and announced: "Now we speak about sex."

This was the first time I had heard her refer directly to sex, although it had been the basis of all our talk. It was typical of Arlette to introduce a change of manner in this uncompromising way.

"You seek sex, William?"

I nodded. I had never felt less sex-conscious in my life; only my memory informed me that it was so.

"But do you want it enough?"

She might have been a novice-master in a monastery, challenging my vocation: "But do you love the Lord enough?"

"It's all I want," I said. "At present."

"Not friendship? Not love?"

"Just sex, madame."

"Why so?"

"Because it is simple."

She nodded several times, apparently satisfied.

"Sex is simple, but it is not easy. Nor is it natural. This is one

45

of the great heresies, that the enjoyment of sex is natural. There is the impulse, yes, which perpetuates the species, as there is for all animals. But no animal enjoys sex, just as no animal enjoys food. For the animal, it is no more than the satisfaction of a need. The human capacity to delight in sex must be carefully developed. The pleasure increases with the understanding. One requires to be trained."

The perfection of sex: I had never thought of it as a process, always as an irresistible event. I had wanted in one sense to be raped. Arlette now presented me with a safe equivalent, which was sexual schooling. I did not at once recognize the source of my eager response, but there it was, not far below the surface, as in the psychotherapist's game of word association: lesson, pupil, disciple, discipline, obedience.

"You are offering me training in sex?"

"If you want it."

It should have been straightforward. I had read manuals on sex technique before, and I had no suspicion then that Arlette's "training" extended beyond technique. But there was something about the way she was looking at me: patient, quizzical.

"You may call it a course of lessons. I have formulated a series of stages, which must be approached in their due order. I call them levels."

"This is what you are teaching the American girl."

"Just so."

"And how many levels are there?"

"There are seven."

"I have never heard of any levels before," I said. At the back of my mind was Mr. Akaçan's warning. It could be that this was one of the old lady's eccentricities, a means of clinging to past glories.

"Of course not. The seven levels are created by myself, and by Schuman. But the reality in which they deal, that is not our invention. You have seen how long has been my apprenticeship. I am first a collector, I have collected secrets, wisdom, insights about sex and the purpose of sex. And I am second a clinician; I have tested, tested, tested. All the years in the Rue Seguier, all

46

the years here at the château. Out of this labor I evolved the seven levels. No, William, you would not have heard of them before."

"So what are they, these seven levels?"

"I cannot tell you. Such experience cannot be transmitted in such a way."

"Then how am I to know?"

"If you so choose, and when you are ready, you will meet each level in its proper turn."

"Does Mr. Akaçan know about your seven levels?"

"Bulent?" She smiled gently, as if inviting me not to think too harshly of the Turk. "Bulent would never understand. Poor Bulent is too shrewd to understand. No, he knows only that I have my own private ventures, which he approves of, because they keep me out of the way."

"I take it I am not, in your opinion, too shrewd."

"No William. You are not shrewd."

"What makes you think I am suitable for your levels, then?"

"You must not be angry if I tell you. It is because you are still a boy. A hurt, angry boy. But also, you have the capacity to be honest with yourself, and that is essential. For my levels I need only an eager willingness to accept new experience, in whatever form, and a commitment to honesty. It is like teaching a dancer to dance. I must catch her young, before she has tried for too long to dance the wrong way, and while her limbs are still pliant. The difference is that for my lessons the pupil must be physically mature, and must possess at least a little self-esteem. So it is not easy."

"And it takes a long time?"

"A long time, yes. But you do not need to concern yourself about that. You may proceed only as far as you wish."

"But if I begin on your levels, surely I will go all the way to the seventh level?"

"Ah, no. Very few choose to go on to the seventh level. None of this is what you now think it to be."

"You make it out to be so mysterious."

"It is not a mystery. But I cannot tell you now. If I were

teaching you arithmetic, calculus would be a mystery. But in time, when you have ascended the necessary grades of understanding, it is no mystery."

Arlette knew, of course, that I would accept the offer she was making me; she would not have risked telling me about the levels without that certainty. She required from me an assent based on little more than blind faith: faith in her as a teacher. Throughout her explanation I had felt a trembling in my stomach, which was a sign I was coming to recognize as an expression of my body's will. This was as it should be: one of the insights of the levels is that it is the body, rather than the subconscious mind, which speaks for the repressed majority of the self.

"So what do you want me to do, madame?"

"I want you to trust me, and to put yourself in my hands."

"I do."

"Come, then."

She beckoned me to her side. With her dry kiss I received the imprint of her personality: powerful, loving, and as a mother can be who has no favorites among her children, indifferent.

I wondered at my good fortune that I should have found, in Arlette, so exactly what I had sought. But it is not so surprising. Those who are unsure of what they want do not want it, and accordingly do not find it; whereas those who know what they want have all but found it already. A little application, and the search is over.

At Arlette's bidding I stayed for the rest of that day in her lodge in the Forêt de Soignes, and she questioned me at length about my past life. Since my very presence at the château was an admission of failure, I did not find it difficult to be honest with the old lady about other equally humiliating aspects of my unsuccessful life.

When on the following morning I returned to London, I had no instructions and no knowledge of what to expect, except that there I was to be introduced to the first level. Because it contained the waiting unknown, the familiar city, banked at an unnatural angle below my jet window, now became for me an undiscovered continent, a new-found land.

48

The First Level

6

"Be patient," Arlette had said.

It was a week after my return to Abinger Road that I received my orders. During that time, hanging irritable about the house, unable to summon up enthusiasm for any other venture, I was sorely tempted to telephone the château.

"What on earth are you so edgy about?" said Louise.

"It's some work I'm doing. Someone has to contact me."

She gave me a curious look. "So you're back at work. That's good."

At least it put Jeannie out of my mind. I was not sure whether the orders would come by phone or by post. The rattle of the letter box early each morning woke me, as it had never done before, and whenever the phone rang I became very still, lest I should miss Louise's call; which came at last.

"William! For you. A Miss Andrews."

The voice on the line was pleasant, familiar. I scrabbled for a pen, wrote down an address, a phone number. "Come around whenever you want," she said, as if we were old friends.

"Like when?" I spoke low, not wanting Joseph or Louise to overhear the arrangements.

"Like now." It was eleven in the morning, Saturday. "Or after lunch. Or this evening. Whatever suits you."

So I went after lunch.

o

Arlette's organization had many employees, if they can be called that, in London. She selected Jilly Andrews to introduce me to the first of the seven levels in the knowledge that her personality, sexually speaking, would complement mine. More than that I did not know at this point, because Arlette's method was: experience, analysis, experience. The insight sandwich.

Jilly Andrews lived in Queens Gardens, Bayswater, a stubby tree-crowded street mainly given over to small hotels. Her flat was above a newsdealer. To get to the apartment you had to go through an arched tunnel which led to a Post Office parking lot full of red trucks; on the right, a flight of steps climbed to her door. No absurdities beneath the bell about "French Lessons" or "Artist's Model;" just her name.

There was an intercom and a buzzer, but on that first occasion Jilly came down and opened the door herself.

"William? Hi." She gave me a great big smile, turned her head, swirling waves of chestnut hair, in order not to blow cigarette smoke in my face. "Come on up. Good to see you at last."

She was wearing a cream-colored shirt with loose puffy sleeves, and a skirt that danced below the knee. She went ahead of me up a flight of stairs. My eyes followed her soft boots, calf-hugging and hemline high. A necklace of pale wooden beads clattered at her throat.

Music met us on the landing, soft lyrics issuing through a half-open door: *Do what you gotta do* . . . "Isn't she just beautiful?" said Jilly about the singer.

The flat was large and friendly, a home rather than a place of work. Unexpectedly, the main room contained a grand piano, a Bechstein. Otherwise, an impression of expensive disarray: bottles of brandy on the floor, used glasses making sticky rings on back copies of *The New Yorker*. I fingered the empty record sleeve by the turntable: Roberta Flack.

"Brandy? Scotch? I'm a brandy freak, or had you guessed?"

I accepted Scotch. While she was breaking out ice in an unseen kitchen I sat down in the corner of a rock-hard chesterfield. The door to the bedroom was open; as far as I could make out, it was a conventional bedroom. The quilt was a Provençal cotton print, tiny blue flowers on white.

When Jilly returned with the drinks she sat down not beside me on the adamantine sofa, but facing me in a black canvas chair. This showed perception: I was not yet fit to be touched. To show bona fides I smiled relentlessly as I sipped my whiskey, but my palms were misting the glass. I was suffering from a species of stagefright. I need not have worried. Jilly had learned from Arlette the art of timing: not an instinctive skill at all, but the fruition of acquired psychological perception. Her mastery of the situation was total, but discreet.

"So here's to the first level, William."

"I'm afraid I don't know what I'm supposed to do."

"What do you say we worry about what you're supposed to do later? Like maybe after you've done it."

Roberta Flack and J&B were the opening barrage, what artillery men call "softeners" or "tenderizers." Jilly did not join me in my awkward pretence that we were friends. She was cleverer. She spoke openly of her business, and so by implication maneuvered me into a special category.

"I only work when I want to, which is less and less these days. And for Arlette, of course. But no more cock-and-wallet for me."

"What's cock-and-wallet?"

"When you turn a trick and you literally can't face the man, I mean literally can't *face* him, then you lay your head on one side and think of the money." She mimed it for me, turning her cheek, rolling up her eyes in comical resignation. "That's cock-and-wallet. But not any more. Oh brother, not any more. There isn't the money in the world would make Jilly go back to that jerkdom."

This was Jilly's way of leading me to suppose that she found me attractive, which every professional woman of any quality must quickly establish. What might not have been credible in its direct form ("You're special") was gratifyingly convincing in its indirect form ("Everyone else is not special"). It was flattering to be singled out and flattering not, apparently, to be flattered.

"Not at all."

"That's nice."

She lit another Winston, almost a chain smoker. We talked a little about Arlette, and her eccentric clothing; and about the château. Jilly had seen a great deal more of it than I had, and assured me it was "unbelievable." It had been built, she said, by a nineteenth-century carpet tycoon.

"He had these carpet machines, and he was really proud of these giant carpets they could weave, and he had them weave him a real monster. The ballroom is designed around it, it goes on for miles, all dragons. What no one told the poor jerk was that you don't dance on carpets, so every time he had a big do it had to be rolled up."

She laughed often and freely, throwing her head back so that the long curls swept away from her face. She liked to tell jokes, which seemed to come to her on chance impulses of memory.

"Hey hey, William," she would say, waving one hand at me as if to say, "Wait, wait for this," and rocking with contained laughter. "I've just remembered this great joke. Let's hope I don't ball it up, it's a great joke."

It was part of her complex technique that all her jokes were dirty.

"One upon a time there was a beautiful princess with an itchy cunt."

This joke, the bent cunt joke, was the first one Jilly ever told me, and is a good example of her method. It was not chosen at random.

"Now the princess didn't mind having an itchy cunt, because she had all the lovers she could possibly desire, and everything was fine. But then one day she was out riding her Arabian mare, she had only the best of everything, you see, when the horse stumbled and threw her off onto this twisted gnarled old tree stump. Very unfortunately, this bent her cunt. Bent it completely at a right angle. From that moment on, as you can imagine, her sex life was ruined. Her lovers couldn't get their cocks in more than an inch or so, which was no use to her at all. For a while she found she could masturbate with an umbrella handle, but somehow it just wasn't the same. So, the princess makes this proclamation, that if she can find a man with a cock strong enough to straighten out her bent cunt, she will marry him, and he will get to be prince. As you can imagine, men came from the length and the breadth of the kingdom, and the princess lifted her royal skirt and dropped her royal panties and they had a go. Busloads of them. They pushed and they prodded and they poked, but it was no use. The cunt stayed bent. So the princess had herself strapped down on a billiard table, and the snooker champion of the kingdom drove a billiard cue up her cunt. But the wood splintered and gave way, without straightening it out. So that was no good either, and the princess's royal randiness got worse and worse. Don't worry, there's going to be a happy ending."

"There'd better be."

"Well, how it went is that one day along to the palace comes this little old man in a turned-up raincoat and dark glasses, and he says, Which one is the princess with the bent cunt? Me, says the princess. I am the only man who can help you, says the little old guy. Naturally everybody has a good laugh, but the princess says: How? Well, says the little old man, I have a bent cock. And he takes it out, and sure enough, it's bent at a right angle. Like a water tap, only pointing upward." Jilly demonstrated the shape for me, as if the organ were protruding from her own belly: straight out, straight up. "Get the picture?"

"I get the picture."

"So the princess thinks, You never know, I might as well give it a whirl, so she spreads her royal thighs, and down she lies. And to general amazement and applause, the little old man's cock goes up her cunt, around the corner, and all the way in. Bingo! My prince! cries the princess. So the little old man takes off his raincoat and his dark glasses and he marries the princess and becomes a prince. For a while they're as happy as can be, until one day, the princess is out riding her favorite Arabian mare, and the horse stumbles and throws her off onto the same twisted gnarled old tree stump. She thinks nothing of it at the time, but when she and the prince tuck themselves in for their four o'clock fuck, it turns out he can't get his cock in. Her cunt is straight

55

again. Well, he knows right away that that's the end of being a prince for him. So he puts on his raincoat and his dark glasses and prepares to leave the palace. Just before he goes—almost through now—the princess says to him: There's something I've been meaning to ask you. You don't have anything wrong with your vision, so why do you wear dark glasses? Well I'll tell you, sweetheart, he says. That is the difference between men and women. If you're a woman with a bent cunt, you can only wank with an umbrella handle. If you're a man with a bent cock, you can wank how you like, but it goes in your eyes."

I laughed so hard at the unexpected punch line that I bruised myself on the chesterfield. Jilly laughed with me. My slightly hysterical response was not to the joke alone: it was the cumulative effect on me of hearing Jilly say so many times the word 'cunt.' Each time it hit me like an electric shock. I had never before heard a woman use the word in a context where it carried specific meaning, and so had never before appreciated its full power of arousal: a function of its very ugliness. It is well known that dirty jokes are a mechanism for coming to terms with unacknowledged fears and unpermitted desires; and more than dare admit it fear that nether mouth.

I at least was cunt-shy: because it was unknown, and capricious, and judgmental, and—who knows?—because it swallowed penises. Jilly's joke acted not only as a liberator, introducing sex between us in a casual and unthreatening manner, but also as a cunt-crusher, a term I compile from 'ball-crusher,' which put her on my side against the shaggy smiler. It was a sex-hate, woman-hate joke, for all that the final victim was a man, and it was the perfect bridge to physical contact.

Jilly had got my measure.

One further paragraph on "cunt." Because of its taboo characteristic, this word has power, more than any occult incantation, and to use it for mere anatomical reference degrades its status, acts as a form of castration. We have no terminology for it, but there is such a thing as female sexual potency, and subsequently a desire in some men to emasculate—spay?—those women who make use of it. I will need to refer many times to the female genitals. To my ear the word "vagina" is too medical and the word "pussy" too coy, so I propose to adopt an older term which is still in use: *quim*, which derives from *queme*, which as a verb originally meant "to join or fit closely, to slip in," and as an adjective meant "of pleasing appearance; closed against or protected from the wind; snug." The word *cunt* itself is a corruption of *quaint*: "skillfully made, so as to have a good appearance; hence pretty, fine, dainty." There are other options, mainly short-voweled words—bag, box, bush, can, crack, gash, muff, slit, slot, snatch, twat—but they lack either the force of *cunt* or the charm of *quim*.

So Jilly was laughing on the floor, and it was easy, perhaps she drew me down from the chesterfield to join her there.

"I love it when people laugh," she said. "People always look beautiful when they laugh. They go back to being children." She kissed me. "You're nice, William. Arlette told me I'd like you."

She ran her hand down over my chest, down and down, to stroke me between the thighs.

"Soon, huh?"

Again, perfect timing. When she kissed me, it was quick and easy, because I was near. She had only to lean closer. When she felt between my legs I was relaxed, and did not jump; for sexual arousal and physical tension are fully compatible. When she said, with unmistakable intent, "Soon," it was exciting, but it was also safe. We had been introduced.

Why should it not have been safe? Because of everything she knew about sex that I did not know. Because of all the men who had made love to her better than I would. Good reasons; but they did not survive her assault.

The record ended.

"You like Janis Joplin? Not everyone does." She crossed to the stereo while I remained on the floor, my back propped against the sofa. "Listen to this track. You're going to like it."

We listened together, leaning close against each other. It was Kristofferson's song *Me and Bobby McGee*. She was right, I liked it from the first. Since that day, that song as sung by Joplin has become special for me. Our tune, if you like.

I asked her to play it again. This time she stayed over by the speakers, swaying slightly in time to the music, slowly undressing. She unbuckled her belt, stepped out of her skirt; and her pants. My heart hammered.

She roamed about the room collecting up the used glasses with deliberate unconcern. Had she been fully naked it would have been ridiculous, but she still wore shirt and boots; and moved as if her creamy thighs were not exposed to my view, as if each time she turned in my direction I could not see the dark triangle of hair. Once as she stooped to sweep up a glass from the floor I caught the pink grin of her quim. Then she was gone, clinking in the kitchen, and Janis Joplin and I were alone.

Feeling good was easy Lord when Bobby sang the blues
And feeling good is good enough for me.

•

She stood in the doorway, unlatching the beads from around her neck.

"I'll need help with the boots, William, honey. Hey, does anyone ever call you Bill?"

"Not really."

I rose and followed her into the bedroom.

"No, you're not a Bill. Bill's are dumber, and fatter."

"How do you know I'm not fatter?"

She unbuttoned the lower half of my shirt, looking for herself.

"I don't call that fatter."

"It's all held in by my belt."

So the belt was undone, and the trouser zipper.

"Like hell it is." She slapped my stomach, as stand-in for my vanity. "You're a fucking wasp, William. Check out some of the men I've known."

I looked down at my paunch with diminished dislike. Because of this innocent exchange, when I rose from the side of the bed to help pull Jilly's boots off, my unloosed trousers slid to the ground, and without thinking much of it, I scuffed them to one side. Now, long after the event, I pay tribute to Jilly's attention to detail. It is very difficult to remove a pair of trousers in a sexy or even a dignified way; when that necessary moment comes, both parties usually avert their eyes and pretend it is not hap-

58

pening: an unpassionate hiatus. Now that condoms are so rarely used, trouser-removing has taken over from rubber-fumbling as the regular cock-collapser.

I was in no such danger. Heaving on a boot, I found myself staring down a long and shapely leg at Jilly's bushy quim. I tried not to get too excited. I did not want, to borrow an image from moviegoing, to take my darkened seat too early; lest I caught the end of the earlier show, without discovering what the film was about.

Jilly patted the bed beside her. Naked from the waist down, we lay together looking up at the ceiling and talked. She smoked another cigarette, and every now and again she felt for my sagging penis, and gave it a friendly squeeze. She was slowing the pace. Throughout she treated me like a timid animal, a puppy in a new home, that has to be coaxed, then calmed, then coaxed again.

She talked to me about how she liked London, how she preferred it to Paris. I asked her how long she had lived in London, and she said six years. I asked her how old she was, and I think she told me the truth: thirty-one. I would have put her at twenty-seven, twenty-eight.

She reached across me to stub her cigarette out in the ashtray. The ashtray was on the window side of the bed, where she had placed it before I came; and on that same side, with a pat on the quilt, she had placed me. The action of disposing of her cigarette could so easily have been the prelude to an awkward who-moves-first dead spot. Instead it became the movement that carried her body over mine. Her reaching arm remained across me, embracing me. Her perfectly positioned lips brushed my cheek. The advance preparation, the skill in execution of this maneuver, was necessary to disguise from me the fact that she was directing me. She wished me to believe that I too was playing my part.

We lay close and still. My tardy body became aware of a new alignment at groin level. I held my breath, clenched my eyes, did not move: yet felt my trembling penis begin its slide into sleek warmth. The engulfment proceeded slow and unresisted, until

59

Jilly's furry belly chafed on mine. Only then did I release my breath and open my eyes. Jilly smiled down at me; and commenced the equally slow withdrawal.

I had just become accustomed to the patient pace when without warning she swooped. I cried out. It was so quick, so much sweet heat so quick.

What I cried out was, "I love you Jilly."

I cannot explain this. I had not thought it or intended it. Immediately afterwards I no longer meant it. But that is what my voice cried out. They were the only words adequate to the sensation.

Slowly, ah so slowly, she withdrew again. I tensed myself for the swoop, but the return was equally gradual. Steady retreat, steady advance, like a lawnmower. It was after the third withdrawal that the attack struck again. I very nearly came.

The cycle was: three slow, one fast. Every time the same giddying impact. I did not cry out any more, not in words. I gasped, as if I was being punched in the belly.

"Slow, slow, slow, quick, slow," murmured Jilly. "What do you say, William? The Jilly Andrews School of Dancing."

"I'm afraid I'll come too soon, Jilly."

"You won't come, darling. Jilly won't let you come until she's ready." She ceased her movements and rested on me, my penis nestled tight within her. "Now I've taken you off the boil. Think of yourself as a pan of milk."

This elementary method worked. Jilly was able to freeze the frame with some accuracy, and to begin again after just the right interlude of suspended animation.

"How do you like my fucking, William?"

"Love it, Jilly. I love it." I spoke a little breathlessly now. The dive-bombing was getting to me.

Detecting that with or without the static intervals I would not survive many more of her swoops, Jilly now switched rhythms. The pace became slow and measured; all that varied was the depth of penetration. Shallow, shallow, shallow, deep: regular and soothing. My fear of imminent orgasm receded.

Without losing her beat, Jilly removed the rest of her clothing and unbuttoned my shirt. I wrapped my arms around her as she lay upon me, skin to skin, and she rocked in my embrace. When we rolled over it was as if it had not been intended by either of us, as if we had overbalanced; but we did not disengage. By the time we were comfortable again, Jilly was beneath me. We had achieved the missionary position.

I was now necessarily in charge. Ever unadventurous, I proceeded with the thrusting pattern into which we had settled: shallow, shallow, shallow, deep. It was very agreeable. The preliminary thrusts tickled the penis's sensitive head, while the fourth thrust fulfilled the mounting promise. Twice I withdrew too far, slipped out completely, and could not find my way back. Each time Jilly's hand was quickly there to guide me.

After some little time, when I felt more established in my role, I attempted the earlier pattern: *slow-slow-slow-quick*. This simple, more or less metronomic, change induced in me a new personality. By the bodily motions of restraining myself for three strokes and then striking with vigor on the fourth, I assumed a mental posture of controlled domination. No doubt it was an illusion; but it was an unfamiliar and gratifying one. I was doing little more than following dance steps. Yet it is a perception not exploited in the West, where we assume thought dictates deed, that the performance of a physical action can create a state of mind.

I followed the drill, and found I was a soldier.

Jilly played her fingers lightly over the backs of my thighs. As my excitement grew, I felt the temptation to override the three slow strokes. Jilly's fingers traced spirals on my buttocks, winding inexorably downwards. My rhythm faltered, became two slow thrusts before the swoop. I did not dare to think, to fear, to hope, where the probing finger was reaching. *Slow-quick, slow-quick*. Soon I abandoned all restraint for the prelude to climax: *quick-quick-quick*. Jilly's finger found the taut skin of my anus, crying out not to be touched, to be touched; and with a small decisive pressure, penetrated. The violation precipitated my orgasm, which I announced with a long groan, as if I had died.

It is a widely practiced method of intensifying sexual pleasure, and where necessary, of inducing orgasm; but I had never experienced it before. Jilly, fulfilling the requirements of the first level, was drawing for me the sexual map of my own body.

With the return of consciousness, I felt a cool breeze blowing onto my right cheek. I had sweated; the breeze was timely. Lifting myself up on my elbows I discovered its source: Jilly was blowing on me. I blew back. We cooled each other, brow and cheeks and neck, where the sweat had formed.

She smiled up at me, her big brown eyes so friendly.

"How you doing?"

"Couldn't be better."

"Don't say that. Wait and see."

I kissed her hot face. My penis was shrinking within her. In recognition of this Jilly made a little joke, which I did not at first understand.

"Now's the time to show how liberated you are, William. You know what the graffiti says: stand up for women's rights, make him sleep on the wet side of the bed."

I smiled because she laughed. Her laughter caused her to contract her diaphragm muscles, and so pushed my soft penis out. It has not been one of my problems, but apparently some men feel rejected if asked to withdraw, even a long time after orgasm. Jilly was playing safe: this was a disengagement joke.

Only after she had moved did I feel the wetness beneath her. I blushed not to have been made aware of it before; and to think how rigidly I must have kept to my own side of the bed.

Jilly concluded this first session by reassuring me that I was a good lover. The statement was concealed, which permitted the sensor that screens emotional meanings to pass on the benefit of the sexual compliment before my mind, ever on guard against patronizing (or matronizing) intent, could perceive what was going on.

"Times like this," she said, "I really believe I could give up smoking." She was drying my penis with a tissue. "I guess it proves I only smoke when I'm tense."

7

I visited Jilly Andrews in Queens Gardens twice a week through January and February 1975, in much the same way that I might have visited an analyst or a physiotherapist. I asked her once how long the first level was to last, but she said only that Arlette would be told when I was ready. I examined myself regularly for signs of progress, and became anxious that I might be falling behind. Jilly said; "You don't know what you're supposed to be learning, so how do you know whether you're learning it or not?"

Money was never mentioned. After a while this began to worry me, so I wrote a letter to Arlette reminding her of my limited funds. In return I received a scrawled communication with no opening and no closing which read: "Special arrangement with Ms. Andrews, also Mme. Harkishin. Do not think of this again. Do you have photographs of your wife? Please send."

I had never heard of a "Mme. Harkishin;" and I could not imagine what Arlette wanted with photographs of Jeannie. But such was my confidence in her that I forgot my mounting debt and hunted out the photographs.

This obliged me to visit Pickford's in Munster Road, where our mutual belongings were in storage; something I had been refusing to do, despite hints from Jeannie via Louise that it was time we agreed on a division of property. The business of searching through the trappings of my marriage was more arduous than painful: furniture in storage is not arranged to be accessible. Eventually I found the album where it had always been, in a drawer of the stripped-pine Welsh dresser, which now formed one buttress of the refugee huddle. I laid it open on a tea chest and one by one removed the pictures of Jeannie: Jeannie with her father, Christmas 1970; Jeannie in Corfu, summer 1971; Jeannie at the Burns wedding, April 1972. I had never owned a camera myself. There were only photographs from occasions when others had been present, no more than a dozen or so. They did not make a very big package.

Louise was encouraged by this development.

"Soon you'll be up to being civil to Mr. Wilcox next door."

Mr. Wilcox was the BBC executive who had bought 47 Abinger Road.

"I don't mind about Jeannie any more," I said. "I looked through all those old photographs, and I just didn't mind."

"So what's the secret of all this newfound strength?"

"Being occupied, I suppose. Not looking back."

Tom, the six-year-old, was sitting on a stool up against the television, which on Joseph's strict instructions was never to be turned up above a low murmur. Now he turned around to me and asked:

"William? Do you go to work?"

It had evidently just occurred to him that I did not lead my life quite like other adult men.

"Sometimes, Tom."

"But you're always at home."

"Not always."

"Oh. So you do go to work. I'm glad." He turned back to the television.

"Why are you glad, Tom?"

64

"I just am."

"As a matter of interest," said Louise, "what are you up to?"

"Oh, you know, research," I said, keeping it vague. "I'm thinking of doing a book." I disliked telling outright lies, if only because of the complications it led to later.

Louise has since told me that at the time of this conversation she had already guessed the nature of my "research." It is true that she did not question me about it. She did no more than tap me lightly twice on one shoulder as she crossed the room behind my chair, a momentary physical contact which seemed to contain a message I had not quite caught, of greater significance than her actual words, which were:

"Tell me about it some time."

Meanwhile, my education at the hands of Jilly Andrews continued. At the first level it was necessary that I discover the various sexual responses of which my body was capable; and, just as important, that I acquire a degree of sexual confidence. Without this, I would not be able to proceed to the second level and beyond.

There is, however, one particular lesson that deserves expansion, if only because it is the continuation of a trend I have already described. This is foul-mouthing.

Foul-mouthing is hardly a technique. Like pornography it is for a while an enabler; and for partners in a long-term relationship, an indispensable part of their mutual communication. Jilly had been accustoming me to foul-mouthing ever since she had told her first joke.

I should explain that with Jilly there was no question about how many times I could repeat the cycle of erection and orgasm. "After a good sleep, you do not go back to bed. After a good meal, you do not sit down again at the table." Arlette preached quality over quantity. Her methods were all designed to delay the single male ejaculation, because, as I was to learn, Arlette rated the moment before climax more highly than the climax itself.

I had therefore become sensitive to the warning signals, and had learned to restrain myself, until by some small pressure, an offering of her pelvis, Jilly let me know that I might release myself for the descent. (I have experienced the approach to orgasm as descent because of the slow early acceleration, and the final uncontrollable plunge; like cresting a hill on a bicycle and waiting, not pedaling, feeling the force accumulate for the giddy drop down the other side.) On this occasion, when Jilly decided it was time to cast me loose, she communicated her permission in a new way.

"Talk to me," she said. "Tell me you like fucking me."

At first it put me off my stride. Jilly drowned my hesitation with repetition.

"Tell me you like to fuck me. Tell me you like to fuck me. Tell me you like to fuck me . . .": a litany of arousal. Pace-conscious as ever, she introduced me to foul-mouthing with full sentences, which slowed the delivery and padded the key words.

"You know I like to fuck you."

I offered this in my normal conversational voice. Nevertheless, I felt a small jolt as I formed the word *fuck:* it was the coincidence of the word and the act. I have experimented since on a more everyday level and found there is an odd satisfaction to be had from touching objects while attentively naming them: table, spoon, door, radio, shoe. Reassurance and excitement together, that the word is the thing, that the name is plump with thingness, that it is I who makes the contact. In a foreign country, clumsily handling a foreign language, this pleasure abounds: in the shop, the unfamiliar word so timidly framed, *timbres,* actually directs the woman to the book of postage stamps. The uttered name, so close to the utterer that it is little more than a vibration of his mind, has become the created thing. So in a sense to name is to create; but first contact between name and named must be made. The spark must fly.

"You *know* I like to fuck you."

My tone was more definite this time. Also I paced the operative word *fuck* to coincide with a thrust. I was rewarded with a thrill of pleasure, all over my chest.

"I could *fuck* you all day, could *fuck* you all day, could *fuck* you all day. . . ."

Now I had the timing. My voice was firm. Only the statement remained hypothetical. It did not take me long to cross the next frontier, and voice not what I might do, but what I was doing.

"I'm fucking you, Jilly, I'm fucking you. . . ."

The contact was now complete: word, act, person. Present word, present act, present person.

"Fuck me, William."

"Fuck you, *fuck* you, *fuck* you. . . ."

My brain hurtled down to my penis. I became cock-headed. The process cannot be called subtle, but the results are sensational.

"Fuck me, William. *Fuck my cunt."*

Cunt? With that, the last permission was granted, and I needed no more guidance. My vocabulary ran riot.

"Fuck your *cunt,* ram my *cock* up your *cunt,* ram my *stiff cock* up your *wet cunt . . ."* And so forth.

On the page these utterances appear boyish, redundant. I can only say that in context they are sexual magic. Partly this is the release of inhibitions; but I believe the stronger element to be the making of contacts. For me, foul-mouthing is a force of integration. It integrates the word and the act, so much so that I have never since used sex words as insults; and it integrates the secret imagination with the penis. Much sexual energy exists in a disembodied form. For a man the female bodies, more truly disembodies, kidnapped from films, magazines, daydreams, and stored in the warehouse of the imagination, have no direct connection with his physical penis. He is correspondingly disempenised. Foul-mouthing reverses this process. It rears up the cock as high as the head.

Alas, its power to excite does not last forever. The returns do steadily diminish. But for a while it makes the eyes bright and the muscles springy. We have the habit of treating pleasures which do not last, love affairs, marriages, as traitorous; as if a joy must be eternal, as we are taught heaven is eternal, to be acceptable. Retrospectively vindictive, we say: it did not last, so what was the point? The error needs no elaboration, and I mention it now to point out that though the potency of foul-mouthing will fade, in its moment it is a heady joy, and ever after, a fond memory.

°

Now the first level had so far exceeded my expectations that I wondered very much what sexual sophistications could remain for a further six. When Jilly informed me that her lessons had come to an end I told her, a little mournfully, that I did not see how it could get any better. She promised me I was still only at the beginning.

"I don't want perversions, though, Jilly."

I was afraid the remaining levels would involve strange implements, little boys, animals.

"There won't be any perversions, William."

"It's just that I don't see how it can get any better."

"Well, it can." And seeing my anxious frown, she pronounced the following widsom: "Just because you can't see outside the beam of your own headlights doesn't mean the sun isn't going to rise."

I was impressed. "That's very good, Jilly."

"Go on, you prick, say it. I'm not just a dumb cunt after all."

I put my arms around her, beautiful friendly Jilly with her kind brown eyes and her perpetual Winston. Janis Joplin sang in the background. I always put the same record on after we had made love, while we dressed, talked, brewed tea. She knew I was sad to be leaving her that afternoon, so she said as we parted, "We'll be meeting again, sweetheart. Just you wait and see."

I took it as a conventional amiability. Nobody likes to think that a parting is final, it is too like death. We leave little doors open: "We'll meet again. Some sunny day." Only we never do.

But Jilly knew about the third level, and I did not.

The Second Level

8

I am not an orchid lover. I pinned my complimentary orchid onto the back of the seat in front of me, where the tiny Filipino child found and despoiled it. A steward made his way down the narrow aisle of the DC8, handing out hot scented washcloths with tongs. Gratefully I swabbed my face and neck. No dinner until after Karachi. Not that I was hungry; I was bored.

Flight TG422 Royal Orchid Service of Thai International droned over the Iranian desert into Baluchistan. There were eight long hours to go before we landed in Bangkok. Beside me slumbered a pregnant girl from Taiwan, her earphones still clinging to her jowls, sweat gleaming on her waxy cheeks. The Filipino child peeped between the seats in front and threw a toy truck at her, which I deflected. I gave the child a motion-sickness bag to play with.

When Arlette had told me that for the second level I must fly to Bangkok, it had been a surprise of the most agreeable kind. Not yet educated out of my faith in geography, I fancied the Far East to be the Harrods of international hedonism. I quickly learned that it was for this reason alone that I was to travel so far: that I was sending myself to Bangkok.

"The second level, like all the levels, may be experienced anywhere in the world," Arlette told me. "In Brussels. In London. In your own bedroom, if you wish. But I must consider other things, also, and there is the matter of the images."

What Arlette called "the images" were what I would call fantasies: intensified pictures of how much more satisfactory sex might be under different circumstances. For a man, the images might be of a pubescent schoolgirl, or of a woman with outsize breasts. Commonly no attempt is made to realize the image; it is retained as a reassurance that the unsatisfactoriness of actual sex is finite. So the image is the spring of hope. It has power so long as it is not too nearly approached.

Arlette's levels are a graded ascent into sexual reality, and so these images are more than irrelevant, they are obstructive. Collectively they act as a "false level," a set of fantasy circumstances which so long as they are not attained appear to be more desirable than the seventh level itself. A wise teacher like Arlette is careful therefore to ground the images even while exploring the reality.

She would tell me nothing about what I was to do in Bankok, except that I would be looked after. When I pressed her for information she shut her eyes tight and shook her head back and forth until her unkempt gray hair was flying about, and said, "Journey like a child, William." I think she believed that children passed their days in a state of pleasant bewilderment.

A flight had been booked from Amsterdam and a room reserved at the Oriental Hotel, Bangkok. My time had been predisposed for me. It was like being back at boarding school, where at the beginning of each term I would find my name tag attached to a new locker, a new dormitory bed: unseen power had condescended during the holidays to reshape my future. It was institutional, yes, but it was also evidence that somebody somewhere had a plan for me. It was the model on which I used to presume the existence of God. All I have ever wanted from God is for him to know what is going to happen to me, and to have intended it.

I experienced the same frisson of security as Arlette handed me the purple-and-gold air ticket with my name printed inside it. Journey like a child: it was almost possible.

There was nothing childlike about my weary droop as I stepped into the arrivals area of Don Muang airport after fourteen hours in a DC8. No one was waiting for me, so I took a taxi to the hotel. It was the early morning rush hour in Bangkok. I lay back in the air-conditioned Toyota Crown with my eyes closed, but was not spared impressions of the city: vicious bounds where the road crossed minor canals, rally bursts of acceleration on the approach to traffic lights, and on every side the screaming of unmuffled exhausts.

By contrast the lobby of the Oriental Hotel was quiet, spacious, bright. A respectful bellboy in white jacket and gray breeches took my suitcase. I fumbled with money for the taxi and, hungry for sleep, baffled by the ratio of thirty-three baht to the pound, I overpaid. There were no messages for me at the reception desk, but my reservation was all in order. Thankfully I followed my suitcase to my room. I let my clothes lie where they dropped, and my body rest where it fell across the wide bed. My last conscious thought was: does jet lag affect sexual performance?

°

Later the room became brighter of its own accord. The light leaned politely on my sleeping face, nudging me awake. I lay for a while with my eyes closed, husbanding the slow somnolent breaths, in no hurry to establish such distant details as where I was and what time it was. It was good to be naked in the cool of the air-conditioned room. I stretched my limbs, enjoying the sensation of physical invisibility that comes from being alone.

Only I was not alone.

I saw her when I first blinked open my eyes, but because I shut my eyes at once, and because she was not moving or making any sound, she became confused with the fading images in my head, and I did not think she was real. She stood by the window, so that the bright light was all behind her, and she was in silhouette. Although my first glimpse was momentary, her form printed itself on my retina in reversed darks and lights; and in studying this I saw that the thin dress she was wearing was

73

translucent, and the clearest form was the outline of her slender body. With peaceful satisfaction I contemplated the faint light between the vision's thighs; but memory tugged at me.

I looked again and, suddenly fully awake, pulled over me a covering sheet.

"Aurora?"

"Hello William."

"What are you doing here?"

"Waiting for you to wake up."

"Oh," I said, as if this was a sufficient answer. Her appearance was so completely unexpected that I did not know what next to say. I lay back and shut my eyes.

"Aurora? Are you really here?"

"Yes. Really."

To prove it she left the window and sat beside me on the edge of the bed. The shock of discovering her must have made me flush, because when she touched me her fingers felt cold. She laid a hand on my shoulder.

"See."

"Arlette never told me you'd be here."

"I'm a surprise. Do you mind?"

"No."

"And you don't mind me opening the curtains? You've been sleeping so long."

"No." I opened my eyes and there she was, looking down at me, her luxurious lips grinning out of her skinny face. She was so beautiful I groaned.

"Hungry?"

"What time is it?"

"Five in the afternoon. Bangkok time."

"Five." The information meant nothing to me.

"Are you capable of getting up?"

"I think so." It occurred to me that Aurora might be the bearer of my instructions. "Do you have any idea what I'm supposed to be doing?"

"Certainly I do. I thought maybe first a good long soak in the tub; then maybe cocktails; then maybe a meal; and then maybe a show."

74

"What is this? A guided tour?"

"Sure. And I'm the guide."

She left me to my bath. Her room, I learned, adjoined mine, and there was a connecting door. This arrangement must have been specified from Brussels. It seemed possible that at the second level I was to enjoy a more intimate knowledge of Miss Aurora Miller. Greatly invigorated by this thought, and by my sleep, I sang as I soaked in my bath.

At dusk we drank cocktails on the River Terrace, near the green awnings of the landing, where the orange flowers of a pecan tree trailed down over the canvas. Behind us was the white front of the tiny original hotel in which Somerset Maugham had stayed, complete with shutters, lace curtains, and a design representing the Orient: a sun rising from a wavy sea. Before us flowed the brown waters of the Chao Phya, with the old city of Thonburi on the farther bank.

"I should tell you right away," said Aurora, "I am only your guide."

"Fine. But why you?"

"I'm working my way through school."

I took this to be a joke. I had not yet realized the extent to which Arlette used students to teach students. She no longer traveled herself, and it was an economical dispostion of resources.

We ate in the hotel restaurant, much as we would have eaten in any good hotel restaurant anywhere in the world. Toward the end of the meal a Chinese cab driver presented himself to Aurora, to let her know that he was ready.

"Thank you, Mr. Shing," she said.

Like all big hotels, the Oriental maintains its own fleet of numbered cabs. Mr. Shing drove Car No. 9. As we emerged from the restaurant into the lobby he began apologizing incomprehensibly, and when we reached his car we found the rear seat was jammed with an entire Chinese family. An uncle of Mr. Shing's had been taken ill, and Mr. Shing was conveying him and his relatives to the clinic. After some patient probing Aurora learned that he proposed to drive us to our show, remain with us through the evening, return us at our pleasure to the Oriental, and only then attend to his unfortunate uncle. "Now Mr. Shing," she said firmly, "you go to the clinic right away. We'll wait here. Then you can come back and drive us. Okay?"

Mr. Shing's gratitude was only surpassed by his fear that we would commission another car. He opened the rear door so that his relatives could be heard thanking us also.

"Won't we be late for the show?" I asked Aurora when he had gone.

"It runs continuously. All night."

Mr. Shing was radiant with relief to find us still waiting on his return. He drove us with particular ferocity, as a mark of his esteem, through the motorcycle-infested streets of the night city; and at the club itself, which was called Siam Nights, insisted on handling all financial dealings for us. He paid a three-hundred baht entrance fee to a man in a tunnel, and beckoning us to follow his broad stubby back, vanished up a flight of stairs into darkness.

The clubroom was unexpectedly large after the narrowness of its access. It was arranged like a miniature stadium: packed benches radiated out from an elevated stage, which was brightly lit by red and purple spotlights. Hundreds of mirror-spheres dangled from the ceiling, reflecting the stage lights. There was no other illumination whatsoever in the auditorium.

Mr. Shing powered us a path through the predominantly Thai audience to some spaces near the stage on the far side. Aurora came behind him, and I stumbled after Aurora, my attention held by the stage act. It was a live sex show.

There are some common human actions that remain forever private, and which each one of us may for all we know perform in an abnormal fashion: the business of wiping the bottom after going to the bathroom for example, or the means a man adopts to deal with the semen when he masturbates. Sexual intercourse was not as regular an event in my life as excretion or masturbation, but I had never yet seen anyone else doing it. Unlike all other important social accomplishments, it cannot be learned in childhood by observation and imitation; not in London at least. On various occasions, in various subterranean cinemas, I had sat through "uncensored" pornographic films, but had never seen

76

anything more revealing than the fillings in an actress's teeth as she gaped in unexplained ecstasy. The show in the club called Siam Nights presented me with my first ever complete picture of the sex act, and in breathless silence I stuffed myself with the novel information.

The couple on the stage, as if aware that they were demonstrators in a learning process, conscientiously made sure that everyone in the audience could see as much of what was going on as possible. Their exertions appeared to cost them no effort, but the accompanying music, which was *Je t'aime moi non plus,* heaved and puffed on their behalf. Thought had gone into the routine. Minor adjustments of posture, a twist of the body here, a lift of the leg there, kept the view unobscured; and where only one half of the audience could benefit, the action was dutifully repeated from the beginning facing the opposite way. Motionless with concentration, I pursued the slim Siamese penis in and out of the sleek Siamese quim.

Aurora whispered to me.

"Do you see how he never takes it right out?"

My admiration for the performers grew. Each change of position was achieved without disengagement. As the demonstration became more athletic than erotic, my interest was retained by wonder at this penis, which could be bent in any direction without either losing its rigidity or reaching its climax. My own penis began to ache in sympathy, impatient for the moment of release.

"What's the matter with you?" said Aurora, seeing me worming in my seat.

"I wish he'd come." I said.

"He won't come. They never do."

The climax to the act was not an orgasm, but a spectacularly difficult feat of balancing copulation. The man stood on a chair, holding the woman impaled at hip level, her legs hooked about his back, her arms hooked about his neck. Then one by one, with little cries, they unlatched their various limbs, until the man's arms were raised above his head, and the woman was stretched out almost horizontal: a human cross. All that kept the woman from falling to the ground was the fierce grip of her quim on his

77

penis. The tableau was held for a few moments, during which time I clenched my legs and sweated. Then to a burst of appreciative applause they separated, and took a bow, the miraculous member still sturdily at attention.

"Is it a trick?"

"Not at all. They'll be back in a couple of hours to do it all again. They do that four or five times a night."

"How can he keep it up so long?"

"I think he lets it down between acts."

Several bikini-clad Thai girls were now dancing languidly on the stage. The audience paid them little attention, and they paid the audience little attention. On their shoulder straps were pinned red numbered discs. Mr. Shing, who had been to a distant bar to bring us drinks, now said to me, indicating the dancers, "If you like, I fetch."

"He doesn't want a woman, Mr. Shing, okay?" said Aurora. "You keep them away."

This was a necessary request. When not on stage the dancers hustled up business by depositing their bodies on potential customers. Mr. Shing spoke a few words to each importunate face, and we were left in peace. Later I learned that he had been saying, "He does not want a woman. He likes only boys."

"Are you sure I don't want a woman?" I said to Aurora.

"Not these," she said.

In the wake of the dancers a small table bearing props was placed on the stage, as if in preparation for a conjuring act. The artiste, a little square-faced Thai lady in the regulation bikini, was greeted with knowledgeable claps and cheers. Her flat features were composed in an expression of serene self-absorption. She discarded both halves of the bikini without ceremony almost as soon as she had reached the center of the stage, and taking a banana from the prop table, proceeded slowly to peel it. When it was half-peeled she sucked it; and when it was well-sucked she inserted it into her quim.

I thought to myself, she should not have peeled it first. And sure enough, when she withdrew the banana, the end of the soft fruit was missing. Evidently it had broken off and lodged itself out of sight. But she continued to mouth her reduced banana,

78

apparently unaware of this fact, and even strode in a domineering way about the stage. When she came to a halt, it was right on the lip of the stage, close to the front row of the audience, whom she addressed with words of international bonhomie: "Hello. Okay. Pretty pussy." This was met with enthusiastic applause. Planting her legs firmly apart, she pointed at one man, leaned over backwards until her hands were touching the boards behind, and with a sharp shout, shot the lost portion of banana straight out like a bullet. A moan of admiration squeezed from a hundred mouths.

Portion by portion, she broke the banana and projected it about the auditorium; and portion by portion, the romance of genitalia faded. I gasped and I goggled, but even as I did so my sympathy for the plucky little pussy was aroused. She obliged it to smoke cigarettes, two, three at once, inhaling and exhaling with contractions of her diaphragm. It was not dignified. She gave it a felt-tip pen, which it seized eagerly, and as she squatted over a sheet of paper it wrote a message in English that I read as a cry for help: I LOVE YOU. How did she teach it such tricks? Surely she used cruelty. Finally she took from among her props an unopened bottle of Coca-Cola, which she shook vigorously before feeding it to the performing quim. Gamely it locked onto the crinkled bottle top, and did not let go, as with merciless wrenches she twisted and tugged the bottle beneath. I and the audience held our breath. At last, with a ghastly burp, the cap came off, and cola froth bathed the heroic organ. How we cheered. But I, I clapped not with wonder so much as with relief, that the ordeal was over.

Aurora asked me how I liked it, and I said I did not. In Mr. Shing's car on the way back to the hotel she suggested to me that I examine what it was about what I had seen that I did not like.

"The vagina is a working part of the body as much as the foot or the hand," she said.

"I know that."

"Do you, though, William?"

She was right: I did not. This secret corner of a woman's body, unparalleled in my own body, forever concealed except in circumstances of heightened expectation, was to me no merely

79

physical accessory. It was semisubstantial: a mysterious mouth, a sacred slit. When encountered, was it not unlike all other material objects? Was it not both space and closeness, both solid and liquid? I venerated the vagina as if it were the Madonna herself, and was scandalized that it should be taught to open bottles of Coca-Cola.

I explained this as best as I could.

"That's okay," said Aurora. "Women have some pretty weird ideas about penises, too. I thought maybe it was something else."

"Like what?"

"Like that you were scared of the sight of an aggressive vagina. Like that you see the vagina as passive, and want to keep it that way."

"Well," I said after a little thought, "I have to admit that's true as well."

"You're going to be okay, William." She spoke with an unexpected tenderness in her voice. "You're going to be okay."

o

In the western courtyard of Wat Po, the most extensive monastery complex in Bangkok, lies the great image of the Buddha attaining Nirvana. It is the largest reclining Buddha in the world, forty feet high and four times as long. It fills the great viharn in which it is housed. From no position can all of the mighty image be seen at once.

Because it is the foremost tourist attraction in Bangkok, Aurora took me to see it so that I would have "something repeatable about Thailand" to tell my friends at home. The value to me of these few days of acclimatization, before the business of the second level began, was that I came to know Aurora. As we visited the temples, so we visited each other.

In Wat Po, on either side of the great Buddha, run colonnades of pillars supporting the roof. Between the pillars stand altars and lesser places of worship. Strolling silent and shoeless down the wide aisle, we came upon an altar at which sat a keeper of prayer fortunes. He was an old man, surrounded a little like a newspaper vendor by strips of printed paper. Petitioners knelt before lighted candles and clasped in both hands a cylindrical wooden box containing slender sticks like jackstraws. They prayed silently, facing the towering midriff of the Buddha, and as they prayed they shook the wooden box. The jackstraws were packed tight, but after steady shaking one stick would emerge ahead of the rest, and in time fall to the ground. Each stick bore a painted number. Each number had its counterpart among the ribbons of paper around the altarkeeper; and these were the prayer fortunes.

"Why don't you try?" Aurora whispered to me.

"Am I allowed to?"

"Sure."

I took the wooden box out of curiosity and knelt down. Once I was on my knees I found myself inclined to treat the matter with more respect. The Buddha was sufficiently outside my own culture to retain a certain majestic credibility. I did not seriously expect an answer to my prayer, but in its way it was a serious prayer. I shook the box.

A single stick began to jerk its way out from among the rest, very much as if some unseen force had selected it. I was impressed. No other stick moved, but this stick, my stick, worked itself all the way out and fell with a click to the stone floor.

My prayer fortune turned out to be printed in Thai.

"We can have it translated," Aurora said.

"No, I don't think I want it translated," I said. "So long as I don't understand it I can believe it."

"True, O wise one." She slipped her arm through mine and we returned to where our shoes waited, among the sellers of postcards and plastic Buddhas in the temple forecourt.

"What did you pray for, William?"

"I prayed that I wouldn't make a complete fool of myself."

"Why should you?"

We sat down on the stone base to one of the many pagodas in the courtyard.

"It's all right for you, Aurora. But I'm not exactly in the same position, am I?" I found it easy to talk to her, knowing that she was under no illusions about me. Arlette had not permitted me to construct an acceptable image. "I mean, look at me. Not exactly a wild success at work. Dumped by my wife for a man called Donald. Practically a virgin. Spending my savings buying what I'm too scared to ask for."

"Okay, but so am I."

"I don't understand that. I never have understood it."

"Let's just say I need something to believe in."

A cluster of Australians passed by, shepherded by a Thai guide. "The marble scenes from the Ramayana," cried the guide, "were transported from the old capital Ayutthaya, after it was destroyed by the Burmese in 1767."

When they were out of earshot Aurora asked: "Why do you say it's all right for me?"

"Because you're beautiful."

"Because I'm beautiful." She stretched out her legs before her, and resting her elbows on a higher ledge of the pagoda, tilted her head back so that she was looking at the sky. It was pale blue and cloudless. "How would it be not to have an appearance at all?" she said. "Just to be space."

"Don't you like being beautiful?"

"I need it."

"You don't sound very pleased about it."

"What is there to be pleased about? It's a trap. I need the admiration, but it doesn't give me what I want."

"What do you want?"

She laughed at the perplexity in my voice. "You really can't see the problem, can you, William?" A passing breeze lifted the light cotton of her skirt. She smoothed it down again over her long brown legs. "Just about a year ago, I was a total wreck."

"What was the trouble?"

"Lack of faith, I guess." She pointed to her breast. "If you could see behind these tiny tits, my friend, you would discover a whole underground parking lot of self-contempt. Self-hatred. Maybe without good reason, but who needs good reason? What you need is reassurance. And take it from me, being beautiful is about as much reassurance as a mink coat."

All this was of great interest to me. As a general hypothesis I would have accepted that "everybody has problems," but secretly I was unable to believe this of beautiful women. Did not all problems spring from the longing for recognition? And was not the ultimate source of recognition beautiful women? A ridiculous male fantasy, of course; but I was learning that what was ridiculous in me occupied as real a space as what was sensible.

When Aurora told me that she had been in a "self-destructive mess" I found it difficult to match the meaning of her words to my overwhelming prejudices about her life, in much the same way that it is hard to credit the millionaire who tells you about his money problems. I asked her to expand.

"Okay," she said willingly enough. "Here I am in Los Angeles, and there are a lot of men spending a lot of time with me. Only I know they're all stupid, because they can't see me for what I am, because if they could they wouldn't waste time on me. So I despise them. I don't want to despise them. I hate despising them. I hate myself for despising them. But I just do. And the meaner I am to them, the more despicable they get. Then there are these other men who aren't so interested in me, and I don't despise them, but I don't let them near me either, because I'm terrified of not being in control. So I'm either mean or I'm cold. I think: how can anyone want to know me? How can anyone give a shit about me? I wouldn't give a shit about me. So I get lonely and I get depressed and I go into analysis, and the analyst tries to get me to forgive myself, but the nearest I can get is to pity myself. I was really in a bad way. And knowing how it was all about nothing, and how I was so lucky, and how didn't everyone envy me, that made it all one million times worse. You know how it goes: I was so worthless I couldn't do anything more worthwhile than cry about how worthless I was. Is all this making you sick?"

"I'm fascinated," I said. "Is everyone in California like this?"

"Oh, sure. None of it's original. It's our leisure industry."

"So what happened then?"

"Okay. One day I met this woman and we got talking and it seemed like she actually understood. She said my problem was that I didn't value myself, which I already knew, so I said, What's to value? She said, Isn't there anything about yourself you're proud of? So I thought about that and said, When I'm in the mood I'm a good fuck. And she said, So go with that. Get to be the best fuck in the world." She grinned at me. "Just about as dumb as that."

"So you came to Arlette."

"This woman in L.A. turned out to be a sexologist, would you believe. She knew Arlette. A lot of people do, you know. So she put me onto her. I thought it was going to be another junket like analysis, gestalt, encounter therapy, I don't know what. But once you get going, it kind of changes."

Another party of sightseers approached. "These pagodas are towers of the dead," their guide informed them. "For one thousand baht a year a place may be purchased for a box of ashes in a pagoda in the great temple of Wat Po."

We stood up hastily, ignorant until that moment that we had been sitting on a tomb. As we walked arm in arm out of the temple precincts Aurora said to me, "I hope I haven't disillusioned you too much. I am supposed to be directing you through the second level."

"I was wondering when that was going to happen."

"How about tomorrow? I'll fix it up with Mme. Harkishin."

"Ah. Mme. Harkishin at last."

"You've heard of her?"

"Only the name." I told Aurora about Arlette's letter, and how she had wanted photographs of Jeannie. "Do you have any idea what she wants with them?"

"I can guess."

"What?"

"She'll tell you when she's ready."

"So who is this Mme. Harkishin?"

"You'll see."

"You've gone very cryptic all of a sudden."

"I'm only obeying instructions. You know about Arlette's insight sandwich: experience, analysis, experience. I'm the filling. First you have to eat the bread."

9

The boat was moored by the river landing, at the end of a line of four lying cheek to cheek. All were of similar design, shallow-drafted craft with flat wooden canopies above cushioned seats. Aurora went barefoot, her rope espadrilles in one hand, stepping with confident agility from prow to prow. I followed more cautiously, holding tight to the low roofs of the intervening boats.

The boatman waited until we had lowered ourselves onto the seats, and then jerked the outboard motor into life. He appeared to know already where we were to be taken. Balancing himself against the canopy, he poled the boat out from the landing and we made for midriver in a slow arc.

"How far is it?" I asked Aurora.

"There's a rule for this trip," she said. "The rule is: you're to ask me no questions."

"Ask you no questions? Why not?"

"That's a question."

"I don't understand."

She nodded encouragingly at me, as if to say: that's right, do not understand. A tiny skiff bobbed up alongside us selling fruit. Aurora bought a bag of rambutans, an unfamiliar yellowish fruit covered with soft red spikes. She showed me how to peel away the pithy outer layer. Within sat an egg-shaped berry the color of canned pear.

"Try it. There's a stone in it."

"What is it?"

I bit at the translucent flesh. It had a delicate refreshing taste, a little like a litchi. We were now cruising on the Thonburi side of the river, where tile-roofed houses leaned out over the water on forests of gray wood piles. The narrow verandas were crowded with washing, water vats, kitchen pans, hanging plants.

"Am I allowed to ask what I'm to do when we get there?"

"No."

"Then how am I supposed to know?"

"You're not."

It was like an after-dinner game: I was not to be helped. I was to work it out for myself.

"It's very difficult to speak without asking questions."

"Then don't speak, William."

On the page Aurora's brief replies appear aggressively off-hand, but this was not her tone. She spoke unemphatically, almost apologetically, as if on behalf of an absent third party whose hard line she sought to soften.

The boatman steered us from the river into the *klong* Bangkok Yai. A longboat shot by, jetting water, rocking us on its swell. Black heads of Thai boys swimming in the *klong* bobbed on the wake. Waterside workshops now pressed closer. From the saw-mills came the sweet scent of fresh-sawed teak. We were headed into the heart of the old city.

I was legitimately curious about the nature of the second level; perhaps also anxious that I might misunderstand what was expected of me, and so delay my progress. Phrasing carefully to avoid the question mark at the end I said: "I don't think it's helpful to keep me totally in the dark."

"I'm not keeping you in the dark. I'm stopping you from asking questions."

"It amounts to the same thing."

"No it doesn't," she said. She had just peeled herself a rambutan, but she handed it to me. I ate it and dropped the stone over the side into the water.

"No question," she said pointedly. "No answer."

"Oh come on, Aurora," I exclaimed. "That's completely different." It annoyed me that she should treat me as if I were stupid. "If the only way we could ever know anything was by direct sense experience, we'd still be monkeys in the trees. That's what language is all about: sharing experiences."

But she would not enter the argument on my terms, and I had no choice but to relapse into silence. I stared at the rickety buildings sliding by. The houses looked poor, but on the rusty roofs were television aerials. We throbbed past a temple, its laptiled roof gleaming orange and green, the colors of the nearby pecan trees. Coconut palms began to appear between the houses. My eye was caught by a line of children on a jetty buying slabs of ice: the iceman cut with a saw at a glistening block that sat in the well of his boat. The children waved as we passed by, and I waved back.

The houses were not as shabby as I had at first supposed. Among the gray piles the *klong* water was crusted with refuse, but in the living quarters I caught glimpses of sofas, televisions, photographs in silver frames. I began to distinguish the old gray plank from the newer amber teakwood. A surprising number of the huddled dwellings were new, or recent.

We were forty-five minutes from the Oriental Hotel when the boatman cut his engine and drew us in to a landing stage. I wondered how many men he brought here, and how often. The steep wooden steps climbed to a narrow roadway; the roadway led to black wrought-iron gates, bearing a yellow tin box for delivery of *The Nation Review*. Bells suspended along the bottom of the gate jangled over macadam as we entered. A white dog chained within began to bark.

Before us stood a beautiful private house. Its steep-pitched roofs were clad in pink laptiles, and from each ridge-end there reached out, in the old Thai style, the characteristic wooden horns. The house stood on pillars, so that the ground floor was a series of shady bays without walls. In one bay was parked a powder-blue Mercedes 220S. Beside the car stood a row of big-bellied water vats, three and four feet high.

A middle-aged Thai rose from a cane chair in the cool, dark living area beneath the house. He greeted us with the *wai*, which Aurora returned. As my eyes adjusted, I saw antlers hanging from the pillars, and antique clocks. A porcelain elephant on a low table issued smoke which at first I thought to be incense, but the elephant was an ashtray, and the smoke curled up from a fresh-stubbed cigarette.

The Thai offered us tea.

"Is Mme. Harkishin expecting us?" Aurora asked.

"She is waiting now."

"We'll have tea later then, thank you."

"I will tell madame you have come."

Aurora sat down in one of the cane chairs. I strolled about, feeling excited, but not wanting to show it. From above us came the sound of footsteps, and water running. My curiosity overcame me at last.

"Aren't you going to tell me what's happening?"

Aurora shook her head. "Just let it happen."

"I'm sure all this mystery is simply making me more nervous."

"Let it happen," she repeated. "Don't interrogate it."

"You can't interrogate an experience."

The Thai returned.

"Off you go, William," said Aurora.

I was led up bleached wood stairs to a wide veranda on the first floor, where like a little village of huts was built a series of rooms. All around them ran the warm gray boards. The gurgle of water was loud.

A screen door was held open for me. I entered alone, and the door banged in its frame behind me. I found myself in a white-walled bathroom. The tub was almost full, but water was still gushing from the single silver spout. Through a frosted glass panel before me I could see a figure moving.

I stood still, uncertain, waiting for instructions and watching the bath. Soon it would overflow. The white enamel tub, its chrome mixer unit, were out of place in this period house. Even more incongruous was a blue plastic air mattress which lay inflated on the tiled floor. My ignorance of what to expect irritated me. I was uneasy; robbed of the pleasures of anticipation.

88

Just as I had decided I must turn off the taps myself, the glass panel opened and a small shy woman in a terry-cloth robe presented herself to me. This was presumably Mme. Harkishin. She embraced me, wordlessly but very sweetly, pressing her cheek to mine. In appearance she was not a typical Thai, her face oval rather than broad and flat, her skin far darker, the shade of a Brazilnut.

I pointed to the bath, to draw her attention to the fact that it was now full to the brim. She inclined her head gravely, but took no action. Instead she proceeded to unbutton my clothes. I did not speak because she did not speak, and I assumed that she did not understand English. As she drew off my clothes the water slurped onto the floor.

Once I was naked she instructed me by gesture to climb into the bath. The water I displaced in doing so flooded the tiles. Gazing anxiously over the side I discovered a drain in the corner down which the overflow was running. Reassured, I lay back in the tub and found a cushioned support ready to receive my head; and on looking up was startled by a watery white corpse, which was my own body reflected in a great mirror screwed to the ceiling.

I had never before seen my body from this angle. I liked it more than I would have expected. Just as hills viewed from an airplane directly above seem not to swell upward, so the mirror was ignorant of my paunch. Into this flattering aerial view reached Mme. Harkishin's slim brown foot, feeling for the narrow harbor between my legs. I paid close attention to her every move, because I was not sure at what point the preparations were ended and *it*, the act, about to begin. I wished my enthusiasm to be correctly timed.

I have sometimes wondered if I am a latent homosexual. Certainly for me Mme. Harkishin's boyish body was the shape of perfection: sleek legs, slim hips, small round breasts. Her skin was flawless. Neatly she fitted herself between my legs in the squatting position. I watched her in the mirror above reach out for a sponge, and for a bar of soap; and so she began to wash me.

She cleansed me meticulously, limb by limb, attending even to the cuticles on my fingers. I have never believed or been asked to believe that "cleanliness is next to godliness," but I was unable to prevent this purification from raising my moral tone. Fortunately her ministrations did not bypass my penis. Gently, playfully, she tickled it underwater with the sponge. Her soft caresses brought it to a hopeful erection; but for the moment she carried the arousal no further.

By the time she was through with me, I was immaculate. She rose gracefully from the bathwater, an oriental Venus, and allowed me for a moment to worship her divine form. Chiefly I noticed that her pubic hair grew or was shaved into a narrow vertical tuft. We were both clean enough now, it seemed to me, to proceeed to the main business; but Mme. Harkishin indicated that I was to remain in the bath.

She herself squatted on the flooded tiles beside the tub and set about thumping and sloshing in a red plastic basin. She was beating up soap suds. The water from the mixer unit was still flowing ceaselessly into the bath, and from the bath onto the floor. I could see no purpose in this, and wanted to turn off the taps to save waste. My mind could not help metering it.

When the red basin was full of foam Mme. Harkishin poured part of the contents over the blue air mattress, and summoned me from the bath. By pressing her palms to her breasts she showed me that I was to lie on the air mattress face down. I settled myself with my head resting sideways on my forearms, from which position I could see nothing but the paneling of the bath. A warm creamy flow spread over my back. I guessed, correctly, that this foam was to act as lubricant for our engage-ment.

I have never been to a western "massage parlor," but I know as do most men that the service offered is "hand relief," masturbation by the masseuse. I think I was expecting Mme. Harkishin to be skillful in this way with her hands. I was not expecting what, following the same euphemism, might be called "body relief."

The first pressure came on my upper back. What it was that rollered me I could not make out. Then my right thigh was seized in a smooth vice, and squeezed, and burnished. After careful debriefing of these sensations I established Mme. Harkishin's unseen posture: she was kneeling over me, her knees

90

gripping my right thigh, and her forearms tramping over my back.

Now that I had a picture of her activities on my behalf, my penis began to stir again. Fortunately the air mattress was of the ridged kind, and with a small adjustment I could fit my swelling erection into a groove. In this frothy comfort I monitored our engagement with vigilant accuracy, updating the battle map with every additional caress.

At intervals I was resudsed. Several times Mme. Harkishin slipped a lithe hand between my thighs, wedging into the air mattress to check the state of my erection. I think these forays were also carried out for the sake of penis morale; for my penis stiffened valiantly each time.

There was a light diffuse tickling just below my shoulder blades which baffled me for a while. Only when it ceased, and she lowered herself onto me, did I establish by elimination that she had been brushing me with her nipples. I regretted not knowing it at the time, because I had not appreciated it.

Now her whole body clung warm to me like a washcloth. The sensation was peculiar. She was not heavy, but no parts of her were easily identifiable. She soaped herself back and forth over me, her breasts sliding down my foamy back as far as my buttocks, and up again until they pushed about the hair on my head. I was able at last to fix my co-ordinates, and so to track her position relative to mine, by taking as a marker her brush of pubic hair. It scraped pleasantly and locatably over my skin.

It was this fuzzy ridge which first caused me to abandon my mental map. With a series of mock-copulatory thrusts she forced the projecting brush some little way between my buttocks, while at the same time running her fingers over my penis. I was suddenly tense with arousal. The combination of scratchy and soapy strokes together, the delicate cockwork, the warm slurp of her breasts on my back, prodded me into the sexual present. I sighed. I closed my eyes.

Judging by my response that I was ready, she turned me over onto my back. Nothing was now hidden from me. Aided by the overhead mirror, I became participant and voyeur together. The idea of what was taking place was as exciting as the physical sensations, so there could be no more satisfactory arrangement.

Fresh suds streamed over my chest and stomach and groin, followed by the smooth heat of Mme. Harkishin's body. She lay full upon me, except that her legs were parted wide. As she tracked up me, my delighted penis found itself slipping between her breasts, silkily rubbed by her stomach, and chafed by her crinkly bush. On the downward journey at first she raised her hips slightly to ride over the erection; but her dark face, gazing at me so grave and intent, promised more soon.

As passive pleasures go, the body massage must be supreme. I lay still and did nothing and was gratified in a hundred ways. I looked all the time into the mirror above, glorying in the sight of her body on mine. Then her hips were lifting no more as she slid down my body; and the head of my penis was pressing each time against the door to her quim. Over several downward strokes she encouraged me to penetrate her, little by little, deeper each time, aiding my entry with spasms of muscular vibration in her pelvis and upper thighs. The observing mirror showed me all. Breathing faster with every incursion, I did not take my eyes from the sight of my own cock nuzzling closer and closer into the golden nest.

When I was fully and firmly ensconced Mme. Harkishin raised herself upright, still kneeling astride me. I looked at her brown body dripping with white suds and felt her quim muscles milking my penis. The mirror no longer gave the best view. In this position, my eyes faithfully fixed on her dark-angel face, she lured me to orgasm. The motions were imperceptible: no jerks, no thrusts; a little sideways rotation; but mainly a succession of squeezes. I tried instinctively to thrust, but she restrained me with unexpected strength. I was to lie back. I was to let it happen.

Mme. Harkishin tickled and sucked the sperm from me. It was an odd orgasm, almost painful, because it was gradual rather than explosive. Afterwards my penis itched and frowned.

°

These were the days when sex for me was orgasm-centered. Ejaculation marked the finish line of the race; beyond it there was nowhere to run to and nothing to do but flounder and gasp. The Bangkok tradition was different.

92

Mme. Harkishin roused me and led me to a high linen-sheeted bed beyond the frosted glass partition. Here I lay obediently while she dried me and sprinkled me with powder. As she rubbed the powder in, a pleasing coolness spread over the surface of my skin. I read the label on the can: it was St. Luke's Prickly Heat Powder, and was made in Hong Kong.

The Bangkok body massage is not strictly speaking a massage at all, but in the better establishments the sexual caresses are followed by the real thing. Mme. Harkishin's reputation was built as much on her skills as a masseuse as on her desirable body. She worked methodically over my powdered body, stressing each muscle and cracking each joint. When she relinquished a limb, allowing the blood to flow unrestricted again, it shivered and floated. She even extracted a loud click from the vertebrae of my neck. There was more power in that little body than I would ever have believed, had she not bent me and stretched me until I was crying out with the surprise of it all.

The massage is surely the sensible sequel to sex. The body has spent itself and surrenders easily to the manipulation. The heavy languor which so often follows orgasm is gradually replaced as the massage proceeds with a tingling vigor. By the time I was released to dress I felt as if I had been fitted out with a new body, which bounced and danced about me.

o

In the dark cave below, Aurora sat as I had left her. On the table stood a pot of tea and three cups. Aurora looked up not at me but at Mme. Harkishin.

"That was terrific," I said. My voice sounded unexpectedly loud; even defiant.

"Drink some tea," said Aurora.

She poured me out a cup, hardly glancing at me. I had expected her to be more interested in what had taken place.

"There's another rule here, William," she said as she handed me my cup. "We drink tea in silence. It's good tea."

It was good tea, light and elusive in taste, refreshing. But the silence was heavy. I looked from Aurora to Mme. Harkishin, but both sat motionless and sipped their tea and gazed over their cups at nothing. My bottom itched. I creaked in my cane seat. Then my legs began to complain and feel restless, so I stretched

93

them out and struck a table leg. The pot rattled. With nothing to occupy myself but the motions of drinking, I emptied my cup long before the others. I was not offered more.

I smelled conspiracy. Aurora and Mme. Harkishin had the air of knowing what they were doing, while I did not. I frowned and became more restless still. At last Aurora put down her cup and rose from her chair.

"Tomorrow, then," she said.

Mme. Harkishin inclined her head.

"Am I coming back here?" I asked.

Aurora did not answer me.

Our boat was still moored to the little private landing. The boatman slept peacefully along one padded bench until we stepped in, when the rocking of the boat roused him. Once we were under way Aurora asked me, "So how did you like it?"

"Very much."

I was ready to elaborate, but she sought no more detail. From her manner I got the impression that she had only asked because she knew I expected it, and that she did not believe my answer. I resented this.

"Why am I getting the feeling there's something going on here that I don't understand?"

"Because there is something going on here that you don't understand."

Seeing my peevish expression, Aurora burst into laughter.

"Now what's so funny?"

"You get so cross when you can't understand something. When you can't understand everything."

"I don't expect to be able to understand everything. I'm not that stupid."

"No, but you keep on trying, don't you?"

I shrugged. "I'll tell you one thing I don't understand. I don't understand what the second level was supposed to be."

"It isn't over yet."

She turned away and looked toward the wide river ahead, and the approaching towers of Wat Arun.

"It's the level of sexual permission," she said.

94

10

Aurora was not an experienced guide, but she had been through the second level herself, and had been well briefed in the basic principle of the teaching method, which was that the core perception must emerge from the pupil's own experience. The pupil is not given an insight from some external store, he is led to uncover a part of what he already possesses.

We settled down to this process after lunch at the hotel; lying side by side on sun lounges by the pool. Aurora's seminaked body aroused general admiration among other swimmers and sunbathers, while mine did not; but I enjoyed a reflected glory in being assumed to be her chosen man.

"Think back to earlier this morning," she said. "What do you remember of our trip up the *klong?*"

"Masses," I said. "Lots of things."

"Tell me one."

I thought back. The odd thing was that although I had a composite impression of wooden buildings and dirty water I could only recall one specific scene.

"I remember the line of children waiting by the iceman's boat, and how he cut the ice with a saw."

"The children waved to us, and you waved back."

"That's right."

"William, all down the *klong* children waved as we went by. They always do. You only noticed those children waving by the iceboat because I had finally forced you into silence."

"I don't follow you."

"People don't listen when they're talking, and they don't look either. When you couldn't talk any more, there was nothing to do but listen, and look. So you saw the children waving."

"So?"

"So you waved back. You became part of the *klong* life."

"But I didn't particularly want to be part of the *klong* life. I haven't come to Bangkok to go on riverboat outings. If I'd been on a riverboat outing of course I wouldn't have asked questions, I'd have listened and looked and all the rest of it. But we weren't. We were going somewhere. I asked questions because I didn't know where we were going, or why."

"What would have happened if I had answered your questions?"

"Then I would have known."

"And what then?"

"Well . . ." It seemed so obvious to me. "Then I would have been able to prepare myself."

"Okay," said Aurora, as if she had been expecting this answer. "So don't you see it? What does it mean, prepare yourself?"

"Just that. Get ready for what's coming."

"Do you have to get ready for the sun to rise? Do you have to get ready to feel good?"

"What's all this about, Aurora?"

"I'm trying to get you to see that when you talk about preparing yourself, you really mean brace yourself, you know, defend yourself, as if what's coming could be a threat. This urge to understand everything—you meet a strange person, a strange place, a strange feeling, and you ask questions—you're saying, Tell me about this strange thing so that I can make it fit what I know already. You're trying to reduce the unfamiliar to the familiar."

"How else am I supposed to make sense of new experiences?"

"Just by having them, William. With all the mess and confusion that brings with it. You're coming up against big things, and here you are trying to shrink them down, trying to make them a lot smaller than you, so that they will fit into your own head. You ask questions not to understand new experiences, but to resist them."

Up to this point I was treating Aurora's statements as a line of argument that was founded more on feelings than on reason. Her attack on intellectual curiosity seemed to me to be an echo of what was then a fashionable contempt for rationality. But as she persisted, I became less defensive.

"There are some experiences that don't happen if you understand them too soon. There aren't any secrets you're not to know, William. But there are secrets you'll never know so long as you go on asking questions."

Our neighbors around the pool, most of whom seemed to be either German or Australian, must have found our behavior puzzling. We lay with our heads close together so that we would not have to raise our voices, and gazed up into the sky, the torpor of our bodies out of keeping with the animation of our argument.

"So what has all this to do with sex?" I asked.

"You are resisting pleasure," Aurora said.

"I am?"

"So long as you ask questions, you're seeking to stay in control. You're accepting what happens to you only on your own terms. So you resist pleasure."

"I've never resisted pleasure in my life."

"It isn't an impulse away from pleasure. It's an impulse toward control. It's fear. Fear that something strange will happen. It can be overcome. You can learn to accept pleasure."

In this roundabout way, in this unlikely setting, I came to the lesson of the second level, the level of sexual permission. It was so far from being anything I had imagined (orgasms in the Orient) that it was at first unrecognizable. Orgasms are deceptive because they are climactic; it was natural for me to suppose that the pleasure goal of sex was orgasm, and that orgasm was the sexual ultimate. How was I to know that it was possible to

97

carry the act through to this near terminus without interrupting the lifelong slumber of my sexual being?

Sexual permission: the best image is a ride on a roller coaster. In pursuit of pleasure the brave child takes the fairground ride, yet when the moment comes and he finds himself rigid in his merciless car at the summit of a violent incline, his stomach muscles tense against the experience. As the car hurtles into the valley he locks himself into a posture which attempts vainly to cancel the acceleration. Despite this resistance, just before the bottom of the slope, where he senses the flattening of the curve, a momentary thrill pierces his defenses, sufficient to persuade him to take the ride again. This time, or the next, he learns to release his muscles, to surrender control and hope of control, and so to discover at last the wild exhilaration for which he has paid.

A certain rashness is required to permit oneself uncontrollable pleasure, as well as a conviction of right. Fundamentally, I did not believe that I had the right to pleasure, suffering as I did from both muscular sexophobia ("It's bad to feel good") and weakling self-opinion ("I'm not good enough to feel good"). Subsequently I have come to realize that the habit of resistance to pleasure, which when pointed out to me by Aurora so surprised me, is so widespread in the Anglo-Saxon culture that it might be called normal.

Those who have never granted themselves sexual permission cannot begin to do so overnight. One essential precondition is sexual self-confidence, which had been the work of the first level. Jilly Andrews had given me sex with a safety net; or perhaps the more precise metaphor lies in swimming: the learner-swimmer wears water wings, which are sustaining, reassuring, and restricting; with their support he becomes familiar with the feel of his body in the water, but in time they must be discarded if he is to experience the joy and power of swimming. In sex also, familiarity must be followed by self-release.

Second-level sex is not exclusively of the kind practiced by Mme. Harkishin; but because her methods offer a high degree of dominant manipulation, they are peculiarly suitable. In the course of many visits to her steamy bathroom, even I learned to distinguish between receiving pleasure and accepting it.

Aurora did initially point the difference for me with the use of a primitive technique. Its purpose was to inhibit my instinctive urge to understand and control. At the start of our second journey in the riverboat she drew a silk scarf from her bag and tied it around my eyes. Such a simple device, a blindfold.

"What's this supposed to do?"

"To give you less to think about."

"I don't stop thinking when my eyes are shut."

"Just try it. Maybe it will work, maybe it won't."

Willingly enough, I settled into my corner of the boat. I had decided to do as I was told; to let everything happen.

"When do I take it off?"

"I'll take it off. Later."

Then she gave me my instructions. I was to concentrate all my attention on sensations of touch; on whatever was touching my body.

"Nothing's touching my body," I objected. "Unless you're going to."

"Not me," she said. "Things. Start at the bottom. What are the soles of your feet touching?"

"Well, the deck."

"No they're not. They're touching your shoes. Your shoes are touching the deck. Can you feel the vibration of the engine through your shoes?"

"Of course I can."

"Okay then. Take it slowly. Work your way up from there."

So I worked my way up from there. Ankles, shins, calves, and knees were barren of touch, but the undersides of my thighs were pressing down on the cushioned bench. Conscientiously I attended to this pressure, but I did not learn anything from it. The boat rocked unexpectedly on a swell, causing me to lose my balance for a second. As I was righting myself I clutched at the wooden rail, but at the same time the material of my trousers, flapping back to rest, tickled the hairs on my legs. I realized I had been overhasty on my journey from feet to thighs. Wriggling my body to locate other areas of contact I learned that my toes had information to give me about the insides of my socks, and that my wrists had opinions on my cuffs. Thus slowly I began to

99

perceive myself as a naked body, a physical self that collided with the world, with the otherness, at an infinite number of points.

The sounds of the *klong* distracted me, but on the whole the simple fact that I was blindfolded enabled me to retain my concentration. I scanned stomach and chest, neck and face, and after I had acknowledged the breeze that agitated my hair, I had nowhere else to go. The exercise produced no discernible results beyond a mild mental stupor. I found myself not thinking of anything in particular, without much difficulty.

In time I heard the engine cut, and felt the boat bump to a halt. Because I could not see I made no move. I waited to be led. I recognized how the technique was designed to work—unable to control, I must let others control me—but it still worked. The difference between the boat and the wooden landing was so great that I was shocked to a standstill. I swayed myself back and forth, absorbing the stability. When Aurora's hand led me away I followed eagerly, adventuring; for although I was blind, I was not lost. I had been here before.

I recognized the bathroom by the turbulence of running water, and Mme. Harkishin by a commotion of the air before me. She undressed me as she had done before, but it was not the same experience. Only my sight was curtailed, but instinctively I became passive. I allowed the commandeering of my limbs. I allowed the drag of clothing over my skin.

I stepped into the rushing waters of the bath as onto a new planet. Submerged in warm liquid, my body scouts reported new species of sensations, and told tales from then on of multiple assaults: the crush of sponge, the skid of soap. Eyeless on the air mattress all my body was hungry for the sexual touch. I was ready for the soak of the foam.

The ceaseless dribble of the bathwater down the drain came to me like the sound of a stream, a river, on which I had cast myself loose and down which I was floating away. Drifting, therefore, adrift, I accepted the press of her body on mine, and sank beneath her sweet weight.

I knew it before I felt it. The straining eye of my penis saw it afar off and leaped to be mouthed. Into the cockpocket slid all of my body, present by proxy; into that snug embrace. By comparison every other mode of touch must be incomplete, the points of contact outnumbered by the pores of space.

When my orgasm came, to which I had surrendered so long before, even as long as when I had felt the river wind on my face, I poured into her like the bathwater streaming down the drain. My happy penis sang for joy. I drifted far away. I slept.

The soft rub of a towel awoke me. Mme. Harkishin's trained hands reintroduced me to my own body. My mind was awake, but at first it was awake alone. All other parts waited for the invigorating touch. Muscle by muscle she worked back into me the strength I had discharged. She did not untie the scarf from around my head until she was finished.

Then, unexpectedly, she spoke to me in English.

"Eyes closed here," she said, touching my eyelids, "eyes open here"—she put a finger to my brow, the third eye, the eye of inner vision—"and here"—she touched the tip of my shrunken penis. It was still a strange concept to me then, that the eye of the soul and the eye of the penis made a pair; but so it is.

Down the wooden stairs tea was waiting. I took my cup and for some moments held it without drinking. My movements were slow, as was my breathing; I sought only the mildest stimulus. The fragrance of the clear tea was exquisite. The pressure of the china rim to my lips, the flow of the liquid onto my tongue, the taste of it as it rolled down my throat, were all sensations to be savored separately, lest my presently relaxed nervous system be overloaded. Quietly, within myself, I praised my guides for the wisdom which had led them to know with such precision what at such a time was fitting.

My temporary blindness had so refined my responses that normal city life, with its chronic overstimulation of the senses, would have been offensive. This sober intermission, and this delicate drink, allowed me time to plug my ears and shade my eyes and pull about me my protective clothing, before reemerging into the violence of the day.

We sat still and silent. The stillness and the silence were bliss.

101

"Tomorrow," said Aurora, later, in the boat, "you can go without the scarf."

I have kept the silk scarf, as a souvenir of Bangkok and the second level; and for when I stop seeing the children waving.

The Third Level

11

As I watched Madame Arlette meddling and muttering over the 8mm projector I began to understand her distrust of electricity: the old lady was frightened of machines. She was attempting to lace up the reel of film with rapid stabbing movements of her hands, as if the projector was a wild animal likely to bite her fingers; and the projector, seeming to sense her fear, had become fractious and obstinate. When it looked as if she might in her frustration pick it up and shake it, I intervened.

"Oh!" she was exlaiming. "Oh, oh!"

"Let me do it, madame."

I completed the loading of the film, and the old lady drew the long curtains. We were alone in a bleak room in the château known as the Upper Library. Its walls were lined with shelves, but there were no books. A small portable screen had been erected before our arrival. A speaker, plugged into the projector, sat on a chair beside the screen.

"You should have an assistant for this kind of thing," I said.

"But the film is private."

I switched on the speaker, which began to hum. Arlette turned out the room lights.

"Ought I to know anything about the film before we begin, madame?"

"No, no. You have only to pay close attention."

Throughout the film, which was not long, I remained standing over the projector. As the leader ran through the gate I adjusted the focus. Where the film proper should have started there were some seconds of flickering light, accompanied only by the hum of the speaker; then the sound track crackled into life, ahead of the picture. The quality was appalling, but beneath the scratchy hiss I could detect a faint voice:

Arlette said I'd like you.

Even on so poor a recording the warm tones were familiar. The words bounced in my head like one of my own memories. My body stiffened. Before I had placed and named what was going on, I had sensed that it was something from which I must protect myself.

There was a male voice speaking, but I could not make out the words. Then a picture jumped onto the screen. It was as dim and grainy as the sound was distorted, but the scene was instantly recognizable. It was Jilly Andrews' bedroom in London. The camera must have been fixed above the door. Even in murky black-and-white I could distinguish the pattern of little flowers printed on the down quilt. Jilly was on the bed, and beneath her was a man, both of them naked. I could see only his legs, the rest of him was masked by her raised back, and for a moment I thought that it was me, that we had been clandestinely filmed.

Hey, did I tell you this one? Jilly's spirited voice rose through the crackle to the microphone on the camera. *Hey, Cubby, this is a good one.*

She altered her position and I saw the head of an unknown man. He was big, broad, pale-haired. I caught odd words in the joke she was telling him. She had told it to me. I watched them laugh together, rolling from side to side. The camera did not move, there were no close-ups. They were not necessary.

Oh Jilly, I said inside myself. Oh Jilly.

Pitilessly the wretched little film rattled on, with the occasional jump cut, mocking my happy memories. The treachery of it shocked me; the treachery of the echoes.

Slow, slow, slow, quick, slow. The Jilly Andrews School of Dancing. He also spoke to her, but his voice was too deep to be distinct.

Now fuck me, fuck me.

I watched the stranger's naked torso jerking over Jilly's generous body just as mine had done; as if he was my understudy, or I his. Afterwards she blew on his face to cool him, as she had blown on mine.

Now he had one arm around her, negligent, satisfied. Even on so poor a print I could not hide from their happy intimacy. With every unthinking touch he was devaluing what had been precious to me. I could not understand how there could be so many echoes. It seemed to have been arranged deliberately to hurt me.

The film ran out of the gate, the reel clattered at a bright blank screen. It had lasted four minutes, but to me it had felt far longer. I switched off the projector.

"Shall I draw the curtains?"

"Thank you, William."

While I was over by the windows I said, "Was that film made for my benefit?"

"No. It is over two years old."

Through the windows I could see the little lake, its surface racing under the high winds. "I didn't need to be told, madame."

"What did you not need to be told?"

"I know I'm not the only one. I know it's her job."

"Come over here, William. Come where I can see you."

I sat down by her, and she took my hands in hers and looked very closely at me. I wished she would not. Her loving motherly old face encouraged in me a ridiculous impulse of self-pity. In order not to cry I exaggerated my irritation.

"Now why are you distressed, William?"

"I'm not distressed." But the shrillness in my voice gave me away. I dropped my shoulders, to acknowledge that I was making a concession. "I liked her. I just liked her. That's all."

"Liked? Not like, but liked?"

"Same thing."

"But you are distressed. The film has distressed you."

"I'm sorry, madame. I'm not a machine. Jilly was good to me, and I liked her. I knew it was her job. I knew there were other men. But I didn't have to think of her with other men, so I didn't. There's no harm in that, is there?"

"No, William, no harm."

"Why did you want me to see the film, madame?"

"For the third level."

"What is it supposed to do for me?"

"What it has done."

"It hasn't done anything for me. Nothing that's good, at least."

"Something bad, perhaps."

It was difficult for me to admit to Arlette how the little film had hurt me, because I knew very well that the terms of our arrangement did not permit me to be hurt. Nevertheless, she seemed to wish to understand my reaction, so I did my best to communicate it. If I understated my sense of betrayal, it was because the film had only just come to an end, and I had not yet fully admitted it to myself.

"The time I was with Jilly was special for me, madame. You chose her for me yourself, you knew how it would be. Now that I've seen this, it's not so special any more."

"Why not?"

"Because the way she was with the man in the film, that's the way she was with me. Almost to the word."

"What does that tell you about her?"

"It tells me she wasn't being sincere with me."

"How was she not sincere?"

"I liked her. I thought she liked me."

"And now you think that she did not like you?"

"How am I supposed to know?"

"But now you have doubts?"

"Wouldn't anybody?"

"You have doubts?"

"Yes."

"Because you have seen her with another man."

"It's the way she was with him, madame. She was just the

108

same with him as she was with me. She even said the same things."

"So if she likes another man, she cannot like you."

"Not if it's in the same way."

"Why not?"

I was sure that Arlette understood what I was saying, but she persisted for her own reasons in pretending that she did not. It was hard to know how to answer. I was barred from using the language of emotions by the knowledge that I had been sent to Jilly for sex, and sex alone.

"It doesn't really matter, madame. It just gave me a shock for a moment."

"I think it does matter," said Arlette gently.

"What do you want me to say?"

"I don't want you to say anything, William. I just want you to find out for yourself what you are feeling, and why."

"All right," I said. "I know what you're getting at. I went to Jilly for sex, but it's true that it got so that I liked her more than that. I don't know why, but I did. I'm sorry. I won't do it again."

Arlette made a little chuck-chucking noise with her lips; as if to dismiss my confession.

"Of course," she said. "That is to be expected. That is natural. Now tell me why you were distressed by the film."

"I don't know what more I can say."

"You are acting as if something has been taken away from you."

"Yes. In a way it has."

"What is it?"

"Being special to Jilly. Maybe it was just an illusion, but it was one that pleased me. It did no one any harm."

"Special in what way?"

"I thought she had a special affection for me."

"And now it has been taken away from you."

"In a way."

"Because you have seen her give the same special affection to another man."

"I suppose that's it."

"Until you saw the film you believed that you alone had her special affection."

"I let myself believe it. Of course I knew it wasn't true, but it made me feel good to believe it. Is that so wrong? Everybody likes to be liked."

"William, you have not only asked to be liked." She stroked my hands back and forth in hers, maintaining our close contact throughout the criticisms she now presented. "You have not only asked to be liked; you have asked that she like no one else. I think this is what you mean when you talk of her special affection. You mean that you have it, and no one else has it. Is this not so? You discover another man is receiving it, and it ceases to have value for you."

"It was Jilly who made me feel special," I said defensively. "She didn't have to."

"You were special to Jilly, William. You are special. But she has taken no rights in you. She has offered you her special affection, but she offers it cleanly."

"So do I."

"No, William. For you, it is not enough that she likes you, she must like you more than others. Do you see it? You are using her affection as ammunition in a battle. You are not secure in her affection unless you see that all others are deprived of it."

"So all this is in aid of improving my character."

"But I am right?"

"I suppose so. I suppose I needed to think I was special to Jilly. But I'm getting stronger all the time. I'll manage."

She chucked in disapproval again.

"You were special, William. You are special. Only, so are the others."

"Everybody can't be special. That's like saying everybody can win the first prize."

"Ah, the first prize." She nodded her head at me with such emphasis that loose strands of gray hair flew over her eyes. "The first prize, for the winner of the competition. Or is it a race? So long as there is a competition, of course there must be a winner, and there must be all the losers. But is there a competition, William?"

110

I was on the point of denying that in my dealings with Jilly I had been in competition with any other person; after all, I had purchased her attentions, and until this morning I had not been confronted with any potential rivals. But something in me responded to the notion of competition. I had had my days of shower-room shame, and the boy who comes low on the cock check tries harder for the rest of his life.

"I think there is," I said slowly. "I feel that there is."

"What do you feel you're in competition for?"

"What for? Success, I suppose."

"Success in what?"

I tried out several words in my mind: potency, adequacy, respect; and so arrived at the embarrassing source. I wanted to be loved.

"I think I feel it's a competition to be loved."

Arlette patted my hands and beamed upon me.

"Just so. Just so. Now do you understand how you have used Jilly?"

"To get extra marks, or points, or something."

"Not really for sex at all."

"No."

"You used the sex for something else. For reassurance that you were lovable."

"I guess so."

"When sex is used for anything but itself, we call it dirty sex. There are so many kinds of dirty sex. You are not alone. Sex is used as a bribe, as a threat, as a tie, as a weapon, as a bait; so many ways. So long as it is used for ends other than itself, it is dirty sex."

This inversion of conventional attitudes was too unfamiliar for me to assimilate all at once. In Arlette's version of Genesis, it was Sexual Desire that walked innocent in Eden, and emotional need that tempted it, serpentine in the tall grass. Passion has long been respectable; but not lust. As I adjusted to this novel perspective, I blushed to realize how consistently I had deceived myself; how in truth I had never enjoyed a sexual relationship that was not, in Arlette's sense, "dirty." I would not have been ashamed to discover this, had I not known that the device was

111

built to dupe myself: my lust a wooden horse concealing in its belly love.

"You came to me seeking the perfection of sex," said the old lady. "So I tell you, William, you must put behind you this dirty sex. Clean sex is nearer to perfection."

"Easier said than done."

"Of course. It is difficult. It takes time. But once you begin to recognize the truth of your responses, it will come of itself."

"I'm not even sure I know what sex used just for itself would be."

"It does not matter. All that is necessary is that you try to live in the sexual present. This is clean sex. This is the virtue of the sexual present moment. This is my third level. Most men, most women, participate in the act of sex incompletely. The greater part of them is not present in the bed. Where is it? It is in the past, remembering sexual failures. It is in the future, fearing sexual loss. Very little attention can be given to the sex that takes place in the present, because the available resources are committed to repairing the past and securing the future. These heavy curtains are drawn across the window, from one side, from the other side, so that there is only a thread of light where they almost meet. And yet this feeble glimmer, this prickle of present pleasure, was the object of past hopes, and will be the material of future memories. Sexual delight cannot be stored. It exists only within its own present. That is certain. But you who make love may choose to enter or not to enter that sexual present moment."

Verbal assertions, as Arlette was repeatedly saying, are useless in themselves. In this case she was framing for me a perception to which she had already guided me; which I had, in a sense, discovered for myself. The process of converting that perception into a felt conviction is still going on today as I write. But Arlette did employ some additional devices, designed to ensure that the perception took root.

"Soon I will send you back to London," she told me. "In London you will visit Jilly Andrews once more; it is all arranged. While you are with her you will not put out of your mind the film I have shown you. You will recall it in detail. You will

112

express to Jilly all the confusion it has caused you. I do not expect you to be free of the emotional games you have played with her; only to be aware of what you are doing."

I helped her to rewind the film and replace it in its box, and to dismantle the screen. Some unknown visitors were awaiting her at her lodge. As she left, she asked me to call on her there the following morning.

"We must talk about more important matters than Jilly Andrews," she said. "We must talk about your wife."

By this stage in my association with Arlette I had been promoted to the status of "family." This meant that when in Brussels I was allocated a room in the château. On this occasion, the room was high in the roof, small and eccentric in shape, like the cabin of a ship. I used it only at night, when I slept alone in the iron single bed.

The château was not as untenanted as I had at first supposed. There was a steady trickle of visitors, who were swallowed up into parts of the building where I did not go; and there was also a small permanent staff. I never learned exactly what any of them did, because the atmosphere of the place inhibited me from asking them. No doubt for the same reason none of them ever questioned my presence in the château, and presumably took me too for an employee of Bulent Akaçan.

In the extensive basement there was a bar used by the staff of the château. On the evening of the day Arlette showed me the film I went down to this bar, having nothing better to do, and disliking my own company. Despite the explanations and the justifications, the film cast a flickering shadow over the evening. I resolved to drink and be melancholy.

There were three men in the low-ceilinged room, all of them, to judge by their voices, American. Two were black, one white. They were arguing about Akaçan.

"That man got no class," one was saying. "He's a fuckin' turkey."

"Since when did you have class, buddy?" said the white man.

"Don't I buy at Brooks Brothers?"

The two black men were dressed in suits like knives; the white

113

man was California casual: cream silk shirt unbuttoned to the sternum, tan chest, golden hairs parted by a golden chain, lightweight beige jacket. I poured myself a whiskey and made the appropriate entry in the account book. As I sat down in a distant corner I realized that the white man in the group was known to me. I stared across the room at his craggy golden face, trying to place him. Seeing my unconcealed interest, he lifted his glass and called: "Do I know you?"

He lumbered to his feet, obviously glad of the excuse to change his company. Once he was upright I recognized him, even though this time he was fully dressed. He was the man from the film. As he swung across to where I sat I had time to reflect that he knew nothing of me, or of my dealings with Jilly Andrews. I searched my memory for the name.

"You're Cubby," I said.

"That's me." He shook my hand in his great fist, and lowered himself astraddle onto a chair. "Pimps," he said in a low growl. "I hate pimps. They think nobody can't teach them nothing."

"They're pimps?"

"Pimps from New York. So how do I know you?"

"You don't. I've just seen you in a film."

"You have?" He seemed pleased. "Which one did you see?"

"With Jilly Andrews."

"Which one is Jilly Andrews?"

"In London."

He scowled in an effort to remember. "A little blonde?"

"No. Brunette."

Once I had got over the surprise of meeting him there was very little about Cubby that I could resent. Seeing that I was drinking whiskey he abstracted a full bottle from the bar and settled down to help me drink it. It seemed I inspired in him fraternal emotions. He told me about himself: he was an actor by origin; I might have seen his commercials; and he knew how to look after himself. I took this to mean that he practiced self-defense, but it turned out that he was talking about bodily hygiene.

"If you were to ask me my secret, pal, I would tell you: odors. Women go for me. But it wasn't always that way. I used to have a lot of trouble. Then one night a lady said to me, and it hurt but

114

I thank her for it, she said, Cubby, bodily odors are anti-sexual. She was right. There's nothing locks a woman's legs worse than body odor. So now the rule is: clean clothes every day, socks, shorts, pants, the whole damn outfit, every day. Shower twice a day. Discreet cologne. Can you smell it? I guarantee you didn't notice it, but it's there. Subtle, easy."

The reality of Cubby was oddly reassuring to me. He was like an enormous child. Once or twice I surprised in his blue eyes the wistful look children assume when they think they are unobserved, as if they are momentarily weary of not being able to make sense of the world.

"You have a lot of girl friends, Cubby?"

"You wouldn't believe me if I told you, buddy."

"How do you do it?"

He did not suspect for a second that my ready awe was anything but authentic. It was not hard to show interest: the question was one I had asked many times before.

"You have to have class. And I'll tell you what else." He confessed this in a lower tone, as if it were faintly indecent. "You have to work at it, without it looking like you're working at it. Me more than anyone. I can never rest up. Never."

"Why's that?"

"Because I have a personal sexual problem."

At this point the two black men rose to leave. As they departed they exchanged affectionate insults with Cubby.

"Be seeing you, honky. Call me if you're in town."

"You think I'd touch your tomatoes? Show some respect."

"Stay easy okay?"

"Nice and easy, buddy."

After they had gone Cubby said to me: "That black dude does all right for himself. He knows how to play the game. One of these days I wouldn't mind trying it for myself. With my experience I could become a pimp easy."

This was an unexpected ambition. "I thought you hated pimps."

"Sure I hate pimps. Some of the easiest guys I know are pimps. It takes class, it takes style, it takes brains. You know Schuman? The old lady's pimp?"

"You mean Arlette?"

"Sure."

"I thought he was her husband."

"So he's her husband. Every girl a pimp runs, he's her husband. But Schuman, he's the pimpo da pimpos. He must be over eighty now. Did you know he was running the old lady before the war? Years before the war. Schuman is the easiest guy in the world in my opinion."

"Where is he these days?"

"Hell, he lives on the other side of the world. Some tropical island." But Cubby was never interested for long in anything but himself. It was not exactly vanity, he felt no great need to construct himself an enviable image before others. It was a real fascination with his own body, which he expressed as selflessly as if it had been his automobile. "I was telling you about my sexual problem. Now this is something of a personal nature. What do you say we put a top on this?"

The whiskey bottle was well on the way down. I listened to Cubby with fuzzy fascination.

"You asked me how I get my women, and I told you I have to work at it. Now here's why. The gospel truth of the matter is, G.I. Joe here don't like to fight the same battles twice." He pointed a finger down between his legs. "This is my sexual problem. The first date, terrific. In like a lion, out like a lamb. But that's it. Old Joe goes for his R&R. And me, I have to look for a new date. Then it's marching off to war, rifle at the ready. I figure that by the turn of the century I will have run through all the women in the state of California."

I laughed, not quite sure whether his ailment was genuine or not.

"Why do you think you have this problem, Cubby?"

"You tell me. Could be God made me with a discriminating dick. Personally I believe it's because I have yet to meet the right woman."

"What sort of woman would she be?"

"That I don't know. But one day the old meat axe is going to wave twice at the same pussy, and then I'll know."

"Have you ever got anywhere near?"

"Not a twitch."

116

Such was our alcoholic fellowship that I felt a surge of sympathy for Cubby and his problem.

"Just a suggestion," I said. "Have you come across a friend of Arlette's called Aurora Miller?"

"I've seen her. Cold bitch, right?"

"No, she isn't."

But Cubby shook his massive head.

"When I want to freeze my meat I'll look her up."

We parted late that night the best of friends. I promised Cubby that I would look out on his behalf for a truly easy woman, and Cubby promised me that when he set up on his own account I could have the run of the stable.

The next morning I knocked on the door of Arlette's lodge shortly after nine, but there was no answer. I looked inside. Benjamin stretched and rumbled, the parrot chattered. I was about to shut the door again, assuming that Arlette had gone out, when I noticed that the kettle was steaming angrily on the range. I picked it up with a dishcloth and found that it had almost boiled dry. It hissed as I refilled it at the stone sink.

"Madame," I called tentatively. "Madame?"

Exclamations filtered through from the next room. Then the old lady herself appeared, in faded yellow flannelette pajamas, her face still baffled by sleep.

"Oh," she said, seeing me. And a moment later, "William?"

"Your kettle had boiled dry."

"Oh." Again a pause. "I thought I had got up."

She disappeared, to return wrapped in her tweed overcoat and shut herself in the bathroom. I talked to Papa, who put his head on one side, narrowed the pupil of his eye, and issued a dark-green semisolid dropping splat into a coffee cup. When Arlette rejoined us, droplets of water were glistening in the fringe of gray hair about her brow.

"When you get old, William, you will find you wake very early in the morning. Sometimes I am halfway through making the coffee before I discover how early it is. Then of course I go back to bed."

"One day you'll burn the house down, madame."

"Benjamin would wake me if there was any real danger."

She set about grinding coffee beans with slow turns at a little wooden mill. The parrot imitated the grinding sound. The collie had been let out, and was barking at cars on the road to Waterloo. I took the hopper and filled it with coal from the big concrete bin behind the lodge. It was heavy on the return journey.

"However do you carry this for yourself, madame?"

"Little, little," she said.

Over our coffee I told her how I had met Cubby in the bar the previous evening.

"And Cubby's problem? He surely told you his problem?"

"Yes, he did."

"It is Cubby's claim to fame."

"Do you know why he has it?"

"Tcha! Of course. He has no interest in sex, that is why. I spoke yesterday of dirty sex; now with that one, it is all dirt, dirtiness, and no sex. He is a good boy, but I am sorry you met him last night."

What the old lady said puzzled me. Was not Cubby's impersonal approach to sex "clean" rather than "dirty"? Certainly I placed his sexual attitudes at the opposite end of the spectrum from mine.

"I would have thought Cubby has just the attitude to sex you want me to have," I said.

"Not at all. Not at all. Cubby is like a professional athlete, he has developed one part of himself and allowed the rest to wither. If Cubby is not sexually successful, he is nothing. There is nothing else there. He is a perfect example, like a specimen bred in a laboratory, of the identification of sex and self. *Copulo ergo sum.* That is why I say his sex is all dirt. He might as usefully for his purposes have specialized in throwing the javelin. He has no interest in sex for itself. But surely, William, this is always the case? Compulsive promiscuity has very little to do with lust; just as compulsive overeating has very little to do with hunger."

"It's so hard to keep up with you, madame. One day you seem to be preaching total sexual liberation, the next you're attacking promiscuity."

118

"What I preach does not matter. All that matters is what you find within yourself to be true."

She had asked me to her lodge that morning to present me with a picture. She now fetched it from her inner room: a stiff card within a foolscap manila envelope. Before drawing it out for me to see, she prepared me by asking me some questions.

"Now William it is necessary that we consider your wife."

"If you say so, madame."

"I have looked closely at the photographs. She is, I think, unhappy with her body. Yet she has a good body."

"Yes," I said faintly.

"Tell me what part of her body she was most dissatisfied with?"

My mind jangled with panic. I took a deep breath to calm myself. Jeannie's body flickered before me, the parts disconnected one from another.

"Her thighs."

"What did she not like about her thighs?"

"She thought they were too thick."

"Did you think her thighs were too thick?"

"No."

"But they are thick. I have seen the photograph where she lies in a bikini on a blanket."

Of course Jeannie's thighs were too thick. I had always thought it; and had always repressed the thought, out of loyalty to Jeannie. The old lady did not press the point.

"Now tell me what part of her body she was most pleased with."

"I would say her breasts."

"What did she like about her breasts?"

"That they didn't sag."

"And you also liked that?"

"Yes."

"Did she like to display to you her breasts?"

"Yes. In the beginning."

I tried to answer Arlette's questions without picturing Jeannie; as if she were a dismembered jigsaw. The subject was still painful to me.

119

"And you, William. What part of your body was she most pleased with?"

"She used to say she liked my hands."

"Your hands?"

"Not very intimate, I'm afraid."

"That depends. And what part of your body was she least pleased with?"

"I don't know. That wasn't the sort of thing Jeannie would have told me."

"Then let me ask you. What part of your body do you suspect your wife was least pleased with?"

I shrugged. "The obvious part."

"Your penis?"

"Yes."

"For what reason?"

"Well, it's not the world's biggest."

"How big is it?"

"I don't know. Not exactly."

"Yes you do. You know exactly. All men measure their penises at some time or another."

She was right; about me at least. I was ashamed to admit to my secret acts of mensuration, because by the fashions of the time size-sensitivity showed both ignorance and immaturity.

"From where to where, madame?"

"From the point where the shaft joins the belly on the inside, to the tip."

"Five-and-a-half inches."

"Fourteen centimeters. Not big, not small." This was the only comment she had to make on the subject which had given me so many hours of anxiety. I wondered where all the questions were leading. "Your wife has a lover, I think."

"Yes."

"Your wife and her lover, they make love together of course."

"I imagine so."

"Do you ever think of this?"

"Not if I can help it."

"It is hurtful to you."

"Yes."

"That is natural. But I want you to teach yourself to think of it, William. Not to like it, nor to cease to be hurt by it, that would be absurd. But I want you to gain access to your feelings about your wife. At present you cannot do so because the dominant picture of your wife is this: she is in sexual embrace with her lover. Of course your mind flinches from it. But even as you turn your back to this picture, it remains dominant. It occupies much space not only in your perception of your wife, but in your perception of sex. That is why it must be included. I have no reassurance to give you. I cannot tell you that your wife's lover has a smaller penis than your own. I can only say to you that this picture will distract you from your own sexual present moment until you begin to contemplate it. Then, slowly, you will find that this simple process of contemplation will release her. For she too lives in her own sexual present moment."

"Might it not be too early still, madame?"

"I think not. Every day you are burying her deeper. But she must be dug up, you see. Exhumed."

From the manila envelope Arlette drew the white card, which for the moment she held face down on her lap.

"This will shock you, William. But it is necessary."

She turned it over, handed it to me; and yes, I was shocked.

It had been well done. Arlette herself could never have worked so neatly with scissors and gum. It was a picture cut from a pornographic magazine: a naked woman, facing the camera, seated on a man whose upper body was obscured behind her, her smooth legs wide apart over his hairy legs, his penis plunged halfway into her. She leaned back on her arms. Her head had been carefully excised, and there in its place, perfectly to scale, was Jeannie. She was laughing, face lifted, so that her hair fell to one side. I remembered the photograph. The Xeroxed head was mat on the glossy body, but the transplant was sickeningly convincing.

My eyes were drawn to the center of the action, to where the stout shaft forced the secret door, by concentric triangles superimposed on the picture in black ink. The triangles were five in number, equilateral, pointed downward. The largest of the triangles touched with its three corners a circle, also in black ink,

121

drawn around the couple on the card. Arlette did not tell me at this point, but the diagram was a Kali *yantra*. The unmarked *bindu* coincided as was proper with the center of the vagina.

My hand shook as I held the card. I tried to anesthetize the fear by focusing on the mechanics of the illusion, as I had done as a child at frightening moments in movies. I studied the line of the collarbone, where the transition from Jeannie to magazine model occurred, remarking to myself on the skill of the collage. But then the technical appraisal faltered, and I saw my wife laughing as she made love, the prodigious penis thick within her as my wrist.

I started to speak, and found the tension had affected my voice. I cleared my throat.

"It's . . . very clever," I said. "What am I to do with it?"

"What you have already done. Be hurt by it."

"I am to take it away?"

"It will lose its sting soon enough, William. Now is its hour of power. Yes, take it with you. Contemplate it from time to time. Meditate upon it."

"It's so ugly."

"It is as ugly as you need it to be."

I slipped the monstrous image back into its brown envelope. "I actually feel weak," I said. "Just looking at a picture has made me feel weak."

"Not looking at a picture," said the old lady. "Looking inside yourself."

12

Photographs change with time. As the moment they have frozen recedes into the past, the meaning behind the smiles and the waving arms becomes lost, and new meanings form. The pictures in their albums age alongside their owners; so that a poorly framed flash photograph of the family at Christmas, remarkable at the time only for the red pupils of the startled eyes, becomes years later a stimulus of sweet regret, the very lacquer of the snapshot seeming to have softened with the expressions of the gaping children.

I have several photographs from the spring of 1975. Joseph Rosenthal was not a family-album photographer, but over two sunny afternoons on their London backlawn he shot some film of Louise, and the boys, and myself. At the time, when we went over the contact prints together and later admired the enlargements, the pictures struck me as nothing more than my own memory of the scene in two dimensions, revealing no hidden truths. But today, when I draw them out and spread them over the table, they tell me so much about that time that I did not then know.

The sequence of the boys and me playing Lionhunters is a silent witness to the change that was coming over me. In the game I am pretending to eat the hunters, I am plunging my face into the boys' flanks with a greediness, an unwitholdingness, that is quite unlike myself; myself as I then thought myself to be. The boys are contorted with terror and laughter in my imprisoning arms. My limbs are flung out in clumsy eagerness as I attempt wildly to catch them. My face is open.

So too in the photographs of Louise and me. Joseph must have seen it through his lens, but I did not: my body's accessibility, Louise's wary fascination. When she stands beside me, in her tight Fiorucci jeans and her soft tee shirt, although her eyes look at the camera, her body looks at me. And I, I am oblivious of the power I am radiating, the power of physical ease. In another picture I am behind Louise, with my arms around her waist and my chin hooking her shoulder, happily unaware of the flood of touch I am releasing over her; but the impact is written on her face. Her eyes are closed, she frowns, she holds her breath.

It would have been at about this time that the subject came up of "mummy's week without the little buggers." The Rosenthals owned a small house in Normandy, and arranged for one week each April to go there without the boys.

"You can't stay here," Tom assured me. "We're all going away."

"Yes he can, Tom," said Louise. "If he wants to."

"Can he?" said Tom, astonished.

"The boys go to Joseph's mother for the week."

Tom whispered in my ear. "You can't stay here, William. Everybody has to go away. I promise."

"But where am I to go?" I whispered back.

Tom considered this. "Mummy," he said aloud, "can William come to Granny Rosenthal's?"

"No, Tom. You know there isn't room. But I'll tell you what, William, if you've nothing better to do, why not come with us to Normandy? There won't be any sun, there never is. Just rocks and gales and miles of gray Atlantic. But we usually come back feeling much better."

I would not have considered intruding on their private holiday, but Joseph appeared, and was unexpectedly insistent.

"It's very simple, William. If you don't want to come, say so."

"It's not that. I'm thinking of you two."

"Right, then. You're coming."

Louise gave him an admiring kiss on the cheek. "You're so decisive, darling." It sounded as if she was being sarcastic, but I caught an agitation in Joseph's beard as their eyes met, a quick smile at some private joke.

           °

My return visit to Jilly Andrews took place as promised. I remember it was a poor sort of day, blustery, rainy, in spite of the convention that it was now spring in England. The drab trees in Queens Gardens had at last squeezed out some gray leaves. The news dealer's shop beneath Jilly's apartment was displaying its wares in racks on the open sidewalk, mainly the new breed of men's magazines then recently launched, with names like *Playbirds* and *Park Lane*. Beyond the high wire gate the same red Post Office trucks still huddled together, as if they had not moved since my last visit.

I climbed the short flight of steps to the white door, trying as the moment approached various expressions with which to greet her. In my mind danced the monochrome bedroom, Cubby bounding on the bed, blown up by the intervening days into widescreen, panavision proportions. Promptly from the intercom came her crackly faraway voice: "Come on up, William." I did not look ahead of me as I ascended the stairs until I heard from the landing above, rasping through the banisters to meet me, a familiar sound:

> *Busted flat in Baton Rouge, waiting for a train*
> *Feelin bout as faded as my jeans*
> *Bobby flagged a diesel down just before the rain*
> *Took us all the way to New Orleans*

She must have had it set up on the turntable waiting for me, my special song. Then there was Jilly herself, framed in her doorway, and I knew it was going to be easy after all.

"William honey."

She took me in her arms before I could speak to her, and her

125

friendly eyes searched my face as if the sight of me was a satisfaction in itself. She kissed me lightly and intimately on the lips.

"I didn't think I'd see you again, Jilly."

"And you saw my movie."

"Oh Jilly, how could you." But there was no sting to my reproach. The film had ceased to be real.

"Honey, that was my star performance." She performed a little parade into the flat. "I'm going to be a movie star."

The speakers filled the room like the old days: *Feelin good was good enough for me.*

"I didn't like your movie at all, Jilly."

"Next time I'm going to insist on Marlon Brando."

"I wasn't sure I wanted to come."

"I knew you'd come. Not lust, maybe; but curiosity."

"And lust too, Jilly."

She put on a Mae West voice: "Wanna come up and fuck me some time, big boy?"

It was then that I touched the source of Jilly's power. It was sex, of course, but not all sex is powerful. When I had described to myself her effect on me before, I had used the word "generosity," a moral attribute, the will to give. Now I saw that it was both less personal and less deliberate. She was, quite simply, fully present. She held nothing of herself back from what Arlette called 'the sexual present moment.' I had made the mistake of presuming that because she gave all she had to give I was the sole recipient.

Outside the tall window rain began to fall with sudden violence, drumming on the news dealer's awning. Jilly and I sat on cushions on the floor and Jilly drank Hennessy and I drank J&B and we listened to the songs. At other times, in other places, was wind and rain and regret; not here, not now.

"You know what, Jilly?" I said, as the understanding formed within me. "You're pure."

"Pure what, honey?"

"Without sin. That sort of pure."

"You think they'll let me into heaven?"

"Oh yes. The saints are looking out for you already."

"Those saints. All they want is a fuck." She held her brandy glass up to the streaked white light of the window, as if studying it for blemishes. "That is, if there is any sex in heaven."

This put me in mind of my ultimate destination.

"What's the seventh level?" I asked her. "Do you know?"

"Not me, darling."

"Do you want to get there, Jilly?"

"Maybe one day. You'll be there ahead of me."

"Why do you say that?"

"I've met some. I recognize the type."

"What type?"

"Oh, kind of wild." She caught my surprised expression and laughed. "Not wild like a tiger, lover. I mean wild like not having a home anywhere. Wild like a duck."

"A duck?"

"Wild ducks are beautiful."

Ducks in flight: almost a different species from the same birds awaddle on the land. The image of Jeannie's lover shifted in my mind. I was going to tell her about him, but found I had nothing to say.

Later Jilly and I made love on the soft flowered bed. In the moment of sweet release I cried out, *I love you Jilly.* She answered as she had not answered before, *And I love you too.* I came to her bed alone and I went from her bed alone, but so long as I lay with her I offered myself as devotedly as any bridegroom, and she received me as exposed as any bride. The secret had been whispered in my ear: there can be commitment where there is no duration.

Stolen kisses: the troopship sails in the morning and there may be no future to wait for. Passion need know no limit because the hands of the watch on the heap of clothes by the bed will not stop moving and there is after all a limit. Thinking all gifts are promises, we hesitate to give all until it cannot be taken. But we look back on that grand, that rash night and say, calling it a grace of war: if only I could love like that again.

We have allowed but two conditions for unfettered love: marriage, and imminent parting. The first invokes the rights and accepts the burdens of a prolonged consequence; the second guiltlessly evades them. But one cannot be forever marrying or marching off to war.

127

The problem has sprung from an error in logic. Total love, runs the popular syllogism, is serious; the whole heart is in it. Serious concerns go on for a long time; witness studies, career, mortage. Therefore total love must go on for a long time. But a man may put his whole heart into singing a song without the obligation to sing it forever. Truly love is only identified with duration because people are afraid to be alone, and use the one to secure the other. *If you really love me, you will love me forever.* Real love, runs the popular lie, binds and is bound.

I grew from child to man in the certain superstition that I was insufficient alone. My days were spent in preparation. I conceived of my life as not yet begun, myself as not yet complete, before I married Jeannie. I did not plant a garden until then, because so long as I was alone I could not think of myself as having come to rest. Such dogmas are printed deep in the heart and cannot be erased. At the third level I was introduced to a new concept of love, a love that can only be given and received within the present moment. I cannot say that it released me from my bondage, but it taught me discrimination. There is a love that binds nothing, and cannot itself be bound.

Patter patter patter went the rain outside. We lay with our arms still tight around each other, sheltering in each other from the wind and the rain beyond the door.

"You know what I like best about sex," Jilly said. "I like to hold people."

The Fourth Level

13

I saw Aurora as soon as I emerged from the ticket hall into the main concourse of Paddington station. She was standing under the departures board, deep in her own thoughts, the echoing noise and hurrying crowds seeming not to touch her. People passing by stared and gave her space. Partly this was the common nervous attention given to all attractive women; but partly it was the way she was standing, her feet planted apart, her back straight, her head high. She was contained within an almost visible envelope of confidence.

We greeted each other with affectionate kisses.

"Where have you been since I last saw you?" I asked her.

"I've been home."

"Los Angeles?"

"Yes."

"Everybody seems to have so much money."

"You too, William."

"But it's all I've got."

"So is my money all I've got. I went back home to work."

"I didn't know you worked."

"I get photographed. I model. Maybe you don't call that work."

We walked down the train looking for empty seats, and ended up in the dining car, where lunch was to be served. The steward assured us that we would have time for a comfortable lunch before the train reached Kemble.

"So what's the plan in Kemble?" I asked Aurora.

"We're going for a quiet English country weekend. How's your croquet?"

"Terrific. I'm a fiend at croquet."

"You'll have to teach me. I don't know one end of a croquet stick from another."

"Mallet. Who are we staying with?"

"The family is called Bancroft. There's Colonel Bancroft, and Mrs. Bancroft, and Mrs. Bancroft's mother, and Virginia Bancroft, a daughter."

"And which one invited us?"

"Virginia."

"Do you know her?"

"Arlette does. I've spoken to her on the phone."

Soft damp countryside wheeled by beyond the window. The spring was turning out to be fine after all. Sunlit fields and red wine mellowed my mood. Also it made me happy to be able to look on the lovely Aurora again.

"When this trip is over, will you be with me on the next one?"

"I won't be your guide any more, if that's what you mean."

"Why not?"

"It's different from the fifth level on."

"So will I see you again?"

"If you come to Los Angeles."

"Or if you come to London."

We exchanged addresses.

"I don't want to lose you," I said. "Apart from Arlette, you're the only person who has any idea what has been happening to me."

"Don't worry. You won't lose me."

The train chattered on through Berkshire and Wiltshire into

132

Gloucestershire. Shortly before we arrived at Kemble, just as we entered a tunnel, Aurora said to me:

"You ought to know that for the duration of the weekend you're my husband."

"I am?"

"It simplifies things with the Bancroft parents. Also, they think Virginia is an old school friend of mine."

"So am I to call you darling?"

"If you feel like it."

So as husband and wife we stepped off the train at Kemble. The platforms of the tiny station have changed little since the days of the Great Western Railway: cast-iron benches, a wood-cased station clock, a bleak waiting room in which travelers sat beneath artist's impressions of prewar London. By the time our train had rumbled out of sight toward Cheltenham, we were the only moving elements in a scene like an old-fashioned postcard, the stone walls tinted sepia by the sun.

Virginia Bancroft was waiting for us by the exit on the far platform. She stood leaning against a red telephone booth, her arms folded, her legs negligently stuck out, staring at both of us as we crossed the footbridge with undisguised and critical interest. Her clothes were metropolitan: baggy sweater and jeans, stacked heels and flat tweed cap, all jarringly out of place in the little yellow-stone station.

We introduced ourselves. "Bit of a trek from here," she told us; and stalked out into the parking lot. Her manner, abrupt, uncompromising, contrasted with a certain facial cheeriness she could not dispel: she possessed the rosy coloring and dark-blonde curls of an idealized English country girl. With an arrogance that bordered on defiance she incorporated this natural blush into a high-fashion face, camouflaging it as overapplied cosmetic.

An ancient Land Rover waited for us. I sat in the back and was jolted about a good deal on the long drive down unmarked lanes. Virginia drove recklessly, chasing the cars that resisted being overtaken: "Shuffle along, grandma, you're not dead yet. Gordon *Bennett* you're a perky little bastard!," and so on. Over the roar of the straining engine Aurora asked her how we would find the rest of her family, and she answered with the one extended word: "Grofuckingtesque."

Some miles beyond Tetbury we entered the village of Didmarton, which was our destination. The Bancroft house stood at the end of a short drive, screened from the rest of the village by a beech copse and a high stone wall: an ordered Queen Anne front attached to an older wing, a large house, but almost certainly not the principal house of the village, as its name, the Dower House, implied. The stone face had a scrubbed and well-tended look, the painted trim and the drainpipes were in good condition, and the quince trees trained on trellises on either side of the front door were firmly strapped into place. A fat old Labrador waddled out to greet us. Virginia made much of him.

"Hello Jason, old fellow, old stud." To me she said, "He still gets a bit fruity now and again, and when he does, it's men's legs he likes. If he gets going on you, just belt him on the nose." She ruffled the dog's fur, accusing his mournful eyes: "Who's a toast-colored sex maniac, then?"

We entered the house. I did not feel it at once, but after we had been standing for a few moments in the stone-flagged hall while Virginia located her parents I became aware of the sensation that something here was wrong, was out of order—as in those puzzle pictures in which the artist has included a deliberate mistake, an airplane with one wing, a child on a swing that has no ropes. I searched around for the source. There was a small lacquered wood table on which stood a vase of pampas grass and dried flowers; an oval mirror; three white-painted paneled doors with china handles; and an uncarpeted oak staircase that rose before us in an elegant curve to the first floor. Framed hand-tinted engravings ascended the wall in step with the stairs, an eighteenth-century series depicting the dress uniforms of officers from different regiments. Nothing was unusual in any of this. I wondered if my discomfort might be caused by an unfamiliar smell. There are smells which affect the stomach but are too elusive to be distinguished by the nose. Also smells trigger emotional memories without passing through the intervening stage of mental image. It was possible that the stair polish, or the detergent used on the white stone flags, had awakened in me the memory of some long-past dismal day at school.

134

Virginia reappeared and beckoned us through a door on the left. Here, asleep in an armchair, was a small man with youthful sandy hair and a stubborn clenched mouth.

"Same weight since the age of twenty-one," said Virginia in a low voice. "Hundred and forty-five pounds. No excess."

This was in mocking imitation of her father, who I learned was proud of his physical fitness, and kept in one of the cellars a set of weights, a punching bag, and parallel bars. But his skin had aged, and all around his eyes was a network of fine wrinkles.

He slept before a basket grate in which a fire was neatly made up, in wait for the cool of the evening. Here was the television, and a number of magazines lying half-read on various surfaces. A tea cart bore the remains of a snack lunch or a late breakfast.

Virginia shook him awake.

"Coming," he said. "Coming."

His slightly protuberant eyes surveyed the three of us without recognition, finally settling on his daughter.

"Ginny?"

Virginia introduced us by our married names. Secretly I was enchanted by this, and by the knowledge that to Colonel Bancroft the pretense was a reality. The colonel now shot out of his chair, as if all at once aware of his lapse of good manners, and shook our hands. There was something of Virginia in the brisk fashion with which he exchanged courtesies. It was all very proper, but I felt in his handshake no expectation that he would enjoy our company over the weekend. The only question he asked me was whether I smoked. I said I did not and never had. "Lucky chap," he said. "I've just given up. Hellish difficult. I expect I shall put on weight."

On the way up the stairs Virginia said:

"Hilarious, isn't it? My father."

The room Aurora and I were to occupy was big and square, with two fine sash windows looking out onto the croquet lawn. Between the windows stood a double bed. It seemed I was to sleep with Aurora.

"This is all very snug," I said, sitting investigatively on the bed. Virginia had left us to clean up after our journey. "If I'm to sleep on the floor please tell me now."

"The bed's big enough for both of us," said Aurora.

"Are we to consummate our marriage?"

"Sorry." She laughed at the face I pulled. "Not part of the plan."

Bending over the washbasin set into a corner alcove, she splashed cold water over her face. When she was shrouded in a towel I said, "I'm not sure about Virginia. She worries me."

I was uneasy about the whole arrangement. In the absence of authentic enthusiasm I had found it reassuring to know that I had been paying. This was no longer the case. What if I failed to meet expectations? What were the expectations?

"Mightn't it be rather the blind leading the blind?" I suggested, thinking: the soft-spoken leading the tight-lipped.

"You'll be okay."

We rejoined the family and were introduced to Mrs. Bancroft. Like her husband, she seemed remote even in the moment of speaking my name. In looks she was recognizably Virginia's mother, and still conducted herself in the semiformal mode of those who habitually suffer admiration. Now in late middle age, her carefully preserved face was inert; as if she had been warned in her youth that too much facial mobility caused wrinkles.

The third permanent member of the household, Mrs. Richardson, Virginia's grandmother, did not speak, and seemed to lead a primarily symbolic existence. She spent her time asleep in various armchairs, like those representations of Old Age, unloved and unlovely, engraved in the final panel of a pictorial progress to show the miserable twilight of a mistaken way of life. I had no reason to suppose that Mrs. Richardson was morally responsible for her own senile decay, or was for that matter miserable; but she was wonderfully ancient and shrunken, and could not have failed to exert a bracing effect on her doll-like daughter.

The company was not what I would have chosen for myself, but I played my part as a guest as politely as I was able. With Colonel Bancroft I discussed the state of the nation.

"Perhaps you can explain this inflation to me," he said deceptively. "I'm not saying it's all the unions' fault. One way and another I've had a lot of experience of the working man, more than you, I dare say. I don't go along with this line that the working man is out for what he can get."

I offered mild agreement; but it would not have mattered if I

136

had violently contested his views. Colonel Bancroft possessed only a rudimentary awareness that other people were separate entities from himself.

"What's got into everybody? Forgive me for interrupting you, but can you tell me what it is that's got into everybody these days? I'm not saying the world has become greedier, but I can remember a time when we didn't have all these strikes and inflation."

"You think the world has become greedier?"

"I wouldn't know. All I know is that when a man can get more for sitting on his backside than he can get for doing an honest day's work, well, I'm not saying something's gone badly wrong, but what do you say?"

Mrs. Bancroft did not share her husband's interest in world affairs, and remained silent during these conversations. The only exchange of any length I had with her concerned her children. Virginia had an elder brother, whose name was Richard. A photograph of him stood on the television in the small living room, taken at an age when his primary role was still that of son. Handsome and decorous, the youth smiled out of the frame with that look of curious condescension worn by children who have learned that their parents depend upon their love.

"We hope Richard will live here after us," Mrs. Bancroft informed me. "Of course, there's this terrible business of inheritance taxes. He may be obliged to sell." She gave a tiny shrug. "There's nothing I can do about that. I choose not to think about it."

"How old is your son?"

"He's twenty-eight. He works in Johannesburg, you know. I expect Virginia told you that."

"You don't worry about the political situation there?"

She turned her shiny face to me, eyebrows twitching in subterranean alarm. "Why? Has something happened?"

"I just mean South Africa in general. Apartheid and so on."

"Oh, that. Well, there's nothing I can do about that. We do hope he'll come back to England, though. He's married, you know. No children. I'm not a grandmother yet." And in the same dull squeezed voice she continued: "I do wish Virginia would get married. She's twenty-seven, you know."

137

"I thought she was much younger."

"But you see, she isn't. I know she's very pretty, but there aren't so many men who want a wife over thirty. And I know girls don't need to be as careful as we did in my day, but I do sometimes wonder whethter she might not find it difficult when the time comes."

"Perhaps she doesn't want to get married."

Mrs. Bancroft lifted her eyebrows an indifferent millimeter. "In the end a woman needs a man."

"I don't think all women do. Not these days."

"Of course Virginia is free to do as she likes. But I sometimes wonder if she realizes it won't last."

We sat down to dinner that evening in modest grandeur. The dining table could without inconvenience have seated ten, which meant that there were gaps between us into which the conversation sank every few minutes. I was placed at Mrs. Bancroft's end. Virginia sat opposite me, sideways on her chair, one arm draped over the upright back, as if she had joined us on an impulse and would shortly be moving on. Mrs. Richardson was on my left, her chair tight against the table. For a while I could hear her furtively attempting to escape.

"Save it up, Mother," the colonel shouted over the polished walnut. "We have company."

There was a general reluctance to permit Mrs. Richardson to go to the bathroom. This was because she fell asleep while locked in, no doubt believing herself to be in yet another armchair, and could only be dislodged with difficulty.

"Such dreadful weather," said Mrs. Bancroft. "After such a beautiful day."

The old Labrador wheezed beneath the table, pressing an importunate nose between random thighs.

"Go away, Jason. Away sir! Somebody's been feeding that dog from the table again."

Virginia poured herself a glass of wine from the bottle standing uncorked between us, and slid it unceremoniously over the hard surface to Aurora. Mrs. Bancroft drew in her breath, offended by this display of café manners, and stared expressionlessly down the long table at her husband. I fingered my wine

138

glass. It was hand-cut, etched with a name and a date: Richard Meredith Bancroft, September 1st 1946.

This meal provided me with my first extended opportunity to study Virginia. I was puzzled, and a little dismayed, that apart from her long stare at the station she should show no curiosity about me in return. It was clearly nothing personal. Her lack of interest in the world about her was as marked as her mother's but was expressed in a sullen, almost sluttish carelessness, which was the antithesis of Mrs. Bancroft's remote propriety. It made me want to seize her by the shoulders and shake her violently, "until the teeth rattled," as the saying goes; which is to say that I sought from her a physical, a sexual response, because that rosy face set in an indifferent stare, that graceless sensual slouch, seemed designed to arouse desire even while frustrating it.

"Do you know," Colonel Bancroft informed the company, "that on the liner *France* there are no less than two hundred cooks. Two hundred! And now she's to be scrapped."

The wind began to beat about more seriously in the beech copse outside. Mrs. Bancroft cut up her mother's meat with sharp clicks.

"They even have a hospital on the *France*. With two padded cells. But those days are over, so there you are. No, for heaven's sake don't give Mother any wine."

He arrested my polite arm in mid-tip. Mrs. Richardson's quavering fork pronged a sliver of meat, rose uncertainly toward her mouth, paused, and descended untouched to her lap, where Jason consumed the meat with melancholy dexterity.

Conversation during the meal was limited largely to the colonel's utterances, which were so clearly an audible expression of a private stream of thought flowing within him, no less impersonal for being private, that very little response was possible. However, the more he drank from his commemorative glass the more imperial became his conversational ambitions; until the point came when he looked about him for an enemy to subdue.

"Virginia doesn't really go along with all this family business, of course," he declared without warning. "I can't pretend I know what she does go along with. Something far better, I dare say."

"Leave it alone," said Virginia.

"No, I'm interested. I really do want to know. You don't approve of families, that much I have gathered—"

"Of course I approve of families."

"But you don't want a family yourself, do you? Don't think I'm saying you're wrong, Ginny. What do I know about it? I'm only asking because I've never really understood you on this one. It seems to me to be natural to get married and have a family, but obviously I'm out of line here. You must educate me."

Virginia stared down at her plate, refusing to be drawn. Her father was forced, not unwillingly, to supply his own opposition.

"I expect you'll tell me that you young people get more out of life these days than we ever did. I'm sure you're right. I don't deny it. Life is for living, as they say. So you see, I'm not so out of touch after all. Only, what I'd like to know is, what happens later? I only ask because it looks like a case of live now, pay later. If I'm wrong, then I'm wrong, fair's fair. But all of us grow older, whether we like it or not."

Virginia maintained her silence.

"One way of life may be right for a while," I suggested. "And then as you get older, another way of life may be suitable."

"Is that a fact?" Maddeningly, the colonel continued to direct his words and his attention toward his daughter, as if it had been she who had answered. "So you think, do you, and tell me if I'm getting this right, that after living a free and easy life, and not keeping anything back for later, and I'm sure I don't have to spell it out, you will be able to settle down?"

"Why not?' I said.

"I'm just asking for information. This is all China to me. So when you decide you've had enough, you settle down. Right. I'm beginning to get the picture. Now the next question is only a practical detail. I don't quite see how you work it. Do you keep one of them waiting in the wings, so to speak? Or do you start from scratch?"

"Oh shut up, Father," said Virginia. She did not raise her head, nor did she speak loudly, but there was a compressed bitterness in her voice.

"I am your father, darling. It's natural that I should be interested. Fathers do worry about their daughters. Maybe they shouldn't, I don't know. I only worry because I sometimes ask myself whether times have changed that much after all. I see now I'm wrong. In my day, of course, there were the girls you married and the girls you didn't. Well I see now that everything's changed. That's quite a relief to your mother and me, Ginny, I don't mind telling you."

I had supposed that Colonel Bancroft was airing a further set of opinions for no more than his own satisfaction, like an artist visiting a gallery displaying his own pictures. I now realized that he was baiting his daughter. This was a skirmish in some secret war. I glanced at Mrs. Bancroft to see whether she was enlisted in her husband's campaign, but her feelings, if she felt anything, could not be read in her face.

The restrained unpleasantness of the conversation was brought to an end by the arrival of a spring storm outside. The howling of the wind and the distant grinding of the thunder dispersed the emotional tension into the conflict of mightier elements. The old lady gave up her fidgeting and sat very still, trembling.

"Come along now, Mother," yelled Colonel Bancroft. "There's nothing to be afraid of. People don't get killed in storms any more."

"Of course they do," said Mrs. Bancroft.

"Talking about dying," continued the colonel, "apparently there was this man who died for twenty-three minutes, and came back to life again. I think it was twenty-three minutes. Apparently he saw heaven. I'm not saying he did, but that's what he says."

"What did he say heaven was like?"

"Pretty good. I don't remember the details."

The thunder rolled nearer.

•

Once we were alone in our bedroom Aurora asked me what I thought of them.

"To quote Virginia," I said, "grofuckingtesque. Particularly that monstrous little man."

This seemed to satisfy her, because she nodded and did not ask me any more. Of course I was curious about what this house and

141

this family had to do with the fourth level; but I had learned my lesson, and I did not ask. In the immediate present I was more interested in our sleeping arrangements.

I took advantage of Aurora's visit to the bathroom to change into my pajamas, shy of being seen naked by her. She returned in a long white nightgown, her clothes over her arm.

"Oh, very sneaky," I said.

"Look who's talking."

The storm was now passing overhead. It was only a small storm, but the thunder growled fearfully enough in the attics. Aurora stood by the uncurtained window on the far side of the bed from me, looking out at the steadily falling rain and the occasional flashes of lightning. Her cotton nightgown was sleeveless, tied at the neck with two white laces.

"Do you feel yourself changing, William? I do."

I knew she was talking not about this particular time and place, but about the effect of the levels.

"Yes," I said. "I feel it."

"Does it scare you?"

"Not yet."

"It scares me. There's a big change coming."

"How do you know?"

"I shouldn't talk about it."

She slipped between the sheets and lay on her back, her slim arms behind her head. I climbed in beside her, a discreet few inches between us.

"It's not going to be much of a wedding night," I said; and we laughed together like children at the absurdity of our situation.

"You know something, William," she said, "I like being with you. I don't think I ever really felt comfortable with men before. What I mean is, I've always kept my distance."

"Like you are now."

"That's nothing." She shifted over to my side of the bed and put her arms around me, her head against my shoulder. "I mean the distances inside."

"That's because we're going through the same thing together."

"And it's because there are rules. I mean, take now. Isn't

everything made so much easier for both of us because we know where we are, we know what we can do and what we can't do?"

"I wish we could, though, Aurora."

"No you don't. If this night was open-ended, right now you'd be all knotted up inside, working out how to seduce me, and worrying about failing. Just feel yourself." She prodded my stomach. "No knots."

I turned out the bedside lamp, but for a while neither of us went to sleep. Each time the lightning flickered Aurora pressed closer against me.

"I never had a brother," she whispered to me. "You can be my brother."

"I can't be your husband and your brother, Aurora."

"Yes you can. And my father and my lover."

She fell asleep before I did, and in her sleep turned many times, as if unable to find a position of rest. I watched her in the faint light. Her face in sleep was undefended, lips parted, brow furrowed by some dream. She was right. I was glad that there were rules. The laces of her nightdress were fastened in an uneven bow about her slender neck; a gentle tug would loose the knot and permit me to fold back the upper panels of white cotton, for I longed to see her breasts. But I did not; and because there were rules, had no need to accuse myself of lack of courage.

She slept curled away from me, but once, restlessly reaching out a bare arm, she let her hand fall against my shoulder, where her head had pressed. I was careful not to move, wanting to retain the contact; and when I could hear the slow breathing of deep sleep I unbuttoned my pajama jacket and slipped it over my right shoulder. With a succession of delicate tugs I managed to ease the material under her hand without dislodging it; and so lay still at last with her warm hand resting on my bare skin.

So long as this night touch endured I did not sleep. The point of skin contact between us grew hotter and hotter, until it itched like a bruise. When at last she moved again in her sleep, and the hand was withdrawn, I could not touch my right shoulder or lie on it, it was so tender.

143

14

Sunday morning in the Dower House brought nothing more lively than breakfast and the Sunday papers. The green world outside dripped and glistened after the night's storm. Virginia too looked fresher, dressed in a skirt and a loose bright blouse, quadrants of white, pink and blue appliquéd in one panel with sailing ships. She also wore the baggy leather boots that had just come into fashion.

I struggled with the unwieldy sheets of the *Sunday Telegraph*, taking in very little of what I read. The only entertainment of the morning came from the colonel, who punctuated the silence with snorts of disapproval as he quarried scandals in the *News of the World*.

"Teacher gives lessons in love. Of course discipline is out of date, I know that. But look what happens."

He wore a pair of black-rimmed glasses, which lent to his indignant remarks an almost legal authority. He looked for no response. Speech erupted spontaneously, when the pressure of his astonishment was great enough to force an outlet.

"Ashamed to be a virgin," he read. "Counsel for John Malecki, forty-three, said in court that Maria Williams, eighteen, had asked him to make love to her because she was ashamed to be a virgin!"

Lunch took place at the long dining table, but today, perhaps to distinguish it from dinner, the table was covered by a laundered white cloth, as if it were an altar. Sundays followed a ritual pattern, whether there were guests or not. "The papers" was followed by "the family lunch," which in turn was followed by "the classical hour." This last was a cultural siesta: the fact of sleep concealed and its onset aided by music from the massive rosewood-veneer radio-phonograph in the drawing room.

Between the family lunch and the classical hour there intruded the necessary business of clearing the table and washing the dishes. I did as all guests do on such occasions, and took charge of the dish towel. Colonel Bancroft made the coffee: "That's my Sunday task. I make the coffee." Mrs. Richardson gained possession of the downstairs bathroom. Aurora and Virginia were left in brief command of the dining room, ostensibly clearing away.

Coffee was served in the drawing room. To my great relief I learned that we three "young ones" would not be sharing the classical hour, but would be taking advantage of the sunny weather to play a game of croquet. I had begun to wonder at what point our English country weekend was going to develop into something a little less predictable.

We left for our game when Mrs. Richardson had emerged from her seclusion, and was once more immobilized in an armchair. In order to make sense of what then followed, I must now give a description of the layout of these two rooms, the drawing room and the dining room, and of the position of the furniture in them.

The drawing room of the Dower House, with its large square bay window, stands to the right of the hall as entered from the front door. The elegant Adam fireplace is set into the wall facing the hall door, and around the fireplace stand two wing chairs, a high-backed Knole sofa, and a grandmother chair. To the left, and therefore deeper into the house, is the dining room. Many years ago the dividing wall was taken down to create a large space for dancing, and replaced by folding screens. These screens have for so long been folded back that the hinges are now corroded into place. With modern central heating there is no need to close the screens when dining, and open they allow a pleasant vista from either room.

The dining room is dominated by the long walnut table. Beyond it, looking from the drawing room, is a tall mahogany sideboard and glass fronted cabinet, containing a display of Crown Derby and the set of Richard glasses. To the right a window looks onto the croquet lawn; to the left a door back into the hall, which, by now a dark passage because of the encroachment of the stairs, runs the length of both rooms into the kitchen beyond.

On that Sunday afternoon, as Virginia and Aurora and I left the drawing room, Colonel Bancroft was sitting in one of the armchairs which had its back to the dining room; Mrs. Bancroft occupied the sofa, facing the fireplace, with the dining room to her left; and Mrs. Richardson was in her usual place, the high-seated armchair to the right of the fireplace, commanding a clear view of the space beyond the folded screens; except that her old head was already bowed in sleep.

Once we were safely in the hall, and the drawing-room door shut behind us, Aurora said to me:

"This is where I leave you, William. Virginia knows what to do."

She touched one finger to my lips, either as a parting gesture or to warn me to keep silent, and went out through the front door. I turned to Virginia for instructions, and found that she was staring at me. The indolent manner was gone; her cheeks were flushed, and she was breathing rapidly through parted lips. She hugged her arms around herself, shivering, trying to control the shivering.

"So what now?" I whispered.

For a moment she did not answer. Her stare frightened me, I did not understand it. She seemed to be intent on the space I occupied, but not on me. I had seen such an expression before, but could not remember where. Then she smiled, a smile both

146

mocking and inviting, and I remembered: this was the universal expression of the models in pornographic photographs, the "fuck-me face," intimate but nonpersonal.

"You know what you're here for," she said.

Through the drawing-room door we could hear Colonel Bancroft choosing a record for the classical hour. "The Pastoral. Let's have the good old Pastoral." His precise voice pierced the paneling. "In honor of last night's storm."

The music began. Virginia looked away from me down the dark passageway that ran beside the stairs. She stooped to draw off her boots, indicating to me to remove my shoes. I followed her over the flagged floor toward the kitchen. By the dining-room door she paused, eased it ajar to check that the family was safely settled. It was then, through the chink of the door, that I saw how the dining room had been prepared.

I plucked at Virginia's arm. I formed the words: *it won't work.* I meant as much as anything else the sexual mechanics. Anxiety is hard on (soft on) erections. She made no attempt to convince me that the wild scheme was workable, or the risks worth taking. Turning her head toward me, she shook aside her blonde curls and set her pretty red lips in her parody smile. She even poked out her tongue, and ran it slowly over her lower lip. There was no attempt to disguise the manipulation. Her expression said: just so long as you dance, what do I care if you see the strings? So she stared, and smiled, and waited, very much as if she had set a match to me and knew that shortly the smolder would burst into flame.

I looked back through the crack into the dining room. The dining table at the Dower House is by way of being a family heirloom. Made around 1770 in the Chippendale style, probably by one of the pupils of the master cabinetmaker, it is an unusually large size for its design. The legs, a modified cabriole, are positioned at the extreme corners as in the far smaller card tables of the period, and sustain the table's full length without crosspieces, stretchers, or braces. It is therefore possible as it is with almost no other design of dining table before or since in the history of English furniture for two people to lie side by side beneath it.

147

The linen tablecloth had been drawn down on one side to touch the floor, in such a way that it screened the under-area of the table from the drawing room. There between the legs waiting for us lay a line of seat cushions and pillows, forming a makeshift bed.

As the first shock passed I began to see evidence of forethought in the plan. The crossing to the table could be made without coming into view from the drawing room, because the table had been moved a crucial two feet or so nearer to the door. Once beneath it, the cloth would hide us, and the music would cover our cushioned noises. It was unthinkable, but there was no doubt that it was possible.

We were standing close together by the dining-room door, both very still. Without warning, Virginia's hand pushed between my thighs, making me jump. I locked my body rigid in fear of noise. Her fingers stroked up over my crotch and down again, several times, feeling for the shape beneath in a way that was more possessive than seductive. My penis stirred. The flesh was willing even if the spirit was weak.

Colonel Bancroft spoke from the drawing room. "Hard to believe he was deaf, eh?" And reading from the record sleeve: "This is called 'Awakening of happy feelings on arriving in the country.'"

My eyes met Virginia's: and thus, her hand clasped over my crotch, I entered into her conspiracy. Like a sail boat I caught the wind and began to race: the wind of her emotion, a manic willfulness, as contagious as laughter. My heart beat fast, and a high color burned in my cheeks. *Okay,* I said, mouthing the syllables without sound. She leaned her face close to mine, so that I expected a kiss, and licked my mouth with the tip of her tongue. I was suddenly aware of her as smell, as taste. As if to seal our curious pact she unbuttoned her bright blouse and cupped my hand to one breast. Her breasts were small, as pink and round as her cheeks. *Let's go,* she said; and dropped softly to the floor.

I waited by the door, my heartbeat louder in my ears than the Royal Philharmonic Orchestra. The cushions hissed and rustled as Virginia crawled under the table. Rigid on my hands and

148

knees I followed. Once safe behind the hanging cloth we lay motionless, pressed together, feeling each other trembling. The family in the drawing room dozed on, apparently unaware of our arrival in their midst.

Although our situation was ridiculous, even perilous if social embarrassments can be called perils, and although our movements were inhibited by the groanings of the cushions and the nearness of the hanging linen cloth, the little chamber beneath the Chippendale table was unexpectedly snug. Small enclosed spaces often give the illusion of security, an image of the womb perhaps, sustained through life by the nightly experience of bed, that hot burrow which we must believe to be a fortress if only because there we permit sleep. I now discovered in myself, together with nervous tension, sexual excitement and the impulse to laugh, the conviction of physical safety. Cuddled up to Virginia I was both aroused and soothed, as if, within my dream nursery, she were an erotic teddy bear.

We did not stir until the first movement of the symphony had ended. In the course of the serene Andante that begins the second movement, Virginia rolled a little apart from me and raised herself on one elbow as far as our wooden ceiling permitted. With her free hand she reached for the hem of her skirt. This skirt buttoned down the front; I had assumed the buttons were dummies, a design accessory. I learned they were fully functional as, one by one, she unfastened them from the hem. Beneath the skirt she wore nothing.

This disclosure was not carried out provocatively; or indeed with any reference to me at all. Her hands worked hurriedly, trembling. As soon as the skirt was fully unbuttoned she lay back and closed her eyes, adjusted herself for greater comfort on the cushions, and began to masturbate.

For a few moments, irrelevant, disconcerted, I watched the slow rotations of her finger in the curly blonde bush. Circumstances hardly permitted me to complain; or to demand, as I had demanded before, to know what I was supposed to be doing. I was reduced to acting if not spontaneously at least receptively. The glow of Virginia's slightly parted thighs, tanned and shapely; the disarray of the coarse wool skirt, rucked up over her

149

hips; the steady rocking of her lower body in the rhythms of her self-gratification; awoke in me fellow feelings. Elbowing movements began to take place in my underpants, as my penis pushed at obstructing folds of trouser. It was bolder than I, who did not dare unzip it from its straitjacket.

Virginia's unbuttoned blouse fell away from her breasts as she masturbated. For a while I lay still watching her in the shadowy light. It seemed she had forgotten about me altogether. Slowly the scene began to appear to me to be unreal, or at least, outside all understood codes of behavior: we were in a dream, in a movie, and the Beethoven symphony was the soundtrack which promised the audience emotional adventure.

I lifted my head to Virginia's breasts and touched one nipple with my lips. She gave no sign that she had noticed. Her body rocked steadily beside me, her breath fell warm on my cheek. More boldly I took the nipple into my mouth and suckled it, feeling with my lips the goose pimples all around its base; and then, allowing to swell in me a kind of greed, I mouthed all over her breast, and down into the valley between, and up to the other nipple, feeding on her sweet pink body.

When I came to rest I found that she was no longer in motion. I looked up. She was gazing at me, with that same provocative smile on her face. She made a kissing mouth, pouting out her lips, like a schoolgirl experimenting with basic techniques of allurement. Her eyes were shivery with trapped laughter, flickering over me, transmitting to me her suppressed hysteria. I kissed her. She sucked my lower lip into her mouth as we kissed and bit it, not hard, but I almost cried out.

The second movement of the symphony was by now drawing to its close with the well-known trill on the solo flute. Sleepy words drifted from the colonel in his near armchair: "There she blows. Good old nightingale. Cuckoo coming up."

I froze, held my breath. Virginia, as if reminded by her father of the business in hand, began to forage at my fly. Her fingers made no attempt to work out the lie of the button at the top of my trousers. With one impatient tug she snapped it off, and drew down the zipper. Terrified by the noise this made, I drew back from her in order to be able to see her face, and found that once again her expression had changed. Her eyes were now tight shut, her lips clenched: she had gone far away, forgotten me once more. The grasping fingers hunted of their own accord, found my penis, and squeezed it like pastry, working it firm. When it was stiff she smacked it about in what might have been an attempt to masturbate me, except that it was too sporadic. My penis showed masochistic tendencies, throbbing and tingling beneath the blows.

I do not know why it took so long to dawn on me what was going on; unless it was the simple fact that the role I was playing is in our society traditionally reserved for, one might say consecrated to, women: the role of the sexual accessory. About halfway through the session, shortly after the start of the symphony's third movement, "The Peasants Merrymaking," I awoke to the fact that this scene had not been staged for my benefit at all, but for Virginia's. It was not I but she who was sexually excited by filial ingratitude. My function was purely servile: I was the available penis. The rest of me, the not-penis, was irrelevant. The best that could be said for me was that I was the back-up team, the penis's owner and trainer.

As I have described, the senior members of the household were twelve or fifteen feet away from our curtain. This was the geographic fact. The psychographic fact was that they were very much nearer; under the table with us; staring bulge-eyed at our genitals.

It was an exorcism. Virginia was exorcising herself of her parents. The fact that her parents knew nothing of it was immaterial. They existed independently within her in the form of the fears and the hurts they had fostered. Prejudices which to me were archaic and ludicrous, such as that men prefer to marry virgins, or that women must marry or fail, possessed a vital and rooted existence for Virginia; for once, not so many years ago, this sophisticated woman had been a bewildered child, and the aging bores in the drawing room had been giants from whose faraway heads had descended reports on the nature of the world: warnings, wisdom, truth. Our mutual exertions beneath the dining room table take on in memory a softer tint, a film of poignancy, because we the aggressors, the exposers, the revolutionaries, were also the victims.

As for me, I was happy to wag my cock at the Bancroft family

151

Sunday, as a symbolic assertion of my right to pleasure. It was actually Virginia who did the cock-wagging; for although she could flaunt her cunt (I return to the power word where it is used aggressively) a cunt lacks the combative angry attack of a cock. A cunt can be bared, can be revealed, can be made accessible, all passive verbs. It cannot strike. For she was not masturbating me at all: she was brandishing my penis as one might brandish a sword.

The brisk Scherzo was now in full swing. Virginia began to make noises, little throaty grunts. Her hand pulled at my penis, indicating in the most direct way what she wanted. She parted her legs as far as she was able, and offered up her pelvis with impatient jerks, in the manner of a fledgling bird who reaches and gapes for the worm the parent bird lowers into its beak. Cautiously I shifted my torso, fearful of jolting a table leg, and felt my head strike dully on the table's walnut-wood underside. Even before I was within range she was pushing and fishing at my penis, cross that it should not find its way at once. The sensitive tip grew overexcited at this attention, and just in time was released to a more subtle and yielding pressure. Both of us ceased our movements, as if a sudden and welcome silence had fallen. So aroused was Virginia by our circumstances that my penis slid into her without hindrance, and so lay within, basking in unctuous warmth.

I felt her expel a long satisfied breath, which matched my own sense of patient pleasure, my instinct in this situation for cautious copulation. So it came as an uncomfortable surprise when Virginia's face suddenly contorted as if she were in pain and she began to ram her body upward, and grind her pelvis around and around on me, as if I were an overhead beam. I locked hard, held my position, not wanting to be tumbled out from under the table into the drawing room. Then just as I was beginning to appreciate the hungry way she was consuming my cock, she gave out another long sigh and sank back. From the phonograph, over the slumbering heads of our unsuspecting witnesses, came the low hastening violin chords, the intimations of the approaching storm.

All of this left me and my penis temporarily stranded. I could feel it twitching ominously in its hideaway, threatening (in Jilly's pan-of-milk metaphor) an irresistible overflow of willful foam. But Virginia's attentions to me lacked follow-through. She showed no interest in any needs I might have. This cool breeze of neglect made my cock thoughtful. I continued to hold myself dutifully above her, supported by my elbows, as grave and as sturdy as a laborer leaning on a gate; until Virginia abruptly opened her eyes, stared blank at me, and said; "More." Her expression was so wild that I began at once to move as she instructed, afraid that if I did not she would cry out her demands.

Only then, looking down on her plump breasts, on her entranced faraway face, did I allow myself to see her as she presented herself: as pornography, as an icon of lust. It is a fine act of social indecency to fuck the daughter of the house in which you are a guest: no extenuating circumstances, no love, no liking even; only this furtive and fantastic urge to lay her down, and part her legs, and pierce her sweet heart. The fourth movement's musical storm was building fast, and with it scudded my own livid piling clouds, an uncharacteristic coarseness, a depravity, which with each panting thrust clotted the air more thickly about the snoring Bancrofts. Watch me, cried the dark boy within me, watch me! Am I not wicked? Are you not afraid?

The combination of sex and circumstance overwhelmed me on the third drum-roll. The crescendo had carried me on its rising wave, but the climax like so many of Beethoven's climaxes was multiple. Virginia, perhaps more musically sensitive than I, shuddered violently with the final drum-roll, and shook my shrinking penis with her interior spasms. I laid myself down at last, and let my head fall exhausted over her shoulder, cushioned by her curly golden hair.

The clarinet and the oboe and the strings sang that the tumult was over. Our hearts bounded the one beneath the other, and our lips slowly curved into the same dreamy smile, the outward sign of a satisfaction which reached up from our genitals to flutter over the drawing room like a conqueror's flag. Had Colonel Bancroft been awake, and so inclined, he might have informed his wife and his wife's mother from the record sleeve that this concluding part of the symphony is called by its composer, "Happy and thankful feelings after the storm."

＊

In this way was I introduced to the insight of the fourth level, which may be simply stated: the context within which a sexual act takes place is a part of the sexual act itself.

Under the Chippendale table in the Dower House the full force of this insight was orchestrated for Virginia; but it ricocheted also onto me. The extreme manipulation of a sexual context, of which I was here a part, becomes necessary once it is understood that the most potent sexual context lies in the mind.

The erotic potential of place is now widely appreciated. Every couple who make love on the kitchen floor, who find sex among the saucepans sharper-edged, more specifically sexual, than it has been in the overtolerant bed, are acknowledging in an elementary form the power of the sexual context. But in Virginia's case it was not the physical location of our bed beneath the table that did the work; it was the nearness of the Bancroft parents. Their real presence, the hissing of their breath, the creaking of their chairs, gave her access to a rich store of resentment which could be converted into fuel for the sexual act.

Thus the levels advance, like space voyagers colonizing a barren galaxy. At the first level, the student is shown the body's capabilities for sexual delight; at the second level, he is taught to give himself permission to accept that delight; at the third level, his powers are focused onto the sexual present moment; and at the fourth level, he is taught to utilize within that moment not only the sexual drive but all other concurrent drives, no matter by what they are generated. The process is one of inclusion. Little by little, the scattered personality is being drawn together.

"If you understand the lesson of the fourth level," Arlette says, "you will know that the more neurotic you are, the better." This is because the fourth level is psychologically pragmatic. It does not offer the unlikely and failure-prone promise of the self-improvers: "You too can be free." It recognizes that the fears and the insecurities experienced by most adults are the product of deep breeding, and cannot be rooted out. It teaches instead that they can be harnessed. Neurosis, obsession, irrational fear, all generate their own energy, which is then consumed in muscle

154

tension, nail-biting, restlessness, insomnia. With the right preparation, these tensions can be channeled into the energy stream of sex. All that it takes is an accurate perception of the source of the tension and its juxtaposition with the sex act. It may seem unnecessary, and psychologically unsophisticated, to insist on the actual sex act rather than a sex awareness; and on the physical presence of the power source rather than an intellectual knowledge of it. But this element of actuality is what makes it work. Virginia could have talked to an analyst about her resentment of her parents without coming near the fierce aggression unlocked in her by their actual proximity. Moreover, the object of the exercise is not fewer personality problems, but better sex.

°

The outside world into which Virginia and I crept that afternoon was blinding in its brilliance. I was giddy with relief. Virginia stretched out her arms and began to spin slowly around, laughing to herself. "Gordon *Bennett!*" she cried, "Oh Gordon *Bennett!.*"

Distinctive clicks came from the croquet lawn. There in and out of the sharp shadows of the beech trees moved Aurora in her loose white dress, pursuing the wooden balls. She said nothing as I approached, but grinned and pushed her sunglasses up over her brow.

"Oh Aurora," I said, sinking onto the warm lawn.

"How did it go, William?"

"Why didn't you warn me?"

"Did you do your duty?"

"I feel terrible. I'm still shaking."

I rolled onto my back and spread myself out in the sun. She stood by me, swinging her mallet. "I knew you could do it, William."

"Then you knew more than I knew." From where I lay I could see up her skirt. "It wasn't for me, though, was it? It was for Virginia."

"Did she get what she wanted?"

"She practically went off her head."

Aurora looked across the lawn to where Virginia was still pirouetting. "Then yea for Virginia."

"You sound jealous."

155

"It has to beat croquet."

"What if they'd heard us! That complacent little colonel . . . I can see all the way up your legs." It pleased me to think of Aurora standing here with her croquet mallet gazing at the dining-room window. "Were you really jealous?"

She drew her skirt in and settled gracefully cross-legged beside me. "Don't tease, William."

"Me tease? You're the prickteaser."

"Why? Because you're the one with the prick?"

Virginia spun toward us, laughing and panting. "Gordon Bennett!" she exclaimed again. "That was almost as exciting as running away from the convent." She slumped onto the grass. "Did I cry out? Did I shout? Inside my head I was yelling."

Our escapade had produced an unexpected effect on Virginia. She was no longer the listless slouching beauty she had been for most of the weekend; nor was she manic, as she had been under the table. The years had dropped away from her, and she had become a pretty little girl who hugged her knees in excitement at her own naughtiness.

"So William didn't let you down?" said Aurora.

"No, no, he was perfect. I don't even remember him being there."

"I was there all right."

"I can't remember when I last felt so perky," said Virginia, rocking back and forth, fascinated by the novelty of her feelings. "I could eat a horse. I know what! I'll get the tea. If I go right now I can have it ready for the monsters when they wake up. They'll think I've caught a touch of the sun. Repellent though my mother is, she does know how to make a pot of tea, which is more than most people know. Oh God, I'm going to turn into her, aren't I? I can't bear it. Except she can't always have been so ghastly, or Richard and I would never have turned up. Just think of it! I'm the living proof that those two had sex together, once upon a time. Ooh! It makes my flesh creep." She began to sing to herself as she rocked: "I'm a little teapot, short and stout, Here's my handle, here's my spout. When the kettle's boiling hear me shout. Pick me up and pour me out."

She rose and left us to fulfill her self-appointed task.

"I like her a lot better this way," I said.

"Strong medicine, though," said Aurora.

"You mean sex?"

"Yes, sex. Do not exceed the prescribed dose."

"Keep out of the reach of children."

She patted me with one hand, then began to stroke my forehead, also running her fingers through my hair. "I feel quite proud of you," she said.

"What about you and me, Aurora? When is it our turn?"

"That's not for me to say."

"But will it come?"

"I don't know. It might."

"I hope it does. Do you hope it does?"

"What do you think?"

"I think you do."

"I'm getting very fond of you, William. I hope that doesn't complicate things."

°

Like Virginia, I found it hard to imagine the sex life of the Bancroft parents; but later that day, before Aurora and I departed, I stumbled upon a small clue that some efforts were still being made by them in that direction. During a visit to the upstairs bathroom I chose to read an issue of the *Reader's Digest,* some months out of date, which lay among the magazines there. Glancing down the list of contents on the cover I noticed an article on the S.S. *France,* one of Colonel Bancroft's conversational topics at dinner the previous evening. Skipping through it, I found all the facts he had cited, the two hundred cooks, the hospital, the padded cells. A few pages further on I came across the account of the man who had died for twenty-three minutes. It was as if I had the colonel's mind laid out before me. And there too, as I flicked the little pages, was a piece headlined "Your Sex Life Could Go Up In Smoke." "The nicotine intake," it revealed, "constricts the blood vessels, the swelling of which is the central mechanism of sexual excitement and erection." Several times Colonel Bancroft had said to me, as unaware as I of the source of his image, "I'd give my right leg for a smoke."

°

The sexual context: not only the environment in which sex occurs, but the interplay of energies. It is my experience that

157

places, particularly houses, respond to the spirit of their human occupants. The relaxed generosity of a happy family somehow impregnates the soft furnishings, so that the chairs are more tangibly receptive, while in an unhappy household even the toilet seat keeps its distance. One day biophysicists will reveal to us the truth of it, that the energy that binds, that forms all atomic structures is responsive to the energy generated by human emotions; or some much mystery. At such a time perhaps it will also be understood how sexual energy affects and is affected by the "atmosphere" within which it is created. For just as the context can modify the sex, which is the lesson of the fourth level, so the sex can modify the context. Perhaps at a particular narrow wavelength a house is tuned to the sexual harmony or disharmony of its inhabitants. If this is ever shown to be so, it will confirm a private fancy of mine: that the uncomfortable feeling I had experienced on first entering the Dower House, which I described loosely as a "bad smell," was in fact a ghost, a ghost that in its dismal fashion haunts many a house, the ghost of dead sex.

15

From the fourth level Arlette's training becomes very much cheaper. This is because professional sex partners cease to be necessary, and students may partner each other. The concept of payment for service remains, but the currency switches from cash to kind. I did not know when I kissed Virginia Bancroft goodbye on the up platform at Kemble station that I would shortly be seeing her again; but a moment's thought would have told me that our dealings were only half completed, and that my turn was still to come.

Aurora and I returned to London; I to Abinger Road, she to the Park Lane Hilton, where she was obliged to wait out a further five nights before her charter flight back to Los Angeles.

I entered the Rosenthal house feeling pleased with myself and pleased enough with the world, but this mood did not last. The house was empty. Up in my attic a note from Louise lay on the bed: "Jeannie's Donald rang, wants you to call back, important. Daytime number. No danger J. will answer. Back 7ish." There was a phone number.

I read the note several times, frowning. I could think of no important reason why Donald should need to see me. This did not stop some possibilities forming in my mind unbidden: Jeannie was ill; Jeannie wanted me back; Jeannie had become tired of Donald. But none of these scenarios called for a meeting between Donald and myself.

The note annoyed me. I did not like the possessive linking of the names: Jeannie's Donald. That was insensitive of Louise. I knew no other Donald.

When she returned with the boys half an hour or so later she asked me if I had seen her note, and I said yes, what was it all about? "How should I know?" she said. "Ring him in the morning and check it out." I paced slowly up and down the long living room while the boys watched the murmuring television and tried to explain why I thought this was not necessary.

"I've been going through a lot of changes, Louise. A few months ago a message like that would have thrown me. But I've been changing. I don't say I'm a different person, but I see a lot of things differently now. For a start, I feel comfortable with myself. I feel good about myself. I can be glad that Jeannie is happy with this Donald, for the simple reason that I'm happy with myself. I don't see what's to be gained by a meeting. In fact, it strikes me as a step backwards. We're all in a different space now. It's not that I have anything against this Donald. The fact is I feel very comfortable about everything right now. What I'm trying to say is that I think it would be self-indulgent, even sentimental. Donald is not part of my present moment."

"He would be if you met him."

"But to achieve what? To satisfy my curiosity? To let him satisfy his? Isn't that just a bit sick?"

"He says there's an important reason. I don't see what you're making so much fuss about, William. If it would hurt you to see him, don't see him."

"That's just it. I'm not making a fuss. I'm objecting to a fuss being made."

"Then why not just see him? It can't do much harm."

I looked at her suspiciously. She was sewing up Tom's torn dungarees. "Why are you so keen for me to see him, Louise?"

"I'm not. If it bothers you to see him, don't see him."

"It doesn't bother me in the slightest. Haven't you listened to anything I've said? I just don't see what's to be gained by it."

Louise put the dungarees to her lips and bit off the cotton thread. Then she lifted her calm brown eyes to mine and looked steadily at me until I blushed. "How was your weekend?" She said.

"Fuck you too," I replied.

°

I did not ring Donald the next morning. Instead I rang Aurora at the Hilton and asked her if she was free for lunch. "What do you have in mind?" I said I thought we might get drunk. "Okay. Pick me up here in an hour."

We did our drinking on the hotel premises. Below street level there is a gloomy bar called Trader Vic's, furnished in bamboo to resemble a South Sea island at twilight. Here we huddled in a corner and drank gin slings on empty stomachs, until I became more pleased with myself and the world.

I told Aurora about Donald's message. "He's got nerve," I said. "I give him credit for that." "Don't you kind of wonder what he's like?" said Aurora. "No, I kind of don't." But she pointed a finger at me, and looked down it in an accusing manner, so I said: "All right, maybe I do from time to time wonder what he's like."

We ordered two dishes of spare ribs, and spent much time licking our fingertips. Aurora wanted to know if I was jealous of Donald, and I said not in the slightest, followed by yes of course. "Are you ashamed at feeling jealous?" "I am rather. It seems so feeble. I mean, if she doesn't want me, what do I care who she sees? She's not a nun." "You shouldn't try to stop yourself feeling jealous. Jealousy can be very useful if you know how to use it." "Useful for what?" "For sex, of course." Her wide mouth grinned at me over her gin sling. "Oh Aurora," I said, "If I had you I could laugh at all the Jeannies and the Donalds." "You have got me, darling. Here I am." She put down her glass and took my hand. "You know what I mean, I mean all the way. If I had you all the way. Body and soul." "And what would I get?" "You would get my body and soul. Fair exchange."

161

We looked tenderly and drunkenly into each other's eyes, happy to be close and happy to be unfree. "Maybe at the seventh level, darling," she said, kissing my barbecue-flavored fingers. "If we both get there," I said, but not even in my inebriation believing it, because I knew she was too beautiful for me.

°

In the course of this meeting I agreed to go with Aurora to a show on her last night in London. Her choice disappointed me, but I concealed this, and assured her that I had not seen the show before, despite the fact that it was already into its third year at the Palace Theater. It was *Jesus Christ Superstar*.

In the taxi on the way to the theater she told me she had reserved a box, which also surprised me, since the view from a box is usually poor. It did not occur to me that there might be more to the evening than was listed on the program; not until I entered Box G and there saw Virginia Bancroft, waiting for us.

She was dressed all in black: a black halter-neck top, straight black cord trousers, and shiny high-heeled black shoes. Over her shoulders was draped a leather blouson jacket, also black. By contrast her dimpled face and bare arms looked soft and pink enough to eat.

"Hello William," she said. "Surprise surprise."

She posed for me on the upright plush chair: legs elegantly crossed, one bare elbow on the padded balustrade, golden curls falling coquettishly to one side.

"Virginia!" I said stupidly. "What are you doing here?"

"I'm being sexy," she said.

I turned to Aurora, who was watching me with amusement. "Aurora, what's going on?"

"Virginia and I have arranged a little extra entertainment for you, William. Tonight the show is all for you."

"It's going to be the best fun," said Virginia, and with an exaggerated gesture, threw her arms about my neck in order to kiss me. The cotton of her garment was so thin I could feel her nipples underneath. "I've always wanted to be a vamp," she said, twining her fingers in my hair, "only these days it's so vulgar to look as if you're trying."

162

As she released me I felt Aurora's arm slip protectively around my waist. "No need to look so miserable, William. It's all going to be quite all right."

"But it's not private in here." The audience in the steeply banked Balcony above the Upper Circle had a clear view into our box. "I get very easily embarrassed in public."

"Me too," said Virginia, patting her stomach. "You should feel the butterflies charging about in here."

I looked down at the uncurtained stage, laid out below us like an illuminated chessboard.

"So what am I supposed to do?"

"Nothing," said Aurora.

"Aurora's in charge," said Virginia, "but only I can touch you. Aurora's not allowed to touch you."

I turned to Aurora for confirmation of this, and she made a face.

"I'm the guide, remember?" "But why in a theater?" I asked still feeling that I had missed some item of essential information. "Why *Jesus Christ Superstar?*" "You'll see," said Aurora. "This is the fourth level in action."

When the lights went down I found to my great relief that our box was plunged into total darkness. Through the diamond pane of glass in the door the corridor light glowed, but it was very dim. We sat in a row on the red plush chairs, Aurora on my right and Virginia on my left. The orchestra began to play. Virginia shuffled her chair closer to mine and laid one hand on my thigh. I was not sure whether to pay attention to the show or not. Aurora was watching the stage with apparent interest. Virginia's hand moved lightly but aimlessly up and down my left thigh, showing no signs of venturing further. I permitted my eyes to follow the drama below.

Jesus made his entry with dramatic mystery, through a bank of smoke: an agreeable-looking man with a Jesus beard and a Jesus dress and no shoes, but too short to be divine. Mary Magdalene sang him a song telling him that everything was all right, which it was not, and Jesus sang that they would be sorry when he was gone, which they would. I found myself feeling a certain sympathy for him. Meanwhile Virginia extended her ministry, stroking

163

various accessible parts of my body, concentrating especially on the left side of my neck and my left ear. When her fingers played over the area just behind my ear shivers ran down my flank. Aurora leaned close and whispered, "Don't fight it."

The music was very loud, and the theater was very warm. Little by little the peculiar combination of circumstances became familiar to me, and I found myself enjoying Virginia's attentions. She was not skilled in her touch, as for example Jilly Andrews had been, but through her prying fingers I could feel her excitement, and was aroused by it. As in our former engagement, it was not I who excited her, but the role she was called upon to play. She remained self-absorbed, like a little girl who has been given a nurse's uniform, and in love with herself as a sister of mercy bandages all the family pets. Her role required that she arouse me, and so she was careful to note which caresses had the proper effect, repeating them with many experimental variations. Suspicious as I was, never ceasing to wonder where all this was leading, I allowed myself, at least provisionally, to be seduced.

When the lights came up for the intermission Virginia gazed meltingly into my face as into a mirror and said, "How am I doing?"

"Very nicely, thank you."

"I'm not supposed to be too sexy yet. Just sexy-ish."

"How do you like the show?" asked Aurora.

"I rather like it. Though a lot of that may be Virginia."

"What do you think of the actor playing Jesus?"

"He's doing all right.'

She handed me a program. "Have a look and see who he is."

I read the cast list. Jesus Christ: Donald Cumnor.

"He's a friend of your wife," said Aurora.

My stomach went cold. I stared at the name on the program. "Donald?"

"That's why we're all here."

"Are you sure?"

"Of course I'm sure."

I did not ask how she had found out. The shabby red theater, to which all through the first half I had been good-humoredly indifferent, became suddenly oppressive. I felt claustrophobic, wanted to leave. What's to be gained from this?, I thought. Nothing can be gained from it. Yet this sick fright was itself an indication that the scene had been well chosen for the purposes of the fourth level.

"What am I supposed to do about it?"

"Nothing," said Aurora." "Just put yourself in our hands."

"My hands," said Virginia.

Thus the second half was for me a very different experience. Jesus, betrayed in the garden of Gethsemane, was also Donald. I became confused between his twin roles, both of which held for me the status of myth. My eyes followed him as he crawled back and forth over the stage, fascinated and repelled by the details of his body. His bare feet in particular possessed a horrid materiality. Because this body had pressed against Jeannie's body, and Jeannie's body had pressed against mine, I felt as if the actor were intolerably close, our limbs entwined, and I shifted about on my chair as if to free myself.

Jealousy has always been characterized as a destructive force, yet it is the keenest point of contact short of sex itself with the bodily reality of other people. Commonly we treat people as we treat other objects around us, as transparencies projected onto the retina, possessed of bulk only in so far as they obstruct our movements. Jealousy is the flash of searing imagination that incarnates the world beyond the double bed. In the intimacy of sex we extend our body-sense to encompass this one other beloved body, and so render it real, personal, private as our own. The terror of jealousy lies in the invasion of this personality, the betrayal of this privacy. The alien hand that caresses your beloved's breast strikes your own breast also; the alien mouth that kisses your beloved's lips sucks horribly also on your own mouth. Thereafter that hand, that mouth, bulges with a carnal substantiality not given but seized.

When we choose to daydream about sexual encounters between people other than ourselves, we do not cast our imaginings from among those we know well, our family, our friends. They are too pimply with familiarity. So the friends are cockless, decunted. The menagerie of dream genitals that preen and pout about us belong to a dimly specified tribe which dwells in a far-off land. How helpless are we, then, how utterly unprepared, against the rude truths of jealousy.

I had believed I had surrendered Jeannie, my one-time wife; but my body was not so magnanimous. The sight of her Donald made me sick in the stomach.

It so happened that at this point in the show Jesus was purporting to suffer. Mocked and manacled, his oatmeal dressing-gown replaced by a mucky tunic, he writhed on the stage before Pontius Pilate. Aurora, receiving some kind of cue from the events on stage, now alerted Virginia, who slipped to her knees beside me and began to fumble in my lap. As if anticipating objections, Aurora whispered to me, "All you have to do is watch the show." But I had not the spirit to object. The sickness in my stomach made me feel tired and weak.

Virginia's fingers mastered the zipper and discovered my penis cowering among the elasticized cotton. She drew it out into the stuffy air of the theater. Though limp, its tip was sticky, a relic of earlier arousal. I turned to look at her, and in the light bouncing back from the stage saw that she was moistening her lips. Her eyes were closed, and her catlike face was shining, as in a rapture of devotion. A lash of sound from the orchestra drew my attention back to the stage, where Pilate stood snaking the long lead of his microphone across the illuminated squares. Jesus knelt facing us upstage, his head bowed for the punishment.

"Watch him," said Aurora. "Whatever happens, watch him."

She drew her chair close up to mine and pressed against me, so that when she spoke her lips were so near to my ear I could feel the damp of her breath.

"One!" cried Pilate, and whipped his microphone cord. It did not touch Jesus, but the music groaned, and Jesus buckled as if he had been struck, and one of the illuminated squares went red. In the same moment Virginia lowered her head and took the tip of my penis between her wetted lips.

"Two!" cried Pilate.

Aurora's voice whispered in my ear, so close it was like a voice inside my head, "He fucks your wife."

"Three! Four! Five!"

"His cock fucks Jeannie."

Jesus jerked under the blows. He was only acting, but I was pleased by the sight of his pain. The music pounded in time with the lashes, and at each blow another square of stage turned red. Despite my sick feeling, despite the banked white faces in the balcony above, my penis began of its own accord to swell in Virginia's mouth.

"Ten! Eleven! Twelve!"

The more Jesus suffered under his punishment the more my penis rose, until it felt as if there were a channel of force between us, and his weakness was feeding my strength.

"His cock fucks Jeannie," hissed the vicious voice in my head. "His cock fucks her cunt."

Aggression welled up in me, fed by the steady access of sexual power. The beat of the music, the licking of Virginia's tongue, Donald's spasms of pain, Aurora's secret spiteful words, all bewildered and intoxicated me. I ceased caring who could see us, or what they thought.

"Nineteen! Twenty! Twenty-one!"

Now I moved in time with the whip-cracks, forcing my penis up through Virginia's lips. "You're not to come," whispered Aurora. "You're not to come."

"Twenty-six! Twenty-seven! Twenty-eight!"

"Can you see him fucking her? Can you see how she wants his cock? Can you see how she loves it?"

"Thirty! Thirty-one!"

We were jolted together, Jesus and Donald and I, by the whipping drums. Our cock, Jesus's and Donald's and mine, pulsed with longing and anger in the sucking mouth. "You're not to come yet." But I was locked into my trinity of punishment and would not have heeded the order, except that on the thirty-ninth lash the chastising arm fell still, and the music quieted.

Virginia raised her head, and clasped the moist shaft of my penis with both hands. I hardly noticed the change, lost as I was in my own dark tunnels. Aurora laid her khaki raincoat over my lap. The lights below went out, but for one shaft descending directly downward into the center of the silent stage. Smoke rose up the bright beams, and when the smoke cleared, there hung

Jesus on the cross. The vertical light cast deep shadows into the hollows of his ribcage. A drum began to roll. Virginia's hands moved slowly up and down my straining cock. Aurora whispered in my ear, "Donald fucks Jeannie. Donald fucks Jeannie. Donald fucks Jeannie." I stared at the figure on the cross; he seemed to me to be near enough to touch, or to push away. Between the pulses of lust and revenge I fought back also at Jesus and his crucifixion, gold medalist of merit through pain.

The drums beat louder. An attendant Roman soldier raised a tall spear to the body suspended in the smoke. Virginia's hands moved faster. Aurora pumped her litany into my stunned ear: "Donald fucks Jeannie. Donald fucks Jeannie. Donald fucks Jeannie." The drums climaxed. The spear stabbed. Aurora cried, "Now!" Virginia's hands squeezed. The sperm shot from me into the receptive raincoat.

"It is finished," cried Donald, and died.

"On the button!" said Aurora exultantly.

Jealousy and blasphemy and exhibitionism pumped out of me with the semen; secretions hidden from me until now ejaculated into view. The stage below burst into noise and brightness. Aurora produced paper tissues and mopped up her coat. Virginia crammed my penis back into my pants and drew up the zipper, Donald rose from the dead.

From some place far away I heard Virginia apologizing to me for using her hands at the end: "I just can't stand that stuff in my mouth."

"Leave him be," said Aurora.

Then I felt her take my face in her firm dry grasp and turn it toward her. She kissed me, not hard but lingeringly, as if she wanted to taste on my lips the intensity of my surrender; or perhaps she wished only to reenter my imagination, from which she had been briefly banished.

o

The fourth level concerns itself with the intensity of the sexual experience, but inevitably its impact is felt in the reverse direction, as a primitive form of psychological therapy. Why this should be so is hard to say. No analytic effort is expended in understanding the roots of the fears that are being harnessed; they are merely exposed to view. But this exposition does frequently seem to help, perhaps because part of the fear lies in its very indistinctness.

Aurora revealed to me at the end of our evening at the Palace Theater that the actor who played Jesus Christ, Donald Cumnor, was not in fact Jeannie's Donald at all. Knowing that I had never seen Jeannie's Donald, but that he was an actor, she had studied the casts of all the current West End productions, and so had found a surrogate Donald.

Oddly this information made no difference to what I now felt about Donald. Much of the anger stored in me against him had been drained away by the exorcism in Box G. I was no longer humiliated, for had I not punished him? Had I not triumphed over him? Not the real Donald, nor the Donald on the stage of the Palace Theater, but the Donald in me.

After Aurora's departure, therefore, I called the telephone number Louise had copied down. Our conversation was brief. I agreed to meet him in a pub called the Hollywood, off the Fulham Road, where his play was in rehearsal in an upper room. He said he would be wearing a red check shirt, so that I could identify him.

I cannot pretend that this meeting was easy for me, but I had lost my former rancor. Donald's appearance made it easier: big and clumsy, gingery of face and hair, respectful, almost deferential, toward me. Not once did he suggest that he was afraid of hurting me. Rather he seemed nervously eager that I should like him.

"Jeannie doesn't know I'm seeing you," he said. "She wouldn't approve."

"Why not?"

"She has all this guilt about you."

I shrugged. Donald peered anxiously at me, attempting to gauge my mood. "I think it's her way of holding onto you," he said.

This unexpected remark made it possible for me to like him. As a defensive reaction to his lumberjack bulk I had typed him as amiable but stupid. Now, simply because he revealed to me my surviving status with Jeannie, I could deal with him on equal terms.

"We were together five years," I said.

169

"I know."

He bought the drinks, whiskey for me, Guinness for himself. He had a tab at the bar. We drank each other's health without irony. Then he began to breathe heavily, inflating himself to the point at which he would say what he needed to say.

"Good of you to come."

"I nearly didn't."

"Good of you."

"You said it was important."

"It is. Yes. It is important."

I waited. I was prepared to listen, but not to draw it out of him. I was too busy bracing myself for what I guessed would be a shock.

"The fact is, there's something I want to ask you."

"Yes."

"Jeannie doesn't think it's fair to ask you. I don't think it's fair not to."

"Then you'd better ask me."

"Yes. Since you're here now."

The crucial exchange came and went with the slickness of a vaudeville routine; as if we had both long known what was to be done, and had only to run through the prepared lines.

"Would you let Jeannie have a divorce?"

"You want to marry her?"

"Yes."

"Is she pregnant?"

"Yes."

"Yours or mine?"

"We don't know."

"Okay then."

He closed his ginger-lashed eyes and leaned heavily back against the bar. I wondered why I was so little moved, and guessed that I was experiencing a delayed reaction.

"I can tell Jeannie you'll do whatever has to be done?"

"Yes."

"Thank you. Thank you. I knew it would be all right. Thank you."

He drained his Guinness and asked for another, ordering me a second whiskey at the same time. Then, self-consciously but charmingly, he held out his big hairy fist and we shook hands. There was sweat on his upper lip. I saw all this with a strange detachment, unused to finding myself in the position of power.

"Tell Jeannie I make no claims on the child," I said, speaking a little too clearly.

"Do you want to know?"

"I don't see why."

But then I began to think about it, about how extraordinary it was after all. My immediate response had been to show no reaction at all, as if to do so would be to put myself at a disadvantage. Also I felt an obligation to do the right thing by Jeannie, an obligation more to myself than to her, to demonstrate that I sought no revenge and so was no longer in her power. That achieved, I found myself fascinated by the fact that Jeannie was pregnant. It was not the baby, I had no picture of the baby; it was Jeannie herself, the new light it shed on her as a woman, as a sexual being, as an object of sexual desire.

"You'll let me know when the baby is born?"

"Of course."

"Is Jeannie well?"

"Very well."

"How long will it be?"

"July. If it's on time."

"I don't suppose . . ." But I stopped. It was an unfair request, almost a perverse one. I hardly understood why I wanted it myself.

"What is it?' He was eager to be generous, in return for what he saw as my generosity.

"It's a lot to ask."

"About the baby?"

"Not really. It's more about Jeannie. Under the circumstances it may strike you as, well, masochistic." I stopped again, and met his frank anxious eyes. "I'm ashamed to ask you."

"You want to be there for the birth?"

"How did you know?"

"It's what I'd want."

"It's not important. It just came to me that I would like that. I don't really know why."

"I'll ask Jeannie."

"What about you?"

He considered, thoughtfully and seriously; for which inwardly I thanked him. As I watched his face working away, I blushed to think of the mockery images with which I had overlaid his name. This real Donald impressed me more with each passing minute, for where I was proud and full of fears, he seemed to me to be humble and unafraid.

"I don't think I'd mind," he said slowly. "I might at the time, but I don't think so. The way I see it, I can't have her past even if I want it. I don't want to take that away from her."

"You understand very well," I said.

We drank, once again touching glasses.

"Congratulations, anyway." I meant it.

"Yes. Congratulations."

The Fifth Level

16

Louise and I passed the ferry crossing in the bar, drinking white wine from individual foil-capped bottles, watching the gulls flying in pace with the boat beyond the mud-spattered windows. Only the white chalk of the Needles, retreating with slow dignity into the haze, revealed that we were in motion. Louise chain-smoked duty-free Gitanes.

"Do you miss the boys?' I asked her.

"I should, shouldn't I? When they're there I can't imagine the world without them. But all the way down the highway they fade, you know, and by the time I get to Southampton I can hardly remember their names."

"Out of sight, out of mind."

"Not very maternal, I have to say."

"I think it's natural enough."

"That's because you're a bit that way yourself."

"What way?"

"Out of sight, out of mind."

"I don't think so. I'm always thinking of things that aren't in front of me."

"You mean you're always thinking of yourself."

I looked up, but there was no criticism in her face. She stared out of the mucky window and sighed.

"Don't get me wrong, William. I would too if I could."

The deep throbbing of the engine lulled us over the water to Cherbourg. Joseph was delayed by problems connected with the publication of a book, which had suffered setback after setback. He was to telegraph the time of his arrival to the house in Bretanville, so that he could be met off the Air Aurigny service to the little airport at Gonneville.

We were only to be away a week. I would not have given up more time away from the levels. By this stage I was obsessed by the process of graduation as much as by the sexual liberation. As I look back I do not find this so surprising. All through the long drawn out years of childhood the passing of time is itself a constructive process; nothing is required of you but that you allow time to go by. Today you are seven, tomorrow you will be eight, and that is better. Today you are in the third form, tomorrow you will be in the fourth form, and that is better; merit without tears. But the day comes when the schooling ceases, the grades, the marks, the degrees; the bus stops, you climb out onto a macadam plain, no road or all road, an uncalibrated universe; and for the first time you ask the questions you will never cease to ask from now on: what am I supposed to be doing? Am I doing it all right?

With the levels I returned to school. This is how I now explain my total submission to Arlette's authority. I have observed contemporaries of mine grant the same unearned dominion to other syllabuses which offer them the security of the classroom: scientology, transactional analysis, Zen Buddhism, mind dynamics, transcendental meditation. The rhetoric is for freedom, but the dreams are for structure. Without the formal, perhaps arbitrary structure of the levels I doubt that my first wild impulse would have endured.

What I did not appreciate when I agreed to join the Rosenthals for their week in Normandy was that the levels, far from being an external framework, were carried within me, and not to be put aside for a holiday. It is hardly strange that I should have

176

come upon the fifth level unaided. It already rustled in my pocket like sealed orders, to be opened on receipt of the appropriate coded signal.

From Cherbourg Louise's navy-blue Renault 4 rattled us through Vasteville, Heauville, and Clairefontaine to Bretanville; the scenic route. Approached in this way, from the land side of the Manche peninsula, the tiny port of Bretanville is virtually invisible. The houses fall steeply away from the road to the ocean, as if entrenched against an enemy advancing from the mainland. Approached by sea, from the direction of Aurigny, this defensive posture is even more marked. The tiers of flat gray houses cling tight to the hills, flanked to the left by an abandoned granite quarry and to the right by a worked-out iron mine. The windows are small and the shutters heavy, against the Atlantic storms. Two granite jetties reach out from the high sea wall, enclosing a narrow strip of sand: gray too, this sand, a paler gray, scored grass-green at low tide by the slimeweed on the mooring lines.

All my memories of Bretanville are happy memories: the bleak houses, the wind on the Flamanville cliffs, the spray on the jetty, the tar-stained beach where the rigging of the moored boats rattles so dismally all night; which is a tribute of sorts to Louise.

"Don't say I didn't warn you," she said as the Renault jogged past the old quarry.

"Who's complaining?"

"You haven't seen the house yet."

It was a tall narrow house, one of a granite terrace built on the road out of Bretanville to Les Pieux. Long before the terrace had been completed the iron mine had shut down, and with it the brief prosperity of the town. There were four houses, huddled together against the road, and ours was the fourth. It had no modern conveniences, it offered more or less no privacy, it was dark and noisy, yet from the moment I stepped through its door I felt a physical easement, as if I had passed from cold into warmth. In reality it was no warmer inside than outside, until Louise had lit the butane gas fire; but the house, like Louise herself, practiced the virtue of tolerance.

We stood over the glowing dome of the fire and drank bitter Normandy cider. It was late afternoon.

"I do hope you won't be bored," said Louise. "There isn't really anything to do."

"I'm getting good at not having anything to do."

The kitchen in which we stood was a big square room occupying the entire ground floor. Its ceiling was stained chrome yellow by wood smoke from the old stove, now replaced by an electric stove and an electric water heater over the porcelain sink. The only other signs of affluence were a red Frigidaire and a silver-gray bicycle, on which Joseph went touring.

A child's toy épicerie stood on the deep mantelshelf. Louise pointed out to me the tiny packages on the tiny shelves: Thé de l'Eléphant, Gloria Lait Concentré, Biscuits Pernod, Nestlé Fromage pour Tartines. Instinctively she and Joseph had surrounded themselves with French items, which though indigenous to the house were foreign to themselves, and so formed a parallel world within which they had no responsibilities.

Steep stairs led from the kitchen to the bedrooms: a single room divided by a plank partition. In Joseph and Louise's room there was a double bed; in the guest room, which was effectively a corridor, there were two single beds.

"I'm afraid there isn't anywhere you can shut the door and be private," said Louise.

"I'll survive."

At the top of the house was an attic living room, created by Joseph. Though no bigger than the kitchen, it was far more spacious. He had installed three large windows which looked out over the town to the ocean, to the Nez de Jobourg on the horizon. The view was northwest. The windows framed dramatic sunsets, Louise said.

"If you're wondering where the bathroom is, it isn't. There's a privy around the back."

"I think it's beautiful."

"It's an acquired taste."

"How do you wash?"

"You stand by the kitchen sink in your bikini and slosh water over yourself."

That evening we sat in the attic drinking *kir* and watching the lighthouse on the jetty winking its green eye. We did not feel obliged to entertain each other, and for a time maintained a fuzzy and comfortable silence. I had first come to know Louise through my wife, but since the breakup of my marriage Louise had rarely spoken to me of Jeannie. Now that for one week we were to spend so much more time together than we had in Abinger Road, I felt the need to release her from this self-censorship; and perhaps to demonstrate that I was no longer to be pitied.

"I did go and see Donald in the end," I said. "Jeannie's Donald."

"I thought maybe you had."

"Jeannie wants a divorce."

"Is she pregnant?"

"Yes."

"Does that hurt you very much?"

"I thought it would, but it doesn't seem to. I rather liked Donald. The other thing is, the baby might be mine."

"God, what a mess."

"Not really. I shan't interfere. I know you don't believe me, but I really have moved on."

"So what do you feel about this baby?"

"I don't know what I feel. It's very odd, Louise, it's not that I don't feel something, it's just that I can't make it out. When he told me I thought: Oh. Like a white hole."

"I expect you'll know when the baby appears."

"That's what I'm hoping."

The bottle of white wine and the cassis stood on the wooden floor between us. Whenever she replenished her glass, she replenished mine. There was no electric wiring as yet in the attic; the only light other than the pink night beyond the windows came from the kerosene heater. It cast a wide blue flower onto the slanting undersides of the tiles.

"Where's all this new strength coming from, William?"

"I don't know. Time passing. Getting involved in other things."

"Your research? Didn't you say you were researching a book?"

179

"Yes."

"What's it going to be about?"

A part of me wanted to tell Louise about the levels; but I was afraid. I had no way of knowing how those who did not share my schoolroom sex games would regard my obsession. I was not afraid that she would be shocked by it. I was afraid she would find it pitiful, or dehumanizing, or merely adolescent.

"I'm still feeling my way," I said. "Still a long way to go."

"Is it about how to recover from the breakup of a marriage?"

"You could say so. Indirectly."

Louise wriggled her black-socked toes in front of the heater. "Shall I tell you what I really think it's about, William?"

"What do you really think it's about?"

"I think it's about sex."

My startled silence gave me away. "What makes you think that?" I said at last, as casually as I could.

"Things you've been saying."

"You must have been listening damn hard."

"I've been curious. Sorry. I can see you don't want to talk about it."

That night as I lay in bed awaiting sleep I marveled at Louise's perception; and realized that I did not mind, that sooner or later I would tell her my secret, and that it would be a relief. I could hear her turning and turning next door, every rustle audible through the plank partition, and thought how it would be when Joseph arrived. I would be able to hear them making love. I wondered if Louise knew this, and if she minded.

The next morning I was awakened by the sharp bark of a car horn in the road outside. Louise came padding through my room and down the stairs. I climbed sleepily out of bed and saw through the window a gray Deux Chevaux van, from which she was buying *baguettes* for our breakfast.

Like Colonel Bancroft, I was given the job of grinding the coffee. Unlike Colonel Bancroft, who had only to depress a button on his Braun electric mill, I had to grind the beans by hand in a wooden box grinder. Louise demonstrated the method, sitting on an upright kitchen chair, the mill gripped between her thighs. Fresh bread; fresh coffee; fresh ocean air; so the day began, as did each of the six succeeding days, in an aroma of robust sensuality.

We drove to the market in Les Pieux to stock up for the week. I cashed some traveler's checks at the Crédit Agricole so that I could buy wine and calvados and cassis. The market was not busy. The booth holders sat hidden behind their wares reading the *Presse de La Manche*. They sold cheeses, shellfish, varieties of sausage.

We ate a light lunch, *crudités*, bread, and wine, in the Café du Coin on the main street. The proprietor had been a wrestler in his youth, and all over the café walls were pinned signed photographs of stars of the ring. Louise drew the sleeves of her navy-blue fisherman's jersey up her forearms, as if preparing to wash her hands. The *vin ordinaire* made us lazy, and we sat talking into the afternoon. No telegram had arrived before we left Bretanville, which meant that Joseph would not be on that day's flight. I found that I was pleased. I was enjoying the easy intimacy that Louise and I had established between us.

"Poor old Joseph," said Louise. "That book has been a torment to him from beginning to end."

"It's going to be good, though."

"Yes. I think it is."

"I'll tell you something I've often wondered, Louise. How on earth did you and Joseph ever get together? It's always seemed so unlikely to me, the two of you."

"What's unlikely about it?"

"Well. Joseph's so cerebral, and you're so . . ."

"Don't tell me. I'm so intuitive."

"Yes."

"Men always say women are intuitive. Just like they always say women with big tits are earth mothers."

"You are an earth mother."

"Careful, William. You're on sensitive ground. I shall throw an infantile tantrum, just to break the stereotype."

"You don't throw tantrums."

"Oh no? Ask Joseph."

I pressed Louise to tell me about her past, surprised at the degree of my own interest. Only later did I understand that I was

181

seeking to make real what had no reality for me. Joseph and Louise's sex life. They had been married over ten years; and were still, as far as I could see, very happy together.

"I met him at work, if you really want to know. Joseph was doing photographs of authors for book jackets. He used to come through my office to deliver work to my boss, when I was at the height of my career as a secretary."

"That doesn't tell me much."

"You want all the gory details?"

"Yes, please."

"You'll laugh like a drain, but here goes." She put her elbows on the red oilcloth and leaned her chin in her hands. I could tell from the animation in her eyes that she enjoyed telling me. "Did you know I used to be a Roman Catholic? Well, I was. A cradle Catholic, brought up by nuns. This really is ancient history, you know. The relevant fact is that at the time I met Joseph Rosenthal I was in love with a priest."

"And the priest was in love with you?"

"Potty about me."

"Why a priest?"

"You don't have to believe me, but in those days every man I met seemed to fall in love with me. It really got quite boring. But this man was a priest." She pulled a face at me, apologizing for her psychological predictability. "Unobtainable, right?"

"But not for long."

"Not for long. Oh William, it was simply dire. He fucked me weeping. I don't mean first the sex and then the tears. Both together."

"What a jerky way to carry on."

"He had his problems. Remember this was the early sixties, it was all a very big deal then. Self-denial was still the thing for priests. It was either God or me. Talk about flattery! Every time we screwed it was like I was more important to him than God. Then he said he had to give me up, and that was when I really fell in love with him. I just worshiped him after that. I was twenty-two, William. What did I know about anything?"

"So where did Joseph come in?"

"It gets worse first. I went off sex. Not surprisingly in my opinion. And that was when I got to know Joseph. People send each other signals, don't they? Joseph was just the same then as he is now, all hairiness and black clothes and fake assurance. I think he felt safe with me. He used to sit on my desk and talk about what he was up to. Then one day he asked me out to dinner, and I said, You'll find I'm not worth the effort, and all he said was, I don't mind."

"But you made it into bed eventually."

"Very eventually."

"So then you got married and lived happily ever after."

"I know it must seem odd. Joseph and I understood each other very well from the first. I suppose the truth is we love each other very much, in our own way."

"There's something you're not telling me, Louise."

"Then we're even, because there's sure as hell something you're not telling me."

Joseph's telegram did in fact arrive that day. It was delivered while we were still in Les Pieux, to Mme. Feuardent, the wife of the garage mechanic who lived next door. She brought it around as soon as we returned, and hovered in the doorway as Louise opened it, ready to offer stoic Norman sympathy should it be news of an illness or a motor accident. Joseph wired that he could not come to Bretanville at all.

"Typical Joseph," said Louise.

"Does that mean you want to go back?"

"Certainly not. Not now that I've got myself all the way here. What about you?"

"Oh, I'm fine."

"Then we'll stay, and make do as we are."

That evening, as if it were already an established custom, we drank *kir* and watched the twilight fade into night. Now that I knew we had the rest of the week to ourselves I felt even more inclined to tell Louise about my current concerns. The roomy gloomy attic was custom-built for confidences. So much more can be said, and later if necessary disowned, from out of the shadows. Louise, sensing my mood, led me gently toward self-disclosure.

"You know you never used to be like this, William."

"I never used to be like what?"

"You never used to be so easy."

"Easy." I thought of Cubby. "I'm easy, am I?"

"Loose. Someone has unscrewed your bolts."

"Enjoy it while it lasts."

"Isn't it going to last?"

"Some time it has to come to an end. The money, and everything. The sands of time keep on trickling. But so what?" I stretched and sighed. "So wiggerly woggerly, what?"

"Wiggerly woggerly?"

"Iggerly oggerly. It just came back to me. Higgerly hoggerly how are you? I'm wiggerly woggerly well. You must have had something like it when you were kids. Funny I should think of that now. Miggerly moggerly morning, Mrs. Macintosh. God, I'm reverting to childhood."

"Oh, William. Whatever have you been up to?"

"If you promise not to laugh I'll tell you."

"Why should I laugh?"

"Because it's a sad story about a sad man."

"With a happy ending."

"We don't know the ending yet. It's a cliffhanger."

So I laid my head on the high cane back of the chair, and looked into the mandala of blue light above me, and told Louise about the last few months. It was as safe and as intimate as talking on the telephone. I did not attempt to guess, as I spoke, how Louise was responding to my tale; the telling of it absorbed me, and the discovery that as my adventures passed out of my lips, they became real. Louise, merely by listening, had the power to grant objective life to my enacted fantasy. So I came to know my own secret.

When I had finished I looked down from the sloping roof to the view of the sea at night. The green light on the jetty shone and vanished, shone and vanished; making me think of Gatsby and his green light, which was a fantasy too, but wholesomely symbolic because it was not masturbatory like mine but romantic.

Louise said, "God knows I wish I could do it all too."

In this way she made me a gift of her envy. For rapid reassurance, give envy. Accept no substitutes. My stand-by shame dispersed as quickly as it had formed. I began to feel exhilarated. Louise asked me questions, in particular about Aurora Miller.

"Have you really not slept with her?"

"I've slept with her. I just haven't made love with her."

"But you would if you could."

"Oh yes." When I thought of Aurora, it was always as I had first seen her, mute and untouchable beyond a closed window. "It's as if she's being dangled in front of me. I don't think it's her idea. Arlette's, more likely."

"Near at hand but hard to get. The oldest game in the world."

"Yes, but why?"

"So where is she now?"

"She's with Arlette's husband, so called. A man by the name of Schuman. In Bali."

"Very nice too. What's she doing there? The next level?"

"I imagine so. Schuman lives there."

"What exactly happens when you run out of levels? After this seventh level?"

"Do you know, Louise, I don't actually care. I'll care later, but I don't care now."

"Live now, pay later."

"I'm paying now. Live now, die later."

The future was faint and far away in those days, in the *kir*-warm attic. Now that it is all about me, the future, I am impressed by the degree of self-abandonment I had achieved even before the experience of the seventh level; for after the seventh level, such questions no longer arise.

○

The next morning I came down the stairs to find Louise in her bikini squeezing soapy water over herself. Drops from the sponge spattered and hissed on the mobile gas fire, which she had pulled up close to the sink.

"Sorry," I said, retreating.

When we were both dressed and eating breakfast Louise said, "Thank you for the tact, William, but I think you're going to have to get used to the ghastly sight."

"What ghastly sight?"

"Me washing in the morning."

"It's not ghastly at all. I had no idea you had such good legs."

"Why shouldn't I have good legs?"

"I don't know. I hadn't thought, I suppose."

"I've always had good legs. You should have seen me in the days of mini skirts. I even had a pair of hot pants."

"Hot pants!"

"Try and sound a little less surprised, just to be polite. I'm only four years older than you."

At low tide we went down to the beach for what Louise called a "nasty walk." The sea smelled of urine. The lighthouse on the jetty was still flashing away, even though it was broad daylight. We explored over the exposed black rocks as far as the great beach of Siouville. The going was treacherous. Between the toothed slates and the sudden pools and the green slime there were few secure footholds.

"Why aren't we going along the road like everybody else?" I shouted into the wind. "It's penance," she shouted back, more agile than I over the rocks, several pools away. The wind pulled her hair from her face and neck, streamlining her, returning her to girlhood. A man with a white dog stooped among the rocks collecting limpets watched Louise covertly, and when she was near he called to her, holding out his basket. He had a knife with which he had been prizing loose the brown shells. Now with its point he scooped out a limpet and offered it to her, and when she refused, ate it himself.

We tramped in a great arc over the firm damp sand of Siouville beach, and returned along the quarry road. Louise's face was pink with health. "The great thing about a nasty walk," she said, "is that for the rest of the day you can be a slob." She slipped her arm through mine. "I'm glad you came, William. Are you glad you came?"

"I'm glad."

"Gladder than you thought?"

"Gladder than I thought."

That night, our third night in Bretanville, as we made our way to our separate beds pleasantly mellowed by calvados, Louise paused in the doorway to her inner room.

186

"Have you got enough blankets on that bed?"

"Yes, it's fine."

"Not exactly soundproof, this wall."

"So I've noticed."

"Does it bother you?"

"No." I was sitting on my bed pulling off my shoes. "I did wonder what it would be like when Joseph came. But then he didn't come."

"It wouldn't have been any different."

"I suppose not."

"I mean, there wouldn't have been anything to overhear."

This was the offer, the reached-out hand. I did not have to take it any further. I could have gone to the rear landing door which opened out onto the back garden and urinated from the steps into the nettles, as I had intended a moment before. Instead I said, "Why not?"

"There just wouldn't."

"You and Joseph don't sleep together?"

"We haven't made love for almost five years."

This was so unexpected that I could think of nothing to say.

"You've been married, William. You know how hard it is."

"Yes, but you and Joseph are still married. I'm not."

She came over from the doorway and sat down by me on the bed. "Have I shattered your illusions? The perfect marriage? Well, it is a good marriage. Better than most."

"But no sex."

"Joseph doesn't like sex."

"And yet you've stayed together."

"Not and yet. Because. It's what's made our relationship so strong. We had to come to terms with it somehow. People expect their marriages to satisfy them in every direction, emotionally, sexually, financially, everything. It can't be done. You can't have sexual excitement and security. You have to choose. Joseph and I had to choose a little earlier than most people, maybe, but it works. We've stayed very close."

"What have you done about . . . ?"

"I take what I can get. It's not all that much, but I find I don't need all that much."

187

"And Joseph doesn't mind?"

"Joseph doesn't mind."

The implications slowly penetrated. "Did you and Joseph plan this week between you?"

Louise nodded, avoiding my eye.

"So you knew all along he wasn't going to be coming?"

Again she nodded.

"The telegram even."

"Joseph wants me to be happy. But you don't need to worry about it, William. I didn't mean you to know."

She put one arm about me and hugged me in a sisterly fashion. Her speech now was brisker, more precise, a sign in Louise that she was nervous. "I have to get a cigarette," she said. "You go to bed and tuck up tight and tomorrow we'll go swimming and treat ourselves to lunch in the Hôtel de la Falaise."

"Isn't there something here we haven't sorted out?"

From within the inner room, where she was detained as she hunted her Gitanes and her lighter, Louise called brightly back, "Forget about it. This is your holiday."

"Just forget about it?"

"If you feel like doing me a favor, one of these days or nights, you know where to find me." She reappeared in the pink-painted doorway smoking. "But no acts of kindness. I can't stand acts of kindness. And let's not spoil our holiday, we're being so good for each other."

"Louise," I said, "you're beautiful."

Beneath the fisherman's jersey I could now see (undressing her with my eyes) such generous breasts, such round hips, such sensual comforts, that the Louise I had known until now seemed all at once to be another person, of superficially similar appearance, for whom I had mistaken this restful and seductive woman. I stared at her, and she smoked and stared back, her eyes saying to me with quiet amusement: so you've got there at last.

"Seen enough?" she said.

"How about tonight?"

"You don't have to save my face."

"I couldn't if I wanted to. The boss is down below; he never does anything he doesn't feel like doing."

"And does he feel like doing?"

"He feels like doing."

"Well then. The two of you had better come on in."

We made a pact to undress facing opposite ways. As I removed my clothes I looked dutifully at the map on the wall, a Carte Physique of the Manche district, and read the titles of the books on the little bookshelf: *Le Livre de Cuisine de Madame Saint-Ange*, the Guide Bleu for Normandie. All the woodwork in the room, the window frames, the fireplace surround, was painted baby pink, as if for a nursery. The bed rocked as Louise hid beneath the covers.

"I'm not usually so self-conscious," she said. "But after all your high-class whores."

The sheets turned out to be bright red.

"The first time's always useless," she said. "I'm not saying that because I'm nervous."

For a while we lay quietly in each other's arms. Every now and again a tremor of shyness or of longing ran through her body.

"I've been wanting this for ages."

"You should have said so."

"I did. You just weren't listening."

Under the red sheets she ran her hands all over my body, familiarizing herself with it. Very carefully, as if it might break, she stroked my stiff penis.

"I want to see it. Do you mind?"

"Go ahead."

"Say if you get cold."

She rolled back the bedclothes. "You're not to look at me. Only I can look at you." She studied it at close range, her head resting on my stomach. As for me, I had not adjusted to our new relationship; my responses were out of phase. There had been none of the tension, none of the long expectation, which for me was an integral part of the preamble to sex. I was still acting as if we were in cane chairs in the attic, drinking calvados. Louise seemed not to notice, and my erection vouched for my good faith. She now licked it with the tip of her tongue, a touch so restrained that it was more of a taste.

"Isn't it beautiful? It's so beautiful."

"Could be bigger."

"I love it just how it is."

Instead of proceeding to further intimacies she now lay back and, closing her eyes, crossed her hands over her breasts; like a dead crusader.

"What are you doing?"

"I'm hugging myself. Don't you ever hug yourself?"

"I'd rather hug someone else."

"But that's it." Though her eyes were shut, all the rest of her face was eagerly alive. "I'm lying here thinking, soon now William's body will be on my body. Soon now he'll be entering me. Don't you ever do that?"

I tried it. Flat on my back, hands by my side, I imagined myself making love with Louise. She was right: because it was within my power to convert the mental image into flesh and blood, it possessed a most yearning precision. My penis panted for her, impatient of its tether. But it was Louise who cracked first.

"Come into me now, please. Oh do hurry."

It was so quick, so easy, I grunted with surprise. "You've been expected," she said. We moved then slowly together, strangers as we were, learning to find each other so much nearer at hand. "You won't come soon, will you? I want to feel you in me all night." Later I played with her as Jilly Andrews had taught me: shallow, shallow, shallow, deep. She picked up the pattern and began to anticipate the fourth thrust with soft cries: "Angel. I love it. Oh I love it. Oh you angel." Her delight delighted me. "Come now. I want you to come. I want to feel you come. Talk to me. Tell me how it is." So I talked her through my climax, leaving the channel open, like an unattended microphone, when the words disintegrated. Staccato sounds kept her informed of my whereabouts, by their duration and pitch. She was as enthusiastic over my orgasm as if it had been her own.

"We're going to have a problem," she said as we sat side by side, the bedclothes pulled modestly up to our chins.

"What's that?"

She lit a cigarette. "I'm not going to want you to put your clothes back on. Ever."

"Prisoner of love."

"Prisoner of lust," she said.

◦

From the top of the precipitous granite steps that led down to the beach, winding around the old *auberge* now renovated by a Cherbourg lawyer, the waves looked summery and sedate as they tripped up and down the fingernail of sand. Once among the beached boats and the striped umbrellas they took on a steelier glint. I paddled into the fringe of spume and hastily retreated.

"I shan't swim," I said.

"It really isn't cold."

Louise swam, parting the gray Atlantic with her slow graceful crawl. I lay on the dark sand and built a sand castle. The sand was perfect for my purposes, not too fine, not too dry. The castle began as a mound with three turrets, on no conscious plan, and slowly acquired surrounding walls, roadways with ramps, a moat, tunnels. The construction of the tunnels gave me particular satisfaction. I packed the sand tight with the heel of my hand and then nibbled into it, firming the walls against subsidence as I went. At the later stages I lay on my side with my whole arm eased into the warm sand. When Louise returned dripping and glowing from her swim I subcontracted her to bore the other end of a grand tunnel, which was to pass fully under my castle, and was too long for my arm alone. A small crowd of children formed to watch in respectful silence. Our gritty fingers met in the moist depths and invisibly embraced.

"You know what I'd like to do now, Louise?" I said, hoping the children understood no English.

"What?"

"I'd like to go back to bed."

"Oh good," she said. "Let's go right away."

We shook out our towels. The children stared at the sand castle. "Okay," I announced with a wave over my creation. "Smash. Kick. How do I say 'kick' in French?"

"*Coup de pied.*"

"*Coup de pied!*" I cried, and swung a foot at a section of wall.

191

They leaped shouting onto the castle, and trampled it and beat it with plastic spades. Before we had brushed the sand off our encrusted bodies the castle was destroyed. "Lovely to see children enjoying themselves," I said.

We climbed back up to the house under the midday sun, towels over our bare shoulders. We did not go hand in hand, for Joseph was well known in Bretanville; but we were close linked, by the happy certainty of the pleasure we were about to give each other.

This request to Louise, "Let's go to bed," as direct and unambiguous as "Let's have lunch," now reverberated in my head in its revolutionary simplicity. It struck me that I had not before been in a situation where the simple desire could be so simply expressed. With most other desires there exists a direct link between the appetite and its satisfaction; which is not to say that everything I wanted was available to me, but when my desire was for whiskey or for conversation or for sleep there intervened no anguished introspection. I wanted it or I did not want it. I could have it or I could not have it. In matters of sex this direct link did not exist. I was obliged to operate through an intermediary with caprices of his own, some minor bureaucrat who had to be placated before he would pass on my impulse of desire. The reply, if any, was also routed through his censorious hands, and reached me overstamped with restrictions and qualifications.

At the earlier levels I had bought the complaisance of this intermediary. I was not buying Louise, but the mode of liberation was much the same. Only the trade was in a different currency. The effect on both of us was curious: we played with each other as if it were a game. The matter of our game may have been, as the barbed phrase has it, "for adults only"; the manner was that of children. For example, as we made our way to the midday bed we found ourselves talking about the acronyms children write on the backs of envelopes. "Do you remember Norwich?" said Louise. "What was Norwich?" "Knickers off ready when I come home." "Did anybody ever write that to you?" "Oh yes, when I was about ten. And romantic ones like Holland and Italy." "What was Holland?" "Holland was Hope

192

our love lasts and never dies." "Not as nice as Norwich." "Oh no."

Louise liked to watch my penis actually stiffening, which was also in its way a game. We would converse about nonerotic subjects as I undressed, to keep it small; then I would lie on the bed as Louise sat by my side and cooed to it, "Come on, little cock. Come out and play." She invented restrictions for herself, such as that she must not touch it, but could touch any part of my legs, and could blow on it, or tickle it with a blade of grass. Later she had a rule that it must begin the game in a specific starting position, which was tucked down between my thighs. The advantage of this was that it had to lift itself much farther, urged on by Louise. "Heave. Here it comes. Keep trying. Fuck. Fucky fuck. Don't lie down. It's lying down. Just a little heave. Cunt. Think of nice cunt. There it goes. Whee! Up you come." The obscenities were added with restraint, because she regarded them as unfair encouragement, almost as cheating.

We played the game also with the roles reversed, as a variant of Round and Round the Garden.Louise liked to keep her red-and-blue striped pants on for this, as part of her fond pretense that she was taking a solitary nap, and had no knowledge of my intentions. So as she lay on the bed with her eyes shut and her legs apart I would begin dancing my fingers about her ankles. "Round and round the garden, like a teddy bear. One step, two step . . ." The tickling alternated from leg to leg unpredictably, advancing from calves to thighs. "Round and round the garden, like a teddy bear. One step, two step. Tickly under there!" The walking fingers ended by prying through the striped fabric into the damp slit; at which point Louise would hurriedly remove her underpants and pull me on top of herself.

She showed me how to work the infallible prediction called Love Marry Hate Adore; and in its revelations we were pleased to find a legitimacy for our games together. "It's a way of telling whether people are suited," she said. "I used to do it with all my boy friends. I can prove it works because look what it says for Joseph and me." She wrote out the two names in capitals on a sheet of paper, one above the other:

193

JOSEPH ROSENTHAL
LOUISE MCKAY

"Now you cross out all the letters in the top name that have a
pair in the bottom name, and you cross out its pair in the bottom
name too. Not J. O and O. S and S. Like this."

JØŠEPH ROSENTHAŁ
ŁØUIŠE MCKAŸ

"Now you count along the letters left uncrossed, saying Love
Marry Hate Adore, like plumstones, and whichever one you end
on, that's it. So Joseph goes love, marry, hate, adore, love, marry,
hate, adore, love, marry. He'll marry me. And I go love, marry,
hate, adore, love, marry. I'll marry him. And he has married me
and I have married him, so its all true."

We did Jeannie and me, both as Jean Perry and as Jeannie
Perry. As Jean she hated me and I adored her; as Jeannie she
loved me and I hated her, both of which fitted the case well
enough. So we proceeded to try Louise and me, once with her
married name, once with her single name. As a married woman
it came out hate, hate. As a single woman it was adore, adore.
"There, you see," she said triumphantly, "it's always right.
We're meant just to play with each other. Adore is fun, not
serious like love and marry. You're to adore me."

"And you're to adore me."

"I do. You know I do."

"You're to be my sex doll. Whenever I feel like it, I can take
you out of the cupboard and inflate you and do what I want with
you."

"Heaven! A sex doll!"

This too became a game, that she was a rubber doll. When
playing this game she made herself as floppy and as lifeless as she
could, and did not speak, but the pleasure of it lay in our
conspiracy to pretend that she was an object, and had no other
purpose than to gratify my lust. It took me a little time to learn
to play the game properly, that is to say, to block out all consideration for Louise as a person; but slowly I came to apply to our

194

sexual union the single-minded self-interest I had before only known in masturbation. Louise enjoyed this even more than I did.

"Do you know something, Louise," I said one afternoon. "I have no idea at all whether you have orgasms with me."

"That's why I adore you so," she said.

"So you do?"

"Do you care?"

"I should, but it feels as if I don't."

"That's what's so good about us, William. I care about my orgasms, you care about yours. Why can't all men be satisfied with their own orgasms? They're so greedy, they want two for the price of one. *Did you come? Did you come?*"

All this disoriented me, because it revealed a mismatch between my standard-equipment moral code and my actual moral responses. The code said it was wrong to put my own pleasure first; yet it felt right. Louise tried to reassure me, saying, "If I want something, I'll ask for it. Women aren't so different from men. If I keep on coming back for more, you can take it I'm getting something out of it. It may not be orgasms, but it's something."

It did not take me long to discover that when making love with Louise, the more excited I became, the more excited Louise became; not because of anything I did in my excitement, but because of the excitement itself. She loved me to be out of control with lust. "I want my body to drive you wild with desire," she said, and repeated the line dreamily to herself as if she was the heroine of a romantic novel: "Her body drove men wild with desire."

"Your body does drive me wild with desire," I said.

"That's why I get so turned on."

"Me being turned on is what turns you on?"

"Of course. That's always how it goes. It's the same for you."

I consulted myself and found that she was right. It was her desire for me which liberated my desires. "Do you think it's really meant to be this easy?" I said, "I mean, why has it been such a struggle all my life?"

"People never say what they want, do they?"

195

The more time Louise and I spent in bed, the longer became our nasty walks, as if in instinctive compensation. On our last day, before Louise returned to London and I flew to Brussels, we undertook the longest walk of them all, the cliff path over the Cap de Flamanville. The way up to the top of the granite bluffs winds slowly, at a gentle incline, past the abandoned iron mine, and from there undulates like downland; but all the way on the right there is a five-hundred foot drop to the battering gray sea.

At first we leaned fearfully in to the land, but then we made out other paths running along the cliff face below us, and saw that the granite was terraced like a giant staircase down to the ocean. The illusion of sheer drop was created by the towering cliffs ahead. Before we reached them the path climbed up onto the grassy scarp, and crossed it at a safe distance from the edge.

The wind was off the land, and almost strong enough to lean on. When we reached the cape itself, the crown cliff, Louise wanted to look over it. Afraid that the wind would hurl us into the sea, we crawled on our hands and knees over the scrub toward the edge, and wriggled for the last few yards like snakes. Side by side we lay looking down at the boiling sea far below.

"Don't you love it?" cried Louise, her eyes full of tears from the stinging air. "Isn't it sexy."

Squalls of wind were whipping the sea up into giant waves. The waves smashed against the granite, and heaved back, and smashed again; so much power expended to so little effect, but passionate, like a wild beast in a zoo. It beat the wall endlessly, not understanding.

"Waves are erotic," said Louise.

"What's erotic about them?"

"It's the power. Power is always sexy. Watch this one. Wham! They just don't hold back, do they?"

I saw what she meant. Over the thunder of the ocean I shouted at her a specialized compliment: "You're a very easy lady, Louise."

"Maybe so," she shouted back. "But am I a good screw?"

My ready affirmative was not enough. As we walked home, pressed tight together so that we could hear each other in the wind, she demanded that I mark her from one to ten on a "good screw scale." "You have to be honest. The opposition is professional, so I won't mind."

"Ten," I said.

"How can I be ten?"

"Because I don't see how it can get any better."

"You can't give me ten. You've got all your other levels still to come. And the seventh level."

"I know."

"So am I demoted?"

"No. If I have to, I'll extend the scale."

But I knew that I had arrived at a terminus, and that from now on any development would be different not in degree but in kind. My training thus far had been a progress toward simplicity, an unlearning of difficulties. On Louise's scale, ten was the only possible mark, because with her in Bretanville, even though I did not yet understand how or why, I had stopped waiting for it to be done to me. From now on, I was doing it.

17

It was early afternoon as the taxi deposited me at the tall railings of the château. The iron gate was warm in the sun. The leaves of the beech trees spread lazy above me, reclining on the hot cushiony air. I did not call at the main house, but made my way, bag in hand, along the gravel sweep to the path through the box hedge.

Benjamin the collie lay sprawled and panting before the lodge door. He had not the energy to bark, but rolled his eye after me as far as it would go without obliging him to raise his black-and-white head. Through the open door came voices, and the squeals of children. Within I found an unexpectedly domestic scene.

The kitchen was stiflingly hot, because the coal fire in the range had been stoked up for baking. Madame Arlette stood over the wooden table, her sleeves rolled above the elbows, her hands plunged into a mound of white dough. Beside her in the high-backed kitchen chair sat a woman of about my own age with short straw-colored hair, dressed in denim dungarees. On the other side of the table two small children pounded away with little floury fists at subsidiary lumps of dough, shouting constantly for approval of their work: *"Est-ce que ça va comme ça, mammie? Tu peux pas l'écraser un peu pour moi, mammie?"* And the little girl, who could have been barely three years old: *"Et moi! Et moi!"*

The old lady greeted me with unmistakable pleasure, embracing me fondly, leaving white arm-prints on my brown jacket. She looked intently into my eyes, checking, as I thought each time, the condition of my soul. Then she kissed me, smudges of flour passing from her face to mine. "You are very well, William. I can see that all is well." The little boy came pulling at her skirt, clutching his gob of dough insecurely in one hand for her attention. *"Et voilà mon petit Jean-Paul. Qui c'est le petit à son mammie, Jean-Paul?"* *"C'est moi,"* said the child happily. *"Parle Anglais à William, mon lapin."* To me she said, "He is bilingual. My grandchildren are *petits Canadiens.*"

Since Arlette had a husband it was to be expected that she would also have children, but the possibility had not occurred to me before. In fact she had only the one child, André, now over forty years old and a successful lawyer in Montreal. The young woman in the lodge, Bobbie, was André's wife. I gathered that she had brought the children for a European vacation, and that they were staying at the château. It was inconceivable therefore that she should not know Arlette's business, yet this innocent noisy family seemed to belong to a different universe from the château and all its concerns.

Any doubts I might have had on this score were eliminated when she spoke to me: "You're one of Arlette's disciples, are you?"

"You could say so."

"I hope you realize how lucky you are. You get the mother, I get the son." She drew her heels up onto the seat of the chair and wrapped her arms around her knees. Her voice, her manner, made her appear too young to be the mother of the robust little Jean-Paul. *"Il ne changera pas, ton petit André,"* she said to the old lady. *"Il ne sortira jamais de sa coquille."*

"Deux mois à Bali avec Schuman et tout cela s'evanouira."

"You know he'll never go."

Arlette's hands never ceased their steady kneading. The little girl dropped her dough onto the floor and began to cry. The little boy lost interest in his dough and complained of the heat. Their mother chided them wearily, and tried to persuade them to play outside. The parrot repeated the little girl's insistent whimpers with irritating accuracy. Jean-Paul turned his attention to me. "Do you know my dad?" he said, becoming with his North American accent a different boy. "No," I said. "Don't you know any French at all then?" "Not really." "Do you want me to tell you some?" "No. It's too hot." He nodded his little yellow head in grave agreement. "I guess it's hot enough to scald a cat," he said.

Jean-Paul's interest in me encouraged Christiane, his little sister, who now stopped crying and crawled over to my leg. "You seem to have made a hit," said Bobbie. "Would you like me to take them outside," I suggested, "so that you can talk in peace?" "Could you stand it?" said Bobbie. "You could take them to the lake," said Arlette. Jean-Paul began to jump up and down at this, chanting: "*Schouette! On va nager!*" "Do you feel up to looking after them in the water?" "Can they swim?" "Not a stroke. You'd have to go in with them." "Well, it's the day for it." "Hooray! Swimming!" "You don't know how much I appreciate this," said Bobbie.

The two children trotted off ahead of me along the path to the château. I followed with rolled towels under my arm. Their ragged golden topknots disappeared through the hedge, but their high laughter still shivered the tranquil air, as natural an expression of the goodness of life as the chirping of the birds. I caught sight of them again running down the sloping lawn out of the shadow of the big house toward the reed-screened lake. There brown ducks drifted, and mosquitoes whined over the placid surface. The children knew just where to go. There was a grassy bank at one end of the long bow of water where the lake bed was smooth-pebbled and clear of mud. They began at once to remove their clothes, Jean-Paul by his own efforts, Christiane aided by me. At the lodge I had not thought to ask what the children were to swim in, but the matter was not open to question. They were to swim in nothing.

I forbade them to enter the water until I was ready to join them. They skipped from foot to foot, their bodies gleaming in the sun, chortling with excitement. When I was in my own opinion fit for the water, Jean-Paul pointed disapprovingly and objected: "You still got your unders on. You'll get them wet." This was undeniably true. I took it that he was accustomed to his father swimming in the nude; and as it was a hot day, and we were not overlooked, I shed my pants. Neither child paid any attention to my hairy pudendum.

The shallow lake had had all day to soak up the sun's heat, and was as warm as a bath. I held Christiane's hand, as she clearly desired, but Jean-Paul tumbled free and set up a great splashing all around. Christiane and I sat down side by side on the stony bed and looked at our legs in the water, while Jean-Paul tried unsuccessfully to swim. Their bodies were sweet and fresh as new milk, and all the time their throats were caroling with delight. It was too deep for Christiane to feel safe sitting on the lake's bed, the water tucked up to her neck, so she clambered onto my lap and snuggled herself into the fork of my legs. This made Jean-Paul jealous, and he set about grappling up my back and slithering down into the water. The ducks who had fled at our approach sailed nearer again, perhaps expecting to be fed.

"Ducks!" cried Jean-Paul from my shoulders.

"Diggerly doggerly ducks," I said.

"Diggerly doggerly ducks!"

"Wiggerly woggerly water."

"Wiggerly woggerly water!" he repeated rapturously, falling back into it. "Splash! Splash you! Sliggerly sploggerly splash you!"

"Liggerly loggerly," said Christiane, and pressed her wet face against my chest to hide from her brother's watery attack.

"Piggerly poggerly *pipi!* Kiggerly koggerly *caca!*" He marched about, up to his navel in the lake, shrieking with delight at the new game. Warm and easy in the water, I found myself thinking of Louise, with whom that childhood memory had been recovered, and as I thought of her I chanced upon a likeness between her and these children, between myself as I had been with her in Bretanville and myself as I was now in the lake. The likeness was strong, a mood equivalent of déjà-vu. Mildly intrigued I allowed the recent memories to splash about me with the naked children, waiting for the link to form in my conscious mind. When it came to me I was shocked, and wished I had not pursued it, because it cast a shadow over our innocent afternoon. My body was comporting itself among the children in the relaxed and sensual manner with which I had made love to Louise. Moreover, this bodily delight in the sun, in the warm water, in the smooth and slippery little limbs that tangled with mine, was so close to what I had known with Louise that I could not pretend it was sexless. Some guilty instinct in me, already recognizing this, had caused me to block all perception of their little genitals. The instruction had not been conscious, but until this moment I had treated their immaculate bodies as if they were corrupt, and had scrubbed out one part of their anatomy, just as not so many years ago pornographic photographs were scrubbed to leave a hairless and featureless smudge below the belly.

I was appalled at my self-censorship, at my false guilt; appalled that I should neuter the children in order to protect myself from the prurient suspicions of Colonel Bancroft and his ilk. I looked with remorseful eyes on Jean-Paul's tiny penis, like the nozzle of a balloon, and on his smooth scrotum, as tight as a grape. I admired Christiane's plump pink cleft, so neatly fashioned, so unblemished. I did not pretend to myself as I looked on this three-year-old quim that I was not also seeing the many others which over the years had aroused my lust; but if there was lust it was a tender and protective lust, which enriched and made wholehearted our floating embraces. I could not fully explain it to myself, but I knew that it was because I had made love with Louise as I had done that the children now played so trustingly in my arms.

Madame Arlette and Bobbie found us still prancing in the water, a merman and his merbabies, our happy din prickling the kind blue sky. "Miggerly moggerly mammie!" cried Jean-Paul. I stood up dripping, unashamed in my nakedness, Christiane cradled safe in my arms. Jean-Paul splashed before me to the bank. "All safe and sound," I said to Bobbie. Christiane did not

202

want to let go, so her mother dried her where she hung. "Thanks," she said. "I hope they haven't worn you out."

"Not at all. They've both been very good."

"That's because you don't fuss them."

While I was dressing I said to Arlette: "I learned something strange playing in the lake with those children." I knew that it was not necessary to apologize to the old lady for what I had felt. "Leave out the actual sex, and it felt like my body was making love."

"Ah, William," she said, shaking her gray-haired head. "You are a good man."

"I'm not sure that I know any more what's good and what's bad."

"Well, my dear. You must tell me what has been happening to you."

Bobbie took the children into town to see a puppet show. Arlette and I remained in the overheated kitchen, where the old lady completed her bread-making. The dough had risen well, and was now ready to be spread over the wooden board. The story of my week in Bretanville accompanied the rolling out of the dough, and the bundling up tight like so many little carpets. By the time the baton loaves had been put to prove on a top corner of the range, I had arrived at my puzzle: the apparent fact that in sex with Louise I had been rewarded for selfishness.

"But sex is selfish, William," she said gently. "How can sex not be selfish? Can a man achieve an altruistic erection? I think not. It is the same for women also. A woman cannot abnegate and lubricate."

I smiled at her carefully turned phrases. "You have thought about this before, madame."

"So I have, so I have. This is a most important discovery you have made, William. Please recognize its significance."

"I feel its significance. But I don't understand it."

"Well then. You are like so many others, you have been taught that what you do for your own pleasure is bad, and that what you do for the pleasure of others is good. Is this not so?"

"Yes. Something like that."

"Very well then. We may say that you have been taught not to take responsibility for your own happiness. You have been taught not to ask to feel good, not to want to feel good, only to wait in silence and hope that others will grant you as acts of kindness some feeling good. Tcha! such nonsense."

Responsibility for my own happiness. It was a simple ethical inversion. Arlette took my self-seeking actions and altered not their nature but their name. Thus I could begin to believe that what I had felt to be right was right.

"In sexual matters," she said, "self-denial is sex denial. Nothing has done more damage to the sex pleasure than self-denial. So many people afraid to seek their own pleasure! So many people burdening others with the duty to make them happy! And they call it consideration, unselfishness, love. Tcha! It is nothing but immaturity. When you are sexually mature you take responsibility for your own happines."

"Of course," I said slowly. "And Louise felt it in me, that I was not burdening her."

"There is a greater gift than pleasure. There is the gift of having been pleased."

"Which brings it back to unselfishness."

"If you wish it to be so. If you need it to be so. But it is of no significance, that. It matters only that you deal directly and cleanly with others. I watched you with the children in the water, William. Did you not feel it, the simplicity? Children of that age have not yet learned to be afraid of their desires. When little children play, they are demanding, they are cruel, they are ecstatic, they are grief-stricken, and always their bodies speak their feelings. We cannot be children, we should not want to be children, but it is not necessary that we forget what it is to play. You were playing, this afternoon. You told me so."

"I told you that it was as if I was making love."

"When we are grown-up, that is how we play."

She understood so well what had been happening to me. So it had been with Louise: sex as a rediscovery of innocence, sex as a game. It was as if Arlette had intended it.

"Did you know I would find this out, madame?"

"I thought that it would be necessary to lead you toward it. It

204

is the next level; and you have come to it yourself, without my guidance. I have told you that my levels are no more than names I give to the processes that I have observed to take place. What we are speaking about I call the fifth level."

The fifth level, the victorious fifth: selfish sex, or more acceptably, self-responsible sex. So much pleasure is orchestrated for charity, dinners for charity, dances for charity, premières for charity, ball games for charity, jokes for charity, kisses for charity; no wonder we have also come to make love for charity. The link may not be so direct; no coins tinkle off the jouncing bed into a collecting plate, but the story is the same: "I'm not doing this for me, dear, I'm doing it for you." A lie of course, a self-deception; and hence, bad sex. Somebody has to shoulder the burden of the world's pleasure and say, They did it all for me. At present this function is performed by those too afflicted to resist, paraplegics, mongols, refugees from zones of war and famine, maltreated animals. Ever since the fifth level I have gone over to the cripples. You are doing it all for me.

When the loaves had been proving for half an hour or so, Arlette sprinkled them with a toothbrush dipped into a metal dish of water, and placed them in the oven. The dish of water she laid on the oven floor, saying, "For the crust." Periodically during the baking she resprinkled the loaves with the toothbrush. The water was soon steaming in the baking-hot oven.

"How long have we known each other, William?"

I thought back. "Five, six months."

"So short a time, yet already you are outgrowing me."

"I don't think so, madame. I'm just about as confused as when we first met."

"It is not necessary that you understand something, William. Only that you be something. Yes, yes." She opened the oven door to moisten her batons, releasing into the kitchen the sweet steam of baking bread. As she turned away from the range again she took my hand and drew me into an embrace. She was so much smaller than I, so much more frail, that I was overwhelmed with a protective love for her. "You know me better than my own mother ever knew me, madame." "God grant I may be a better mother to you than I have been to my own son," she said. Her embrace was not the formal smack of continental courtesy: she folded into my body, her wrinkled cheek pressed to my neck, as if we were lovers. "Do you ever wish you were young again, madame?" "No, no. None of that is of importance." The manner of her embrace, a reluctance to release me, warned me that she saw what I could not see: that from here on our ways were to part, that when we met again it would no longer be as teacher and pupil, nor even as mother and son. She separated from me, stepped a pace back, and held out her arms as if proudly displaying me to an unseen audience.

"So. Now you are ready."

"Ready for what, madame?"

"I would like you to go to Schuman. Do you have money still? The flight is expensive. Once you are there it will cost you very little."

"I have enough," I said.

"Yes," she repeated more decidedly. "You must go to Schuman."

Apart from that single occasion when she had shown me his photograph, Arlette had never spoken to me of her husband. What little I knew of him came from such diverse sources as Cubby and Aurora Miller. Tentatively I now asked her what I might expect from him.

"You will think it curious," she said, "that we are as we are, Schuman and I. But one day you will understand. As for Schuman, he is an old man now. He has not always been a good man. So, so, you will find what you will find. He has lived so long he has outlived his own littleness, and now he is big."

The Sixth Level

18

It is no accident that what I have referred to many times as the journey through the levels took the form of a series of actual journeys. The business of learning is also the business of unlearning, and old habits of mind are more easily uprooted in strange places. Schuman lived in a village called Peliagan, near a town called Ubud, at the heart of the island of Bali; where the Indian Ocean meets the South China Sea.

On the flight out from London I had a row of three seats all to myself, and was able to sleep in reasonable comfort. From Singapore the short-haul jet operated by Garuda, the Indonesian airline, was full to capacity. I occupied a center seat between a fat woman and a thin man. The woman was from Fort Lauderdale, Florida, and was on vacation. The man was reading the *International Herald Tribune,* folding and refolding the paper as he read it so that it was never more than two columns wide. Despite my comfortable earlier flight I was very tired, and I found them both irritating. At first I disliked the woman more, because she talked to me without appearing to notice that I was not answering: "They tell me Bali is the most beautiful island in the world. I'll make up my own mind about that. I don't pay no attention to nobody. You know Fiji? There's an island. Fiji is fine. Not one half as spoiled as Hawaii. You know Hawaii? They tell me Bali is real unspoiled. Easter Island now, there's an island that's not been spoiled at all. Not at all. Did you ever go to Easter Island?"

Later I came to think of this woman as the lesser of the two evils, because although she persisted in speaking to me, she was almost toally unaware of me. The man in the window seat did not speak at all, but he was forever adjusting his arms and legs in polite consideration of moves I made. This unnecessary sensitivity toward me became inhibiting. The way he folded his paper was designed to keep his arms out of my airspace. The result was that each painfully elaborate refold somehow involved me, and left me as tense and constricted as the man himself must have been. The few times our eyes met he wore an apologetic look, the kind of inoffensiveness that is provocation to assault.

We were flying over Java, an hour out of Jakarta, when a great volcano came into view. The jagged peak trailed a streamer of cloud, lit gold along the upper surface by the descending sun, reaching all the way to Lombok. Beneath the glowing cloud, barely larger than the volcano itself, lay the island of Bali.

The woman on my right craned over me to see what I was looking at. "Is that a volcano?" "That's Gunung Agung," said the thin man. "Does it ever go off?" "I believe it did erupt in 1962." "Well!" She leaned across the aisle and told other members of her party: "Did you know that was a *live volcano?*"

I spent my first night on Bali, my night of acclimatization, in the Kuta Beach Hotel on the coastal strip. I watched the sun set between the palm trees, and wondered why I was not pleased by it. After darkness had fallen I could not rest for the roar of motorbikes racing along the crescent beach. From my hotel cabin I could see their headlights darting over the spume left by the waves.

It was too early to sleep. I walked into Kuta, a town of tin-roofed houses thrown up to accommodate the influx of surfers. Low voices called out to me from shadowed doorways as I passed: "Grass? Smack?" In the open-fronted *warungs* American and Australian scammers sat around Tilley lamps drinking cold canned beer. Their conversation was all of the deals they were doing, in batik cloths, or carved-horn chess sets, or paintings from Ubud. A scooter rode up beside me, cruised along at my walking pace. The man riding said, "You want girl?" and the girl who clung on to the pillion behind him nodded and smiled, only her eyes and her teeth visible in the darkness. "Thousand *rupiah*," he said. "Stay with you all night." A thousand *rupiah* was less than one pound.

Bali on that first night, shabby and corrupt, "spoiled," as the fat American lady was no doubt concluding in her air-conditioned hotel on Sanur beach, fingered me as I went by, accused me of responsibility. I and the scammers and the American matrons were all stripping our pleasures from the poor, and giving nothing in return but money.

These were dangerous thoughts. I returned to my hotel and bought a map of the island, to see where I was going the next day. I found the road to Ubud, but there was no sign of Peliagan. The hotel clerk marked it in for me with his pen, off the road. "You wanna taxi?" he said. The nasal Americanized voice depressed me further. The boy looked so young. "Is there a bus?" "Only *bimo*." I had come by taxi from the airport. The gross Chevrolet had been in places wider than the road itself.

The *bimo* turned out to be a small brightly painted truck with a canvas roof. Passengers sat clutching their luggage in the back, facing each other in two rows; as it filled up they crammed into the central space, and spilled over the welded rails of the tailgate. It was early morning. I had been warned that *bimo* travel was not pleasant in the full heat of the day. There were already six passengers by the time it reached me, and a basket containing live chickens. By the time we reached the city we could not move. All through Denpasar the roads swarmed and screamed with motorbikes, and once out of the city the *bimo* drove at reckless speed, hurling us about over the disintegrating macadam. Travelers dismounted, and more travelers took their place, and I became worried that the driver had forgotten me, but he said, "Okay, okay." We left the coast behind and climbed the long flank of the volcano into cooler air, and the rice in the paddies on either side changed from dry yellow to gray, from

211

gray to green. Past the village of Mas there was water in the fields, shelf after shelf of shining blue and white reflecting the sky.

At a meeting of three roads, where a signpost pointed ahead to Tegallalang, left to Ubud, and back to Mas and Denpasar, the driver rapped on the oval plastic window and called out, "Peliagan." It was not the village itself; but the road ran no nearer. There was a *warung* here, as there was at every crossroads on the island. After the *bimo* had roared away in a cloud of orange dust the only sound was the grate-grate-grate of ice being shaved into a glass of Coca-Cola. I carried my suitcase over to the shade of the *warung*. On a plank bench beside the rows of sliced papaya and the jars of dried biscuits sat a foreigner like myself drinking a bottle of F&N orangeade. "Going to Peliagan?" he said amicably. "Yes." "If you can hold on while I drink this, I'll take you. You'll never find your way otherwise."

He was an American called Mickey, about forty years old, I guessed, currently living in Schuman's compound. This was no great coincidence. I learned from Mickey that any foreigner around these parts was likely to share our destination, for it was not a tourist area, and we were not alone in making pilgrimage to the old man. At first this disconcerted me. I had not expected to find myself among a flock of disciples.

Mickey had been into Denpasar to send mail home, and had stopped off in Ubud on his way back for kerosene. Two ten-liter cans sat on the hard earth by his feet. "Denpasar sucks," he told me. From Mickey I learned also that Aurora Miller was no longer in Peliagan, or even on Bali, but had flown back to Los Angeles only a few days earlier. Somewhat subdued in spirit, therefore, as well as weary in body, I began the last leg of my journey into the remote valley where Schuman held court.

A beaten earth path led down the side of the *warung* away from the road. There were a few grass-thatched houses, but soon we were passing between deserted rice fields where wind-driven bird scarers clattered over the young plants. On either side ran irrigation ditches ferrying the water from field to field, even at times crossing our path, carried overhead by rickety wooden aqueducts which leaked muddy pools onto the earth track. The sound of flowing water filled the air. I was overdressed for such brisk walking in so humid a climate, and began to sweat. Mickey, more sensibly dressed in cut-off denims and a U.C.L.A. tee shirt, strode ahead of me. By a log bridge over a stream I called a halt, and sat heaving on the ground beside a carved stone altar the size of a bird bath. On the altar lay fresh offerings, red hibiscus petals and grains of cooked white rice, to the spirit of the stream. "You'll get used to it soon enough," said Mickey. I asked him how long he had been here, and he seemed uncertain. "Maybe five weeks. You lose count."

The tree-fringed stream was not wide, but over the years the current of water had sliced deeper and deeper into the soft Balinese sandstone, and now the log bridge passed over a twenty-foot drop. Fortunately I had reached the far side before I discovered this, for the bridge had no railing.

Our path climbed a long hill, curving around its shoulder to the summit. Again we rested, as the next valley came into view. Its steep slopes ran across our way like a green groove in the world, dark sugar palms spiky on the skyline. The valley flanks were terraced and cultivated all the way down to where a river wound between black rocks far below. There in a river pool we saw the tiny figures of villagers bathing; and above the pool a slow-moving column of women carrying buckets of water on their heads zigzagged up the terraces.

Mickey pointed out a cluster of buildings halfway up the far valley side: "Peliagan." It was not a large village, no more than a temple and a run of houses along the line of the rice terraces. The earth of the house compounds was a dry sepia, the thatch roofs gray, laying a faded stripe into the embracing green of the valley.

We descended to the river, where we splashed the sweat from our faces, and so were refreshed for the final climb. Schuman's house was at the far end of the village, on a higher terrace, and we did not pass the temple or the *banjar* or the other dwellings. The first inhabitants of Peliagan that we encountered were not Balinese, but New Yorkers. They were both naked, for the innocent reason that they were taking a shower. A little tributary stream had been ducted out from the overhead rocks by a bamboo chute so that it tumbled down into a natural basin beside the path. Here the two white bodies leaned together, back to back, enjoying the cool cascade that broke over their heads. "Hi, Jerry," said Mickey, "hi, Midge. This is William." They both wagged their hands in greeting, a pear-shaped woman and an egg-shaped man, comfortable if not comely in their nudity. "Jerry's a psychoanalyst," said Mickey. "I guess I mean was. He and Midge are married, but they like for us not to know."

The path wound upward, an irregular staircase formed of tree roots exposed by the rubbing of countless feet. At the level of the next terrace a mud-and-reed wall ran alongside the way, rising at intervals to thatched eaves. This was the perimeter of Schuman's compound. Over the low sections of wall I saw a wide courtyard, containing several mat-sided huts built of coconut wood timbers. Chickens scratched in the red earth. A small group of foreigners like myself sat conversing under the shade of a tree. Mickey dropped his cans of kerosene by what he called "the kitchen house," an open shelter beneath which stood four tables at right angles to each other, the legs of each table sunk in tins of water to hinder the ants. Each table had its *kompor* kerosene stove and its wok. Mickey led me across the baked compound to the largest of the structures, which was known as the long house. "Schuman's out most of the time," he told me, "or incommunicado in his own house. If he wants to be accessible he comes in here." We passed into the cool of a welcoming chamber, plank-floored, thatch-roofed, open all along the face that looked out into the valley. This side had been built out on timber struts to form an extended veranda which overhung the terraces below. Rugs and blankets and sleeping bags lay about, giving the room the air of a dormitory, which in effect at night it became. Several people sat on the veranda, their arms leaning on the single rail, their legs dangling. "Seen Schuman?" said Mickey. "He went out with the Dutch girl," they said. "Here's where you crash," Mickey told me. "Do you have a bed roll? The temperature drops at night up here in the hills." "No, I don't." "We'll find you something for tonight. Tomorrow you can walk into Ubud and pick up a blanket or two."

He introduced me to the others on the veranda: Colin, a one-time Catholic priest, who smiled nicely out of an immense and unrestrained beard; Piper, an Australian lady who had been burned an angry red by the sun; Zig, or Ziggy, by origin a

214

Welshman, deculturized by decades of world wandering; Marta, an ex-actress from what she called "the faggot axis," Los Angeles-New York.

"You guys eaten already?" asked Mickey.

"There's plenty left in the wok," said Colin. "So long as you like fried vegetables."

"You'd better like fried vegetables," said Marta, and they all laughed. Mickey went to fetch us some lunch, and I settled down with the group. It was curious to find myself in their company, for although none of them were known to me, we shared a past. However, I soon picked up the unspoken convention, that the levels were not among the topics of general conversation. This was in acknowledgment of what we had all learned, that to tell the story of certain types of experience flakes away from that experience some of its substance. There was also an element of courtesy here. Some of the visitors to Peliagan had made their way to Schuman along the word-of-mouth trail that exists in the international community of wanderers, and so unknown to themselves were inadequately prepared. Aware of the potential for ego competition inherent in any system of graduation, Schuman limited his discussion of the levels to private dialogues; and we followed suit.

I asked my new companions what went on here and they told me, "Nothing." There was no organization, no school, no lectures, no demonstrations. Schuman permitted those who wished to do so to share the space of his compound, but visitors had to shift for themselves in matters of food and bedding. An informal system had grown up, as it always will, which had achieved a certain continuity. Thus today I was the most recent addition to the group, and the Dutch girl Henrika who had been in Peliagan over three months was the most senior; but within a week Henrika was gone, and a Swedish couple had arrived, and I was one of the established residents. During my time there were never more than twenty visitors.

It is true to say that nothing happened in Peliagan in the sense that there were no formal instructions, but we had all made the journey there to be taught by Schuman, and Schuman did teach. In groups he was silent, or chose to answer direct questions with further questions of his own. Such teaching as he did took place at times and in places of his choosing. This meant that the rest of us knew nothing of what went on, except that he was frequently to be seen walking between the rice fields in earnest conversation with one of our number.

On first sight Schuman did not live up to my expectations. He was little, as little as Arlette, and bald. The skin of his face and neck was shriveled and mottled mauve with exposed capillaries. He liked to wear colonial-style khaki shorts, out of which protruded in a ridiculous manner his sticklike legs. In general there was a sleepy air about him, as is the way with old men, so that you could never be sure he had heard you, or recalled who you were. Undoubtedly he had a certain presence, such that I could always tell at once on entering the long house whether he was there or not; but I put this down to the attentive deference with which he was treated. He did nothing to command this deference and appeared to be unaware of it.

I learned what I might expect of Schuman from the others. He himself did not so much as acknowledge my arrival. "Don't worry," said Ziggy, "he's seen you. He likes to take his time." Schuman's way was to wait until he deemed that a particular individual was sufficiently adjusted to life in Peliagan, and only then to make the first contact. Nobody was very sure what signs he looked for, but it was generally agreed that it was a matter of slowing the pace, or "easing down." Marta liked to say: "This is Schuman's pig farm. We're all little piggies, and he's fattening us up. When you get to be the right weight, zappo! in with the hook."

The pattern of life at Peliagan was determined largely by the sun. We rose at dawn, as the light streamed in over the veranda, when there was still a heavy dew. According to the dictates of our informal rota, I would fetch water from the nearby stream, where I would also wash away the residue of sleep; or light the kerosene *kompors* in the kitchen house, beneath the four black kettles; or prepare the pots of muddy Balinese coffee; or, if all these tasks had been performed by others, I would carry my bowl of heated water from the kitchen house to the low perimeter wall, and standing the bowl and my little round mirror on the mud ledge, would proceed to shave as the mists cleared in the valley below. Breakfast passed slowly, usually silently. Most of us

216

sat in a line along the veranda of the long house, which faced southeast, and watched the sun rising out of the hills. During the cool of the morning we carried out the laborious tasks, the work in the narrow vegetable plots beside the compound, the trek across the valleys into Ubud to buy coffee and candles and kerosene. When the sun had warmed the water we bathed under the stream shower, or in one of the pools of the river where the rocks were worn slippery by soapy feet. According to the local custom we bathed naked, with the left hand covering the private parts.

Through the midday heat we would lie beneath the cool thatch, eating fried vegetables, drinking sweet rice wine, telling each other stories of our homes and our pasts. For the rest of the day I hardly know what we did, but the time stole by, and the sun would be setting, and the candles lighting. Darkness fell at six. Now from the hospitable veranda we looked down on a navy-blue valley, flickering with the yellow flames of lanterns and the dancing sparks of fireflies. Geckoes began to scuttle and croak in the roof. We ate our supper, and drank arak, and Peter the gentle southerner sat cross-legged before the gamelan and played the bamboo bells softly in the background. Schuman too could play the gamelan, and many times I came upon him tinkling away to himself, his ancient face turned out to the sky.

In the village *banjar,* between the community notice board bearing the census figures for Peliagan and a government poster advertising vasectomies, there stood a full-size table-tennis table. Colin the spoiled priest was a table-tennis fanatic, and he and I often strolled down to the *banjar* to challenge the village boys to the best of five games. We never won, but by the time Colin left we had raised our standard to a creditable level. Around us as we played flowed the life of the village, the crowing of cocks and the barking of dogs, the stray pigs rooting at refuse, the murmuring clusters of ducks chivvied along by their duck shepherd with his long feathered pole. The Balinese girls too passed by, and lingered to watch us play; not exotically sensual as their reputation has it, but moon-faced and modest, their behavior characterized by a formal gravity.

I began to notice how Schuman observed us all as we came and went, not with his eyes so much as with an alertness of body.

I suspected he learned more from the tenor of our voices than from anything else, because he would often tip his head to one side, like an attentive bird. When he wished to attract someone's notice, it was with the most economical movement of one hand, and at a discreet moment, so that the rest of us would not see who was singled out. However, we always knew; for we were always alert for the moment when the signal would flash for us.

If he was not with us we often talked about him. Jerry, who was professionally accustomed to assessing personalities, made it clear that he was witholding his judgment. "He acts like he's a nondirective teacher," he said, "but until he condescends to speak to me I have to put my response to him on hold." This attitude irritated his wife Midge. "I don't see the old man losing any sleep over what you think of him, Jerry." "Okay, okay, I'm only saying I lack information, that's all." "But don't you feel the power there?" said Marta. "What sort of power?" said Jerry. "Hell, I don't know. Don't you feel it?" "I'll be frank with you, Marta, all I feel as of this moment is that he has no will of his own. Push him and he folds up. Now that's only a provisional opinion, and I don't want anybody to hold me to it." "He has a will," said Henrika from the shadows. "It's a different kind of will. He lets you have your way because what you want doesn't matter to him." "Jerry doesn't like to admit anyone can teach him anything," said Midge. "I'm here, aren't I?" said Jerry.

As the days went by, and I too felt myself easing down, I came to sense the power Marta attributed to the old man. It was not the power that brings dominion, it was the power that is to be felt in mature trees: strength, stillness, authenticity. Schuman's power in truth was no power, but a self-ease made potent only by the self-doubts with which we assailed him. The more I observed him, the more I learned of myself. Where I spoke and acted ceaselessly in the awareness of how others would respond to my words and actions, and so ceaselessly adjusted my manner to my audience, Schuman lived in utter trust with himself, as indifferent to others as a cat. His power over us lay in the plain fact that he neither sought nor needed our approval; therefore, as if in accordance with some natural law, we sought and needed his.

My education proper began as a result of a cockfight in the

village. By then I had been in Peliagan almost a month, and had not once conversed with the old man except as part of the general group. The cockfight was arousing considerable interest among us. All day Balinese men had been passing our compound wall carrying cockerels in deep beehive baskets. A ring had been erected by the *banjar*, beneath an awning of palm-leaf mats. Small *warungs*, little more than tables, had sprung up along the temple steps, selling sweet soup and rice cakes and roasted pork. As the afternoon began to cool several of us from the upper terrace drifted down to join the gathering crowd. The owners of the fighting cocks squatted around the ring, their baskets between their knees, the air under the awning hazy with the smoke of clove cigarettes. The spectators were all men. The women stood by the *warungs*, or sat along the temple steps. The square was loud with the crowing of the birds.

Before each fight the men around the ring called odds and laid bets with each other in a cacophony of voices, jerking fistfuls of *rupiah* in the air. After each fight the blade man took the defeated cock from its owner and severed its leg, so that he could unbind the blade with which the bird had fought. When he was done he washed his hands in a bowl of water which became progressively discolored with blood. This basin doubled as a clock. At the beginning of each round the timekeeper set a pierced coconut shell to float on the oily surface. The shell took about fifteen seconds to fill and sink, at which point the time-keeper rang the bell a second time for the round's end.

The fights were fast and violent. We stood immediately behind the timekeeper's table. I watched three fights with little understanding, but by the start of the fourth I was able to identify the combatants before they were lost in the thrash of wings. Their owners squatted on either side of the ring, holding them by their breasts and tweaking their ruff feathers to build up their aggression. One cock was ginger, one was black. Both were armed. The gleaming blades projected upward behind their legs like spurs.

When the flurry of betting had died down, and the bell had sounded, the two cocks trembled at each other on the hard earth, beaks extended, ruff feathers erect, no more than a few inches apart. They engaged in midair, wings pumping to gain the ad-

219

vantage of height, steeled claws striking from above. The moves were too fast to follow. As they sank to the ground the bell rang, and their owners snatched them apart. Neither bird seemed to be hurt. The owners groomed them with firm hands and spat into their beaks.

When the bell went for the second round, the ginger cock struck with unhesitating ferocity, before the black cock could leave the ground. Badly wounded, the black cock tottered to a corner and took refuge behind its own basket. There it lay on one wing, palpitating. "They'll stop the fight now, won't they?" said Midge. "They fight to the death," said Jerry beyond her. "It's their virility they're putting out there in the ring. They can't back down." "Oh, Jerry, don't tell me they're penises. Why does everything always have to be penises?" "Come on, Midge. Male fighting birds. Cocks, for Christ's sake."

It was clear now which was to be the killer and which was to be killed. Out of long habit I lent my instinctive support to the victim. But when the two birds faced each other again, as the vibration of the bell died away into tense silence, as water flowed into the pierced shell, in the moment of stillness before the violence, my body went cold and I switched sides. Until that moment I had not known I would do it. From that moment it was irreversible. For the first time in my life I aligned myself with the strong against the weak, not out of admiration for strength, but in recognition of my place. This was my coming of age: I no longer belonged with the victims; I was no longer blameless.

The wounded black cock tried to show aggression, but it could only wobble feebly before sinking to its belly feathers. The killing was quick and mute but for the thrashing of wings. The chop of the knife made me jump. Already, so soon, the pink cotton was being unwound from the black cock's leg. "Why, William, you're shivering," said Midge. But I could not explain, and did not try. Killing clarifies; even the death of cockerels.

A hand brushed at my left shoulder. I turned and saw the diminutive figure of Schuman. "Young sir," he said, "come to the temple steps tomorrow morning, and we will talk a little."

19

Everywhere you go in Bali there are temples. They say the island has ten thousand temples. These places of worship are not enclosed chambers in the Western fashion, but courtyards in which stand many open pavilions, richly ornamented with stone carvings. The soft stone erodes in the rain, and the carvings have to be regularly replaced. It is this geological accident as much as anything which has made the Balinese into a race of artists.

I waited for Schuman by the split column of the temple gate. Brilliant light fell aslant the village, making the leaves glow on the trees and the rice fields sparkle on the farther slope of the valley. In the temple behind me a stonecarver was at work on a pedestal, ringing out his *chink-chink* into the cool morning. Curious children stared at me and went on their way. A line of women stalked majestically up the river path, each bearing on her head a slab of stone for the construction work in the temple. The duck shepherd passed, leading his herd to the flooded fields where the rice had been cut.

When Schuman appeared, comical in his khaki shorts, a wide-brimmed straw hat hiding his bald head, he succeeded somehow in belonging to the village scene. Perhaps it was the unhurried way in which he crossed the square; or the dignified uprightness of his posture, so typical of the Balinese. He had a long stick in one hand, as tall as himself, which gave him a pilgrim air.

Together we left the village by the path through the rice terraces. On this first of our many walks together he led me to the overgrown temple in the monkey forest, for no more significant reason than that few people walked that way. In the beginning he said little, except to ask me to tell him about myself, and about my experience thus far of the levels. We walked slowly, and I talked, and the trees crashed about us as monkeys dropped onto the leaf-strewn path. Unafraid, they loped at our heels like gray dogs. I told Schuman all that I could, and he nodded and nodded. When I spoke of Aurora Miller I added that I had expected to find her still here in Peliagan. "I sent her back," said Schuman. "She is not yet ready." He would not tell me what he meant by this.

Our attendant troupe of monkeys leaped ahead of us through the split gate into the temple. We followed, and settled ourselves on the base of a carved stone stairway, which led up to a doorway to nowhere. Schuman pointed out to me that what we were sitting on was a stone representation of a turtle: "He is Bedawang, the world turtle, on whom the world rests." Reared up on either side of us like newel posts were the wise heads of the twin-headed world serpent Antaboga. I was not sure whether Schuman expected me to treat these curiosities with respect or not. While monkeys crowded around us, tugging at our clothing with their tiny hands, wagging their tufted heads and showing us their pink mouths, the old man told me something about himself.

"What I am now, young sir, such as it is, is not what I intended to be. It has all been an accident. That I live on this island, that people such as yourself come to me. Sometimes when I am lying in my house alone at night I find that I am laughing, *hoch! hoch!*, the way old men laugh. I am laughing to think that I am called teacher. Master. I am only Schuman the Alsatian pimp, grown old, gone crazy, so they say." He pushed the monkeys from his knees, not unlike a monkey himself with his bright little eyes and graying skin. I would not have ventured to

222

ask him about his past, just as I had never asked Arlette; but it seemed he was proud of it. "Before I was as old as you are now I had twenty women on the boulevards of Paris. By the age of forty, four houses. You have been to the château in the Forêt de Soignes. It is mine. I am the owner. Ah, you did not know that. And do you know what it is to be a pimp? You cannot know. It is to be a god. My women worshiped me. I know, I know, it is not easy to believe when you see me now, but so it was. Arlette will tell you. I was father, brother, lover, son, professor, prefect, priest. Everything. How else could I have come to learn what I know today? If I had not been a pimp I would have been a priest, but as a priest what would I have learned? As a pimp . . . I was past the age of fifty before I so much as heard speak the names of the *tantra*, and the *tao*, and yet I had already learned all that they had to teach. Why? Because I was a pimp. Do you know these ancient traditions?"

"No. I know nothing about them."

"Good. That is fortunate. So many like yourself seek to rob others of their truths, thinking it will be quicker work than finding their own. It is all to be learned on the streets of Paris. All men come to the same truth if they only wait, and do not try to be what they are not." He poked me with a bony finger. "I saw you at the cockfight. Arlette has prepared you well."

He seemed then to fall into a reverie. I supposed he was musing on Arlette, his wife, if indeed they were married. They were remarkably alike, not in appearance so much as in presence. When I shut my eyes, and when Schuman was not speaking, it was easy to imagine that Arlette sat beside me.

"Did you hear what he said?"

"Who? You mean Jerry?"

"Our psychoanalytical friend at the cockfight."

"I heard him." I looked curiously at the old man, half expecting to discover some device whereby he had suggested Jerry to me, as magicians force cards.

"It was interesting, what he said."

"Jerry thinks everything is a sex symbol. Midge is right about that."

"And Jerry is right. But he does not know it."

"Right about the cockfight?"

"Of course, that. But more than that. You say he sees the world as a sex symbol: well, so it is, just as sex is a world symbol. Now there is something for you to think about, young sir. But we must go slowly along this path, both because I am old and because you are young."

He would say no more than this, and asked me no more questions about myself, so I gathered that our first session was at an end. He sent me back to the village without him. I assumed he had another private meeting to attend, with another of his self-appointed disciples.

A week went by before I next received Schuman's summons. During that time I thought about what he had told me, but could make nothing useful of it. "Sex is a world symbol": it was the sort of abstraction which may or may not be true, but which makes little difference either way. I need not have troubled myself over it. In saying to me, "There is something to think about," Schuman had been planting a seed of awareness in me, much as the seeds of flowers are planted in the earth. The soil of my mind had been well fertilized over the past months. The seed was left to germinate.

Such gentle growth suited the slow round of life in Peliagan. In the cities in which I have lived most of my life it would have frustrated me, so accustomed are we by now to rapid results. It is easy to see from my present perspective why so many people remain so unhappily ignorant: the knowledge, the happiness they seek dwells like tiny wildflowers in cracks by the side of the road, and they drive by in their automobiles too fast to see it.

A mistaken notion has spread in some circles that Schuman's community in Peliagan exists in a perpetual state of orgy. The fact is that although the visitors to the compound are both men and women, and although all have come to pursue the path of sexual enlightenment devised by the Schumans, very little sexual activity takes place; and such as does is of a highly specialized nature. I had been in Peliagan some weeks before I realized that there was a certain amount of discreet passing to and fro in the dark of the night. It may seem unlikely that such a sex-aware group, rolled up in blankets within feet of each other night after night, should have exercised such restraint; yet my experience has been that the more access a person has to sexual satisfaction, the less obsessed he or she becomes by the whole business. Those of us in particular who had passed through the five earlier levels had no difficulty with this temporary celibacy; which to me further proves Arlette's theory of 'dirty sex,' that most compulsive promiscuity is designed to anesthetize self-doubts rather than to satisfy physical needs.

On our next walk together Schuman took me up the zigzag path to the top of the ridge, from where we could see the hills and valleys undulating into the bright distance. As was his way, when he spoke it was without preamble, straight from the center of his own thoughts.

"Your friend the American girl," he said. "I think you admire her."

"Yes," I said, a little taken aback.

"Have you ever seen her naked?"

"No." Then I recalled the afternoon I had passed lying with Aurora by the pool of the Oriental Hotel, Bangkok. "Not fully naked, at least. I've seen her in a bikini."

"Do you remember what her body looks like?"

"Very well."

"It is beautiful, I suppose, her body."

"Yes. Very beautiful."

"Then we shall play my game with her. It has no deep meaning, this game of mine, it is no more than it seems. For you we may call it *Cherchez la femme,* Find the lady. So now, young sir, if you please to look out over the valleys." My obedient eye followed his stick, which wavered erratically over the expansive view. "You see this ridge on which we stand. And the line of hills over there. You see how they seem to come together? Now picture to yourself your friend's legs, lay her over the hills. Do you see it? Arrange the legs so that they lie over the two lines of hills. Can you do it? Does she lie there?"

"Yes, I can do it."

"It is not easy, I know. Project her there. Hold her there. Do you see her naked legs? Describe them to me."

"They are brown. Slim. Her left knee is raised a little above the right. Her legs are parted."

"Very good. Hold her there. Now I want you to let her body

225

sink into the hills, as if sinking beneath the surface of the sea. Let her sink, slowly, but as soon as the trees have covered her, let her sink no farther. You see her legs? Slim, you say, brown."

"Yes."

"Sink them. They are sinking?"

"Yes."

"Now does she lie there, covered by the green palms as if they are her sheet?"

"Yes."

"Make your thoughts strong. There she lies. She is sleeping. If you were to wake her, these long limbs would stir beneath their thin coverlet. Do you see her there still?"

"I see her."

"Perhaps you can make love to her as she lies there."

"Perhaps."

There was no more to his game than this. He required me to discover in the world about me shapes which corresponded to parts of Aurora's naked body, and to "see" them for a sustained period of two or three minutes. Like all acts of mental concentration, this is harder than it sounds. The old man gave me several pointers, so that I would pick up the quaint little game quickly: the roots of banyan trees, he said, were rich in body forms; and the rocks in the riverbed, ground smooth by the water flow; and the irregularities in the earth paths over which we walked. "Look down as you walk and you will come upon her, lying with her arms flung back, or folded into a bend, as she rests on her side. See, here: here are her little feet, here her buttocks, here her head. Do you see her?" Also I was to look up, and find her body in the formations of clouds that sailed slowly by overhead. "Each day," Schuman said to me, "I want to you leave the compound by yourself for an hour, or for two hours, and go on your own way finding your friend's beautiful body on all sides. Wherever you see her, do not walk on; stand still, and make your thoughts strong. See her with precision. Sink her into the natural shape she has assumed. Believe she lies there. Speak to her. Do not allow yourself to reduce the exercise to an artistic perception, you are not seeing how like the human body is the natural world; you are seeing your friend, who lies naked, who waits for you to make love to her."

Later he taught me to extend this visual identification to the other senses. Walking beside me he would say: "Have you ever felt a woman's breath on your face as you make love? This warm wind we feel now, think of it as your lover's breath. Her face is so close to you as you go along that her breath warms you." So also with the sounds with which the island was alive, above all the sound of running water: "You hear the fall of water through the irrigation channels? Think that she is there, paddling in the water. She is out of your sight, but near. Perhaps she lies down in the water, so that it ripples over her body." Schuman even co-opted the cowbells. The cows grazed with wooden bells around their necks. As they dipped their heads to the grass the bells *donk-donked* across the valleys. "Think that your friend has such a bell around her neck," he said. "It hangs just between her breasts. Each time you hear it ring, think how it falls against her skin."

I carried out this exercise as he wished me to, day after day, and so slowly filled the island around me with remembered images of Aurora. There was no one to see what I did, and so I came to forget how it might appear to an outsider, and the shapes formed before me unsought. Aurora's slender arms reached out for me from the trees, her wide mouth smiled out of the clouds, her angular breasts broke the skyline as if she lay on her back athwart the entire island, her mass of dark hair tumbling down like forests over the hills. This daily meditation, for so it was, had no effect on me that I could discern. It was not especially erotic. Because the process was so gradual I was unable to tell how it was in fact altering my manner in the world.

At about this time I was learning from Peter how to play the gamelan. Gamelan music is a soft trickle of sound, without beginning and without ending. Playing and listening to the gamelan is an act of easing down. We played at night, seated on rugs on the veranda, looking out at the stars. Faint from the village came the music of other gamelans; and on all sides the stridor of crickets. In Peter's hands the hammers danced over the bamboos faster than the eye could follow. I accompanied him slowly, *plink plink plink,* and was carried along by his more confident stream. After some nights of this I found the rhythm, and the music took the place of speech. When I did speak, laying down the hammers after playing for up to an hour at a time, my voice emerged in a soft slur, and the others laughed. The more time I spent in Peliagan the less I spoke; the less need there seemed to be for speech.

We sang songs too, from memory. Piper, whose sweet light voice seemed not to belong to her outsize body, knew all the early Simon and Garfunkel songs, and also the slow ballads of the Mamas and the Papas. Midge sang us Rodgers and Hammerstein favorites, and we all joined in the choruses. Our Balinese neighbors liked these sessions far better than our attempts on the gamelan, and hearing us sing would often slip silently into the long house and sit listening in the shadows.

The Balinese lived and worked all around us in Peliagan, but our way of life was not Balinese, nor did it attempt to become so. Even Schuman, who had lived here on and off for the last ten years, showed no signs of going native. He spoke Bahasa Indonesia, the official language of the country, but only a little Balinese, which was still the common tongue of the villages. He liked to attend the constant religious ceremonies of village life, and accorded them proper respect, but privately he confessed to me that he regarded it as a form of theater. He lived in Bali because "nowhere else in the world is it possible to possess so little, and labor so lightly, and live so well." Now eighty-three years old, he had retired to Peliagan, and did not expect to leave the island again alive.

Inevitably he had come to know the island ways well. When I asked him how long I might expect to be in Peliagan, he told me: "The people here carry their newborn babies everywhere they go, and never let their feet touch the ground until they are one hundred and five days old. They believe the baby must be allowed to enter the material world slowly." And so it was also for me; for I stayed over three months, easing down to the sixth level.

When Schuman saw that I was well established in his game, as he called it, he introduced me to the next stage. "So far I have asked you only to see the woman's body in the world about you. Now you must begin to see your own body as it passes through the world." This was to be my own feet-touching-the-ground, my

228

own entry as an active participant into the physical universe. "Whenever your hand rests on what is soft, or what is warm, think that it is her skin. Caress it as if it is her skin. Whenever you speak, speak lovingly, as if you speak love words to her. Whenever you draw a deep breath, release your breath as if you blow on her face, which is always before you. If you are tired as you walk, and sit down to rest, lean a little to one side and think that you lean on her."

He encouraged me to make noises, little wordless love songs, as I went on my solitary walks. "But you must think that she is listening. You must be talking to her, not the rice fields, nor to the sky." "Should I be directing all this to the one woman?" I asked. "It is an effort of the imagination," he said. "You will find it easier to retain concentration if there is only the one woman, so long as she is a woman for whom you have great desire. As for your friend, you have no need to worry. This is only an intermediate stage. You will have passed beyond it before you see her again."

So I walked the green terraces, chirping and humming to my faraway friend, until the notion that she was beside me became so habitual that I caught myself addressing comments to her in the compound, like a widower who forgets that his wife has died. "Every action that you consciously undertake," said Schuman, "find a way that you can think it is a part of making love to her. Accustom your body to be forever reaching out in the posture of love. When you wish to empty your bladder, stand for some moments until you attain full awareness of what you are about to do, then let the water flow from you like semen." In particular he urged me to make full use of the business of bathing. "Wait until the sun has warmed the water of the pool. Recline in the water as if you are in her arms. Sing to her. Hear her voice in the sounds of the water. Let each breath that leaves you blow warm on her face. Let go your muscles so that she may enter you. Open the door of your penis so that the water flows from you. Let the flow of water about you join the flow of water within you, and the flow of sound from your belly up through your throat join the flow of the sound of the world in through your ears. Make love to her in the river."

All these things I did, and found that so inconstant was my mind that only for a few seconds at a time could I surrender my body to the pretense that I was making love. These brief moments did grow longer, and I found them pleasing, but not in a way that I would ever have thought of as sexual. Never did I have an erection. Instead I experienced a state that I can best describe as an electric restfulness: the surface of my body excitedly alert while within I danced and sang as in a dream.

Schuman gave me no intellectual exposition of what he was doing to me; but unaided, the realization came. One starry night I left the long house to empty my bladder into the uncultivated forest over the back perimeter wall. Since I had begun Schuman's exercises, urinating had become for me an occasion of conscious delight; mildly intoxicated also by the rice spirit called arak, I stood swaying, pissing, and chanting into the black bushes, and so returned across the compound as light as a leaf. Unusually, the old man was sitting alone on the porch of his little house, as if he was waiting for me. His porch did not look out into the valley, like the veranda of the long house. It faced the volcano. Because this night was so clear, the outline of the jagged peak was discernible where it blotted out the dusty spread of stars. Uninvited I came to a stop beside his house, and let my weight rest on one of the wooden uprights supporting the porch roof. I wanted to talk: not to converse, but to vent the thoughts that had swollen inside me, as if my mind too was a bladder to be emptied.

I meant only to tell the old man how well I liked his exercises; and how I now saw that the levels were having a more far-reaching effect on me than I had anticipated. But other words also slipped out, that I had not known were waiting in me. "I've never really known where I'm going," I heard myself say. "I've never known what I was supposed to be doing. I used to think I knew, but I didn't know. It's so much easier if there's someone there to tell you what to do. But I didn't expect this. I never expected it to be like this. And now it's too late, isn't it?"

The old man was silent.

"When I began this whole thing, I thought that what I wanted was something small, and neat, and precious, like a jewel. I thought it would be hard to get, but that if I got it, I'd know I'd got it. I'd be able to feel it in my hands. That was what I wanted, something clear, something simple. Arlette said it was simple. Not easy, she said, but simple. But she didn't tell me it was so big. She said it was sex, only sex, nothing but sex, so I never thought it would be big. Not as big as this. But it's too late to go back now, isn't it?"

"It's been too late for a long time."

"I think I've known it for a long time. Is that possible? I've told myself, all you're doing is enjoying yourself, learning to enjoy yourself, and there's been this question mark all along: is that enough? Is enjoying myself enough? That question always frightened me. I've always blocked it out. I thought it frightened me because the answer was going to be, no, enjoying myself isn't enough; and what was I supposed to do then? But that wasn't what frightened me. I see it now. I've been frightened to find out that the answer is yes."

I did not know how this had come about; only that it was so.

"I so much wanted it to be a small thing, that could be given to me, like sweets. But it's turning out to be so big. It's turning out to be everything,"

"Why does that surprise you?" said the old man.

"What surprises me is that it doesn't surprise me after all. It's as if I've been expecting it."

"It is sex that made you. It is sex that creates life."

I saw now the intention behind the levels; how I had been patiently pieced together like a jigsaw. Schuman did not want to formulate for me what I was discovering for myself, but he did offer back to me, in his own revealing words, what I had so far expressed. "Sex is the power that joins," he said. "We are all alone until we learn to make love to the world."

20

The final stage of the sixth level, which is known as "dark sex," followed shortly after this exchange. It was only now that I discovered how Schuman engineered the specifically sexual element in his teaching. I had not wondered about it before because by this stage in my progress through the levels I had more or less lost the habit of straining at the present as if it were elastic designed to catapult me into the future. Also I was contented. I did not chafe at the conditions in which I found myself, and so was introduced to the subtle pleasures of patience.

Our custom in the long house was to retire to sleep by about nine o'clock, but it was not unusual for members of the group to be out in neighboring villages, or even as far afield as Murni's *warung* in Ubud where other expatriates gathered, and so figures came and went unremarked at late hours of the night. One night, after rain had been falling all day and clouds still shuttered up the sky, the old man took me aside and told me not to go to sleep with the others, but to join him in his house on the far side of the compound.

I had never entered his little domain. It was understood among us that this was the old man's private space; and as its matting walls had no windows, I had not even glimpsed its interior in passing. When I entered it at last I found that the single room, far from concealing anything, was virtually empty. A kerosene lantern stood on a large wooden chest, casting its light over the batik-patterned sarongs that draped the walls. A palliasse lay rolled up on one side. The dirt floor was covered with palm-leaf mats. Such possessions as Schuman had must have been contained within the chest, for there were no signs of any others.

I sat down cross-legged on the mat facing him, there being no other form of seating. "It may amuse you to know," he said, "that what I am about to tell you is what I told to my women in the old days, when they first came to me. I said it then to give them enthusiasm, to make them believe in what they were doing. I was concerned only to make good whores of them, which I did. But that is all long ago now. So to our present business." He closed his eyes but did not lower his face, as if he looked at me still through his eyelids. "First, the silence."

We sat without speaking for a long time. I was well accustomed by now to such spaces, and no longer instinctively crowded my mind with chattering thoughts. If ever something of importance is to be said, this preparatory silence is as necessary as the plain bread with which a connoisseur cleanses his palate before drinking wine.

"For the last several weeks you have been teaching yourself to respond sexually to the world around you. You, a man, have been learning to see all that is other than you as a woman. For so it is. Tonight you will make love with all the world. Tonight you, the man, will make love with the not-you, the woman. It is for this that you must now prepare yourself."

One by one he recalled to me his various exercises, requiring me to awaken each part of my body to the expectation of sexual contact, and to sense in the space around me the female forms of the island. He told me that in order to sustain this effort of the imagination, which was to be that I was making love with the valleys, and the paths, and the streams, and the clouds in the sky,

233

as well as all the women I had ever desired, I must not seek to know the individual identity of the one who was to join me. We were to make love in complete darkness. She too would know nothing of me. "You will be to her what she will be to you, the not-self from which you are both so unhappily separated." I was not to speak to her and she was not to speak to me. Schuman would return before dawn and send one of us away before the other, so that we would never learn each other's identity.

When his explanations were finished, he instructed me to remove my clothes. He unrolled the palliasse, and laid over it a thick patterned blanket. The lever on the kerosene lantern scraped as he raised the glass chimney and held the flame to his lips. The close lantern light on his bald head and beaky nose gave him the air of a wizened baby. So he blew out the flame; and for a moment I saw him in the doorway, blacker than the black night; then he had drawn across the opening a heavy curtain, and I was in utter darkness.

I felt for the blanket and drew it over my shoulders. For a while I saw facing the door, but no one came. I could not help wondering who the woman might be who was to join me, whether she was an islander or one of my fellows from the long house. Then as more time went by this speculation faded from my mind, and I found I was drifting into sleep. The darkness was so total that it was hard to tell whether I was awake or not. Unable to see even my own hand before my eyes, I began to lose my sense of where I was in relation to myself. I tried to repeat the exercises as the old man had instructed me, but even as I populated the limitless night with voluptuous images, I was skimming and ducking below the surface of sleep.

In my half-sleep I dreamed that I lay naked on a well-kept English lawn, and Aurora stood above me, also naked, and when she laid herself by my side the sun which she had been shielding from me pressed down like hot-water bottles. I clambered out of this half-sleep to discover a body creeping warm against mine. I was lying on my side, my knees drawn up in a semifoetal position, and the stranger was shuffling her body toward me, as unable as I to tell where I began and ended. I felt for her, and

234

our probing hands met and clasped, relieved to have gained some orientation.

So she lay beside me, a more substantial darkness among the darkness, invisible, nameless, real. As I explored her with my hands I formed her, woman-form, any woman and every woman, my mind faltering between sleep and waking not thinking to wonder who she might be. At first she was Aurora, kneeling over me on the sunny lawn. Then she was Louise under the red sheets. Then she was nobody, a shape, a warmth beside me in the cooling night.

The blackness banished scale. I might rise so tall I overstrode valleys, or shrink so small I tucked myself between her legs as into the cleft of a peach. I let my hands form the landscape of her body like God molding the world from its primeval clay.

Strange hands shocked my penis with curious touch; and retreated. I opened myself out to make my body accessible to her will. A hand trotted shyly up my chest, fingering for my mouth. I licked the salty palm. Who was she? She was who I wished her to be. So I let her be Jeannie. I furnished the darkness as the bedroom of our one-time home: to my left the window, to my right the bedside lamp, beyond, the door to the landing. And here beside me Jeannie, naked as she had so rarely been, available as she had never been. So strong was the picture I had to restrain myself from speaking to her, saying, "Why was it not always as easy as this?"

I too was an anonymous body, to whom this woman turned seeking only man-form, any man, every man. In this capacity I offered myself to her, and she became Aurora, released from the restraints of her role as my guide, plundering my flesh for grateful sensation. It was Aurora's smooth leg that hooked across me, Aurora's furry crotch that scraped against my cock. I felt her breath on my shoulder, saw her lips part and her eyes close in longing; though in reality I saw nothing. She ground her pelvis against mine, and pressed my hands to her breasts, and I said, "So that's what you've been wanting from me all this time?"; but in reality I said nothing. It was my fantasy, but because I worked it on an actual person, it was also real.

235

I had been blind before, in Bangkok, but this was altogether different. My eyes were free to see. I did not feel helpless, or passive. Once I had overcome the inhibitions on movement, the fear of clumsiness, I felt my power. The mid-world we occupied between corporeal reality and projected dream granted a series of unfolding freedoms. I did not know, was never to know, this woman's identity, and so enjoyed freedom from the consequences of my actions. I was not to speak to her, nor she to me, and so I was freed from all anxiety about her response. I could not see what she looked like, whether she was ugly or beautiful, and so was freed from the stern decrees of my own vanity. I was in all objective terms alone, and so freed from self-consciousness; but I was not alone, and so was spared solitude. My companion performed the function so greatly enjoyed by Louise, the sex doll, with the significant difference that this woman had no known personality to inhibit me in my exploitation.

I did not forget Schuman's more philosophical perspective, that in the blackness I was making love to all the world; indeed, I found that once I had released myself to the freedoms of my situation, the sex doll dream was not so far removed from the creator God dream. The link lay deep within me, in the discovery of my own power. Through sex I voyaged out to touch the world.

Power made me rapacious. Creation made me violent. My companion allowed me to use her body as I willed, and the megalomaniac vision took on the physical form of rough sex. Through her body I raped the valleys, and I raped Jeannie, and I raped the mountainous sky. Dark sex exposed in me a stagnant well of aggression. I made love as if I made war; as if our lumpy palliasse were a hard-earth ring, our engagement a cockfight, and my penis the murdering blade.

Dark is a different country from light. There is no justice there, no accountability. There are no maps. Where you are now you will never be again. Eyeballs roll over in their sockets, and the nothing that you see is the chamber of your skull. The nightmare rules the night. Devils clog the air like bats. Before you in the long hours to dawn there crouches wild possibility.

236

Dark sex, if properly conducted, has the blast of a controlled explosion. Schuman used it carefully, within a specific context, to forge the link between the sexuality of the self and the sexuality of the world. He knew that nothing could be everything. He knew also how quickly we, his students, would run away from nothing, away from everything, to the comforting cubicles of our sometime selves. He took precautions. He never coupled the same pair twice, lest they find out too much about each other; for only so long as the companion was unnamed might the self roam free. My first companion, for example, did not speak, as Schuman ordered, but during orgasm she could not hold back a cry, a shrill squeak which I would instantly recognize were I ever to hear it again. For all I know I too cried out when I came. I remember only the later time, when the old man's crusty hand was shaking me awake, not knowing which of us it was he had hold of, telling me to find my clothes and return to the long house.

°

Over the following days and weeks I continued my meditative walks, and from time to time, according to no regular pattern, passed a night in the galactic embrace of dark sex. The frequency of these nights was dictated as much as anything by the quality of the visitors to Peliagan; for Schuman was not easily persuaded that his eager pupils were ready for his instruction. But I did not know this at the time.

One insignificant incident will serve to illustrate my growing physical adjustment to the sixth level. The old man spoke of "making love to the world," or of "offering a sexual response to all things," phrases that can easily be misperceived as metaphor. The effect of his exercises, and of his dark sex, came slowly, but it came. My sample incident took place after my fifth night of dark sex, some six weeks after I had begun to follow the exercises. I was playing table tennis in the *banjar* against Piper, the over weight Australian. Despite her girth, Piper played a sharp game, and I was losing. After dropping two points in succession through attempting high-velocity services, I switched to slow safe lobs. Piper, hoping to lure me into another inaccurate slam,

237

returned the ball slow and high. I watched it sail over the dark green surface toward me, and reached out my bat to meet it. The ball struck my bat with the usual pop and rebounded; but with the slight impact, a shiver went up my arm. I was immediately aware that this vibration came from the ball, that it was what I could only call the intention of the ball. I did not suppose that the ball had a mind, only that it possessed a simple and separate nature which delivered power when it struck my bat. The bat too had its own nature, its own power. The physical reaction in my arm seemed to be caused by the collision of miniature powers.

I waited for the ball to return, following its bounces with close attention, absorbed not by where it might go when I hit it, but by the moment of meeting it. My play showed a sudden improvement. "Found your eye," said Piper. My newfound eye looked on her with pleasure. I liked Piper. I liked her big generous body, out of which flew like a lark escaping her pure child's voice.

The quality I call "intention" revealed itself more each day, in objects animate and inanimate. It is like a handshake. When you greet a stranger by shaking his hand, if you feel warmly toward each other you experience not only a pressure on your hand but the sensation of the stranger's positive intentions. At the same time you transmit to him through your clasp the goodwill with which you present yourself. Increasingly I found my contact with the world around me took on this intentional character; as if all things wanted to shake my hand.

I spoke of such intimations only to Schuman. When he was satisfied that my response was securely based, and that I would not turn his words into a pattern by which to refashion my own experience, he ventured to give me a wider view of the sixth level. "Because we have genital organs," he said, "people make the mistake of thinking that sex is a partial business, confined to one part of their body, in the way that taste is confined to the mouth, or smell to the nose. But sex is not an accessory, it is of the essence. If you are fully present when you make love, for a brief moment your disintegrated personality integrates, fuses, becomes whole. You cease to be a thought rattling in a body, or a

238

spirit languishing in a prison of flesh. What is not understood is that this is how we are meant to be all the time. Sex is the means to this fusion, but it is more than this. Never forget that it is sex that creates life. We may say sex is the life force, except that without sex there is no life, so it is better to say, sex is life. When I tell you: make love to the world, I am telling you: live in the world." The old man had a saying that most succinctly contained the message of the sixth level, a line I would turn vandal to spray on public walls were it not for the constraint of the insight sandwich. He said, "Sex is the spirit of the body and the body of the spirit."

From this perspective the shames and guilts of obsessive sexual morality merge into the shames and guilts of pornography, allied in their effort to housetrain sex. "We've made about as big a mess of sex as we have of religion, haven't we?" I said. At a later stage Schuman, who was not to my knowledge religious, endorsed this parallel perception when he said, "Just as God is not a pet, so sex is not a pet."

It was now clear to me that the final purpose of the levels was not merely good sex, but a state of being. Yet this is a false antithesis, for I know Schuman would cluck his tongue at me and say, "Good sex *is* a state of being." What now began to occupy my thoughts was the old man's assertion that it was possible to make such a state permanent. He persisted in speaking of it in unambiguously sexual terms, as "making love to all things," so I framed my questions in like fashion, and asked him how it was possible to make love all the time. "It is not easy," he said, "but it can be done." "You don't mean that I am to have a perpetual erection, I hope?" "Not exactly. But it is possible to be perpetually sexually aroused." "I'd wear myself out." "Maybe," he said, "and maybe not. It all depends on whether you are ready. I think you are too young still, but you have learned well."

Some days later, on returning from one of my solitary walks, it came to me that I wanted to go to sleep. I was crossing the village square at the time. Without hesitation I laid myself down on the warm earth in the shade of the temple wall. This was not an uncommon act on my part; my latter days in Peliagan passed in a dream state that dropped frequently over the lip of sleep.

239

When I awoke, perhaps half an hour later, I found Schuman standing over me, leaning on his stick. One of the villagers, seeing me asleep, had gone to fetch him; not because I was lying in the village square, but because I had been joined as I slept by a small herd of pigs. Their plump black bodies lay pressed against mine on all sides, and they snorted softly as they dozed in the heat. Balinese pigs are not much bigger than corgis, and some of them, apparently seeking closer contact, had wriggled under my arms and between my legs. The villagers were both amused and impressed.

I stood up carefully, not wanting to disturb the pigs. "I didn't lie down with them," I said. "They lay down with me."

The old man did not say, because there was no need for him to say, and I would not have understood, that the pigs had been sexually attracted to me; yet such was his belief. So accustomed are we to identifying sexual attraction with the sex act that this suggestion becomes at once repulsive, bestial. It means no more than that the pigs felt the power and·trustworthiness of my physical presence, and sought to share it. No more than this, and no less than this; for it is a great thing. Schuman said only, "If the pigs say you are ready, then you are ready."

I followed him back to his house, where he sat me down before him on the porch that looked out toward the distant volcano. For a while he peered at me in silence, as I had come to expect. Then he laid his hands on me, one to each shoulder, in an uncharacteristically formal embrace. A dry heat spread from his hands over my upper back.

"Across your way there now stands a high wall," he said. "In the wall is a door. When you open that door, if you are able to open that door, pause before you pass through. It is enough at the beginning just to see what the world is like beyond the wall. If you pass through that door, you will no longer need me, and you will no longer need Arlette."

His solemn pronouncement puzzled me. "How am I to recognize this door?"

Schuman's wrinkled face puckered up, and he began to cough. "I am a foolish old man. You must forgive me." His rasping coughs shook him as if he was trying to suppress laughter. "How

240

you all listen to me! You put such temptations in my path. . . "
He became calmer, and patted my shoulders to reassure me.
"Yet what I tell you is true. Where I am sending you now, if you
arrive you will no longer need me."

"Am I to go away, then?"

"I think it is time."

"Where am I to go?"

"That does not matter. Anywhere. Home. But you will need
there the assistance of a friend, a lover, whom you trust."

"As a sex partner?"

"Just so. One you know well. One for whom you feel much
desire. The American, perhaps."

"Would she do?"

"If you trust her."

I considered this. Yes, I trusted Aurora. Also it seemed proper,
almost inevitable, that I should turn at last to her. "I've never
made love with her," I said. "I've no way of knowing she'd
cooperate."

"She will cooperate, if you ask her."

"You want me to go to her in Los Angeles?"

"Where you go is immaterial. If your friend is in Los Angeles,
then by all means go to Los Angeles."

"And what am I to do there?"

"Well now, young sir. We come to the point. What have I
been teaching you here in Peliagan? I have been teaching you to
live as if you are making love to all the world; making love to all
that is other than you. You have asked me, how is it possible to
make love all the time? How is it possible to make love forever?
My answer is that there is a technique. Of course it is more than
a technique, far more, but it is enough for now for you to think of
it as a technique. This technique is not my invention, nor
Arlette's. It is the basic technique of the Chinese *tao*, and of the
tantric *sadhana*. That does not make it more true. But when you
feel its power, if you feel its power, you should not be frightened.
You will be sharing an experience that has been understood and
practiced since the days of the Han dynasty, over two thousand
years ago."

The old man squatted down on his haunches and began to

rock gently back and forth, never taking his eyes off me as he spoke. I listened and was amazed; not at what he had to tell me, so much as at my own recognition of it all, as if the knowledge had been lying patiently within me from the beginning.

Schuman said, "I call this technique, and the door that it opens, and the world that you will enter beyond that door, the seventh level."

The Seventh Level

21

On my arrival in Los Angeles I did not call Aurora Miller at once. She had no warning of my coming, and for all I knew my visit might be ill-timed. I asked the cab driver to drop me in Larrabee Street, West Hollywood, and having located her address I walked up the hill to Sunset Boulevard. There I checked into the nearest cheap motel, which was called the Casa Real.

It was early evening. The flight through the time zones had delivered me unnaturally alert, like an overexcited child, to this unknown town. The clerk at the motel looked at me oddly as I signed in, as if he was unsure whether or not he had met me before. He read my name and address on the registration form. "You been here before, sir?" "No," I said. "We get British television crews here from time to time," he said, as if this explained his mistake.

I dialed Aurora's number from my motel room, but there was no reply. Outside the window cars streamed up Sunset Boulevard. Illuminated signs said Crocker Bank, and Hav-a-Kar Economy Car Rental. After flushing, the pale green lavatory emitted a low groan, which continued for some little time, until it died away in lingering resignation. It was a long way from the murmur of the irrigation channels on Bali, but it was a voice speaking to me nonetheless, and I heard it.

I was not hungry and I was not sleepy, so I descended by the outer stairs, crossed the plastic turf by the motel pool, and found the entrance to the bar. As I sat over my Budweiser a lone drinker like myself caught my eye, a man with white hair and a boyish face. His brown cheeks crinkled in a smile of recognition. "Hi," he said, "how you doing?," and transferred himself to the stool beside mine. The bar was dimly lit, presumably to create an intimate atmosphere, and I supposed he had mistaken me for someone else. "Fine," I said. His name was Skip E. Lowe, and he was the host of the revue that was presented each night here in the bar, a modest showcase for unknown singers and comedians. Skip, a movie actor, had just secured a part in a film to be called "The World's Greatest Lover;" he saw in me one with whom he could share his good news. "I just heard today," he said, laying one hand on my arm, "it's camp but not too camp. I play a wardrobe man. Gene Wilder insisted I have the part. It's made for you, Skip, he said. He's a wonderful man, Gene. Fox will do anything for him. So I heard today." "That's wonderful, Skip," I said, pleased by his overflowing good humor. "What a perfect young man you are!" he cried, parodying his own camp manner. Seeing a young woman enter the bar he sprang from his stool and seized her by the hand. "Precious," he said, "I've found the most perfect young man for you, so you must shack up with him at once. Do yourself a favor, get yourself laid." The young woman, one of the novice singers, was not at all put out by this introduction. She turned upon me a glazed indifferent eye, but then frowned and looked away. Her boy friend and singing partner appeared, and we all talked in a desultory fashion as they waited for the showcase to begin. The singers were listless in voice and manner. They had nothing good to say for the Strip, or Hollywood, or Los Angeles in general. But the girl glanced at me from time to time, and I caught in her eyes a quite different expression, as if she were asking me for something.

Skip vamped his performers to the half-empty bar. "I met an old girl friend today, I have to tell you this, she said, Skip, she said, you're just what I've been looking for, you're just what I need, stay with me, Skip, never leave me, you're the answer to a maiden's prayer. Is that so? I said, how's that? I'm through with men, she said. So don't laugh. See if I care. Our first entertainer tonight comes from Venezuela, he tells me. My friends, give him a break. If you don't laugh, he don't eat."

I found the Venezuelan's routine very funny. The two singers leaned beside me grimacing with boredom. It became obvious that they had sat through this performance several nights running, because as the comedian delivered his lines, they mouthed along in a mocking undertone. In his main monologue the comedian presented himself as a criminal tormented by low self-esteem, which caused his crimes to lack conviction: "I raped but I never came." I laughed easily. Soon he was telling the jokes direct to me, as if we were alone in the bar.

Shortly after this I returned to my room, rang Aurora's number again, and getting no reply, went to bed. The air-conditioning unit made such a noise that I switched it off, only to find that it had been drowning other lesser noises. The striplight in the corridor buzzed, the pipes in the walls sang, and the night beyond the window was restless with traffic. It was as if all around me voices were calling out, and I wanted to say, "Yes, I hear you, but you must not all call at once." It was difficult to attend to so many demands, and I wondered how the people who lived here endured it.

I awoke at three in the morning and took breakfast in the Ben Franks Coffee Shop, three blocks up Sunset, which was open twenty-four hours. The orange juice, "squeezed not frozen" as the signs proclaimed, was so delicious that I told the waitress about it. She stared at me, her heavily made-up face inscrutable. "Is that a fact?" she said. She was a middle-aged lady with hair like nylon, required by the job to wear an ugly brown and orange minidress. I could tell by the way she wiped at the plastic surface on either side of me that she wanted to talk. "What's the trouble?" I said. "Who says there's trouble?" she said. Then she

247

sat down by the cash register, and told me how her husband had gone away. She called herself "a girl." "What's a girl supposed to say when a man comes home all hours of the night and stinking and can't even drop off his own pants? Is a girl to lay there saying Oh hi honey how was the game?" Her husband had telephoned her from Lake Tahoe to say he was not coming back. There was an eighteen-year-old daughter who was "no better than a hooker only she's too dumb to take their money." Once she was talking the waitress began to shake and cry. I took her hands and held them between mine and slowly she became calm. "I guess you're right," she said, although I had not spoken. A policeman came in for a coffee but she ignored him, her streaking eyes on our hands, until he said aloud, "How's about some service here, ma'am."

I waited patiently till nine o'clock, but even so I could hear that my call had dragged Aurora from deep sleep. For a few muzzy moments she was incapable of taking in who I was. When she understood she sounded genuinely pleased. "Give me half an hour to get myself together, okay, William? Come and have breakfast. Did you just get in? We'll talk over breakfast."

At that time her apartment was in a building known as the English Village. A gate on Larrabee Street led into a leafy forecourt, around which was built a low block, consciously old-fashioned in style, with leaded diamond-pane windows and stucco walls. I could hear her voice as I climbed the stairs to the first floor. "This is not a big deal, okay? I'm getting a lot of pressure from you, and I don't need it." I trod more heavily on the stairs to give warning of my arrival, and she came out of the half-open door. "William!" We hugged tight and then stood back to look at each other. She was as lovely as ever, but I was dismayed to see the strain in her face. I kept my hands on her, wanting to ease some of her agitation. "What's happened to you, William?" "Why should anything have happened to me?" "I don't know. You're different." She took me into the apartment, where a man sat on a couch with his head in his hands. "Do you have any plans, Morgan?" She spoke in formal tones. "Not right now," he said. "Then William and I are going out for breakfast," she said. "He's just got in and I want to talk."

248

She drove me to Daniel's on Hollywood Boulevard, fuming at Morgan all the way. "I told him I wanted the apartment. I told him you were coming over. I've had it with his pain. I don't want to know about his fucking pain. I don't want to humiliate him. It makes me feel sick." I laid one hand on her lap. "It's good to see you, William. Good to see you."

Over coffee at Daniel's she told me about Morgan. "You'd think I'd have learned by now. Any sex I have outside the levels screws up on me. Am I supposed to be a nun or what? Morgan's okay, I like him, only he wasn't supposed to be heavy. The whole idea was he was going to give me a good time, and look what happens. I give him a bad time." She smoked fast and looked about her and talked without stopping. I knew that her words did not matter, that they were ballast that must be shed, so instead of listening to her voice I listened to her hands and her eyes. "I've told him I can't give him what he wants, but he says that's okay with him. I don't give him anything, not a fucking thing. I mean, what does he want? What can you do with a guy who refuses to be dissatisfied? Why do I let him come around? It's me, isn't it? That's what makes me so fucking mad, it's not him, it's me."

"Can you smoke with one hand? I want to hold your hand."

"I'm smoking too much. I should just look at you. It makes me feel better just to look at you. Don't pay me too much attention. I know I'm going on about myself. I've been in this town too long. What brings you here? Have you come to see me?"

"Yes."

"I'm glad." She kissed my hand. "Will you come and stay in my apartment?"

"Yes."

"I'll have to get rid of Morgan."

"I'll talk to him."

"What's happened to you, William?"

"I've lost weight," I said. "Does it show?"

We drove back to the Casa Real and I checked out. By the time we had returned to Aurora's apartment Morgan had gone. "He'll be back," said Aurora. "He likes surprise visits." The phone rang. "Oh hi, Melanie. Terrific. So how come we never

249

get together and talk properly? Fine. Let's make a night this week. Name a night. Sure. Or I'll ring you." The apartment was like a sanctuary, cool and dark and uncluttered. The walls were white rough-plaster, bare but for a portrait of Aurora by Theodora van Runkle. In this painting she sat on a blue chair beside a vase of flowers, her face set in an expression of aloof dismissal. Two broad-leafed plants stood by the window. Copies of the *Los Angeles Times* lay over a wicker table, by a portable black-and-white Sony tuned to Channel Z. Beyond this main room was a kitchen, a dressing alcove with a shower, and a bedroom. While Aurora talked on the telephone I turned over the sheet-plastic pages of her portfolio, and saw in pose after pose what the photographers made of her. Smirnoff vodka, Salem cigarettes, Revlon cosmetics; and Aurora, achingly beautiful, unsmiling, unattainable. There was a masochistic quality to the camera angles, always lower than her eye line.

She had hardly replaced the receiver before the phone rang again. With an apologetic smile at me she answered it, and the smile lingered incongruously as she spoke. "Sure I saw her. Why do you want to know? I'd say, average. Average in what way? In looks. Yes. I mean, you wouldn't turn your head if she came into the room." I wandered into the kitchen. Out of the window I saw green-tiled roofs, palm trees, and below and beyond, fissured and gray as a moonscape, the endless city. I remembered our conversation by the pagodas of Wat Po, and how I had been unable to believe that she too had her problems. The signs were clearer now, or my eyesight had grown keener. But there was nothing I could tell her; not with words.

The telephone conversation ended and she joined me in the kitchen. "That phone! They get lonely, they pick up the phone. They've nothing to say. Everybody wants something from me. It never enters their dumb brains that I might need anything—." I pressed a finger to her sweet lips and said, "It's all right now." I put both arms around her and held her tight, breathing deep and slow, forcing her breaths into my rhythm. After a few moments her body yielded, and I sustained her weight.

"Been sleeping badly, have you?"

"Yes. Can you feel it?"

"You're so thin."

"How long have you come for, William?"

"I don't know. Not long. As long as it takes."

I released her and went into the main room where I had left my suitcase. The phone rang and I answered it. It was the James Worsmer agency making an availability check for a job. "She left this morning," I said. "A five-day shoot in Mauritius. Sorry about that." After I had replaced the receiver I looked at it thoughtfully for a moment and took it off the hook. "William," said Aurora, "what are you up to?" "I'm booking you," I said. "I need you for the next few days all to myself." "Do I get asked?" "I've asked you already, and you've answered. We're past all that." She picked up the telephone receiver and turned it over and over in her uncertain hands. "Do you know what's so pathetic?" she said at last. "I can't bear for the phone to be off the hook, but there's no one I want to have call me." She laid the receiver down on its back. "So you've booked me. What's the job?"

There came a soft knock at the door. "Morgan," said Aurora. He entered with the slow reflexes of a drunk, but he had not been drinking. He had forgotten about me, and viewed me with passing surprise. "I have to talk to you," he said to Aurora. "No you don't," she replied. "I've been thinking," he said, as if he had not heard her, "and I realize I make you feel guilty. But you don't have to feel guilty. You don't owe me a thing. I acknowledge that." "Then what is it you want, Morgan?" "I don't want anything. That's what I'm trying to tell you." "Then why have you come back?" "To tell you that I don't want anything from you." He stood stiff across the room from her, visibly trembling. His eyes begged for a kind look, but her face had set like a plaster mask. It was so clear to me how the pain might be grounded.

"Morgan," I said. I held out my hand to him, and automatically, as one does, he shook it. I retained his hand, which forced him to become aware of my presence. Our eyes met. He began to blink. "I'm an old friend of Aurora's. I'm only here for a few days. I know you won't mind." What I said was of no

251

importance: conventional phrases within which later he could find an honorable motive for doing as I wished. To Aurora I said nothing, but I took her arm and drew her nearer, covering my action with more inconsequential chatter to Morgan. "You know how it is, friends never seem to be on the same continent at the same time. I'm not often in Los Angeles. These few days will be gone so quickly." Now I had one of Aurora's hands in mine. Still talking, I pressed their hands together within my own clasp. Because I too was touching her, she did not resist the contact. Morgan stopped shaking. "Anyway," he said, in a quite different tone of voice, "that's all I came for. I'll be in touch soon. Have a good stay, okay?"

After he had gone Aurora said, "I don't believe it."

"His tank was empty," I said. "He wasn't about to go anywhere with an empty tank."

She still held my hand. She drew it closer, and pressed it to one breast. "Don't waste your pity on Morgan." She began to rub herself with my hand, apparently unaware of what she was doing. "That creep is just famous for fucking women over. How was I to know he'd go soft on me? What happened to all the bastards I used to be warned about?" She grinned at me. "You know what that old monkey Schuman said to me. He said, Rape isn't all it's cracked up to be."

"I've been with Schuman," I said.

"So that's it." She asked me nothing about my months in Peliagan, knowing that she would come to it herself in her own time, in her own way. "And now you're here."

"And now I'm here."

"So what's the program? Do you fuck me or don't you? What I need is somebody who'll fuck my body without fucking my head."

"What you need is sleep."

"I'll sleep if you'll sleep with me."

I did not tell Aurora what it was that I hoped to achieve with her, because it was not necessary that she know. All I told her was that from that evening on we would not be leaving the apartment for several days, and that therefore we must get in a stock of food. We drove to Ralph's in her orange Volkswagen

252

and bought a dozen bottles of white wine, two bottles of whiskey, a three-foot-long sausage, ten pints of long-life milk, six packs of frozen home-bake bread, a small sack of oranges, two dozen eggs, a bag of muesli, four pounds of ground coffee, a Dundee cake in a tin, and twelve chocolate bars. Back in the apartment Aurora rang an answering service to have them take her calls, and I wrote on a piece of paper: "Gone forever. Back soon," and pinned it on the door to the stairs.

"What now?" she said, excited by these arrangements.

"How about a drink."

We opened a bottle of wine, still cold from the supermarket refrigerator, and solemnly touched glasses. "What are we drinking to?" "How about Arlette?" So we both drank in honor of the old lady who had brought us together. We took the bottle to bed with us. Aurora wore one of her stock of nightgowns at my request, and lent me a baggy man's shirt that she had purloined from Western Costume. A label in the neck said that it had been made for Lee Marvin.

We sat up in bed side by side drinking chilled Fumé Blanc. "From now on, we live in bed," I said, "but we have to take our time." "That's fine by me." "I want you to sleep tonight, you need it. No sex till tomorrow." "Tomorrow!" It was midafternoon. "What are we going to do till then?" "Nothing. We have to slow down. We have to find each other first, and that takes time." "Okay," she said, "if you say so." She turned her face to me and rubbed her nose on my shoulder, as if to identify me by smell. "We've switched roles, haven't we, William? I like it." "You always told me we'd get together." "I knew we would." "I like your sheets." "I have very good taste, or hadn't you noticed?" "I've noticed."

For a while we talked, and our inactivity felt strange; but as the hours passed we slipped into a different time scale, within which it was difficult to estimate how long we spent talking, or stroking each other, or dozing. In all this I was following Schuman's instructions.

"I'm just letting go," she said. "Is that all right? Just to let go and not have to be strong any more."

"Yes, that's all right."

253

"They all think I'm so strong and I'm not. They all wait for me to say what to do. Oh William, I get so tired. There are times I just want someone to pick me up and carry me, like when I was a little girl."

"You must have got very tired of me, then. Telling me what to do all the time."

"No, not really. That's been easy. Because of the levels, of course. It wasn't me who was telling you what to do, it was Arlette. I was just the guide."

"You were good, Aurora. I was lucky."

"Oh, I loved it. Watching your little face all screwed up and cross! These days there never seems to be time for flirting. I love flirting."

"You were flirting with me?"

"Of course I was flirting with you."

"Did you ever get jealous? I've often wondered that."

"In a way I did. Not at first. When Arlette first asked me to go with you I was happy just to give back some of what I'd got from the levels. And you were so stern, as if it was a matter of life and death. I kept on wanting to laugh at you. But then while we were in Bangkok I got to like you, and that made things more complicated. I found I wanted you to be attracted to me for me, not just for the levels."

"Is there a difference?"

"Of course there's a difference." She was lying curled up tight against me, her head in the crook of my arm. Now she raised it indignantly. "Do you mean that as far as you're concerned I could be just any woman lying here?"

"Any woman I trust."

"And how many women do you trust?"

"For this? One."

"Me." She lay down again, content. "I'm glad."

"How about you?" I asked her. "Do you trust me?"

"Yes." Then, "What does it mean, that I trust you?"

"It means you believe I see you as you are. It means you tell me the truth about yourself, as best you can."

I invented a rule, to prevent our filling reservoir of intimacy

254

from leaking away, which was that we were never to be out of the bed together. If one of us left the bed to go to the bathroom, or fetch the whiskey, or put a ready-to-bake loaf in the oven, the other must stay and maintain the body heat between the sheets. In the evening, having resolutely forbidden any form of sexual contact up to this point, I began the game of body secrets. "I want our bodies not to have any secrets from each other," I said; for in order to make love to her without any holding back, I knew I must expose to her the petty shames which had lodged in creases of my body over the years. I showed her the stunted little toe on my right foot, and told her how when I walked my feet turned out, pigeon-fashion. I told her how I had always believed my penis to be too small. I showed her my tubby tummy, not holding it in; and my unhairy chest; and my sticky-out ears; and the mole on my upper lip which every morning I cut shaving. Her catalogue was as fond and foolish as my own: her breasts too small, her upper arms too thin; her teeth projected; the pale hairs grew too thick on her upper lip; her eyebrows were too heavy. As I write down these lists the exercise appears to be pointlessly undermining, but in practice it was not so. This was an extension of our heart's trust to the further outposts. It cleared the way for that rarest of all conditions for true love, which is body trust.

We went to sleep that night nested in each other's arms, heavy with the convalescent torpor of a day in bed. So safe did we feel that within minutes of turning out the lamps, aided by whiskey, we sank into sleep.

I awoke long before Aurora the next morning, and lay quietly watching her in the striped light that fell through the cane blinds. Already this white apartment had become my universe, this sweeping moment the hem of eternity. I did wonder then how it would be, whether it would fall out the way the old man had promised. But he had also said, "If it is not to be this time, it will be the next. Or the next. You will know it when you find it, there is no mistaking."

I made coffee, and brought it to her with milk and muesli on a tray that said California The Golden State. She woke up very

255

slowly, and clung to me to be sure I was there. She had dreamed she was in an empty house. "Room after room, all empty. I kept opening doors and calling out, Anyone there? They were all empty." But the long drugless sleep had refreshed her. When her beautiful face first discovered me above her with the tray, her smile made me weak with its radiant warmth. I kissed her lips, and they were soft and wriggly as a child's lips whispering confidences in my ear.

After breakfast we drew off our shirts and lay for the first time skin to skin, caressing each other's bodies with curious hands. "I do so want you inside me, William," she said. "Soon," I said. "I do love you," she said. "I love you, Aurora." This was the final freedom we allowed each other; there were no limits set on our emotions. Schuman had said, "You will experience feelings of love that you may consider exaggerated, or unwarranted. Do not resist them. Let all the doors stand open."

I entered her very slowly, and then lay still within her for a long time. We lay facing each other on our sides. Her eyes were open, gazing gravely into mine. The closeness, the completeness of the touch, filled me with silent joy. When she began to move, wanting to feel how I was inside her, I said, "Gently. Only gently. This is the beginning." In a while our slow movements ceased to be the making of love as I had known it. The passion did not diminish, but the urgency fell away, so that it was as if we were rocking together, or were being rocked, in some great cradle by some great hand. The motion was effortless. My erection did not diminish. We looked into each other's eyes so long at a time from so near that I lost the distinction between us. It was more like dancing than sex.

"It's so strange," said Aurora. "How long can you last?"

"I don't know," I said. "We'll see."

We broke to eat and drink at noon, but as soon as we were done with food we settled ourselves into our most comfortable positions and resumed our dreamlike lovemaking. I spoke softly to her about the island of Bali, and how she had been with me on every side, and how I had sung to her; which she loved to hear. I was telling the story also to myself, in order to reverse the flow I had created there, and bring the Peliagan valley into the recesses of our bed.

At times I lay still, and held Aurora still with restraining arms.

"You don't want to come, do you?" she said.

"Not yet."

"When?"

I gave an absurd answer; but it was necessary, because our lovemaking must cease to be a prelude to the little death, must become a prolonged birth. "Never," I said.

"Are we to make love forever, then?"

"Yes, forever."

With any other partner this would have been foolishness. But Aurora was familiar with the language of the levels, she knew that I was telling her to live within the sexual present moment, to relinquish the future, which in lovemaking houses the gift-giver orgasm. As Santa Claus casts his bulgy shadow over childhood Decembers, so orgasm blocks the light that falls on love.

There were no revelations that second day, nor the second night. I was not disappointed. It was remarkable enough that we had been able to be joined for so long without discomfort or diminution of desire. I told her that we were not to sleep that second night, nor ever again; that we were to wake, and make love, forever. Of course we fell asleep, at some unknown hour before dawn; and though I had no memory of withdrawing from her, we woke apart.

Any impatience we might have felt, any awkwardness at our passive days and nights, was now far behind us, or far ahead. The disruption of normal activity had brought with it a suspension of normal divisons of time. The third day merged unnoticed into the third night. By the fourth day, bewildered by the artificial condition of waking sleep, we had entered a slow and precise world in which there was energy but no stress. We lived within a detached and spacious high, of the kind that will be familiar to insomniacs.

The shivers of Peliagan returned to me. Each time I reentered the warm harbor of her body it was as if I was connected to a source of power. Without noticing it, we had virtually ceased to talk to each other. When I was thirsty I brought her oranges. When she was hungry she shared with me her slices of Dundee cake. Through her, my self-love became other-love, without ceasing to be self-love. It is widely believed that to become one with the world the self must be made small, so small as to dwindle from the world. But it must be made big, big enough to embrace the world. Christians are taught to love Jesus the son of God in all men. I have been taught to love myself in all men.

When the shivers came I found that I produced a peculiar sound, a cross between a cry of surprise and a laugh, as if I were being tickled. This made Aurora laugh also. She grew light-hearted, as I had done in Bretanville. She whimpered when I withdrew from her as if I had removed from her clasp a favorite doll, and writhed her body discontentedly on the patterned sheets. She crooned with pleasure when my penis was given back to her and was safely hugged within her private pocket.

This state of perpetual sexual arousal, perpetually reined back from the violent outspill of orgasm, did slowly work its desired effect on me. Like a cloud that grows heavy with moisture but does not precipitate in rain, I became saturated with sex. The promised breakthrough came at an unexpected moment. The term "breakthrough" is here properly used. A barrier does exist, a stretched membrane between feelings generated by outside stimuli on the body-self, and emotions, ideas, beliefs, which seem to be a product of the mind-self. When the taut separating skin is at last pricked, the two realms of sensation flood each other, and the fused self swims in Panthalassia, the universal ocean. It is this state that is called the seventh level.

On the sixth night I left our bed to take a shower. Aurora murmured to me from half-sleep. I ran the water until it was blood warm, and then stepped under it. Ever since my bathing exercises in Peliagan I had learned to find keen delight in the flow of water over my skin, and so was not surprised that the tremors I had been experiencing should return, and should run with the water in a vibrating pulse down the length of my body. I lifted my head, intending to wash my face, and turned it so that brow and eyelids and cheeks received the full discharge of the shower. At the same time, obeying an impulse of release, I stretched all of my body that would stretch. I arched up onto my toes, and reached out my arms in an attitude of physical surrender. It was here, at the shuddering peak of my stretch, that the world stood still.

This discredited phrase describes a precise experience. I guess that the illusion of suspended motion is caused by an intense burst of brain activity, which concentrates a number of perceptions into a microsecond of real time, and so gives the sensation of a greater lapse of time than has taken place. The apparent effect was that the water hung in the air above me; that my body remained lifted up although I was not aware of sustaining it; and that all sound became a deep booming hum. I felt weightless. I felt that I was being rippled.

Then the water struck my face again. I heard its sharp splatter on the tiles. My arms floated down to my sides. My body sailed to earth.

In physical terms this extraordinary moment can be explained without reference to mysteries. No doubt it was a culminating muscular and nervous protest against physical overloading, as are all spasms, palpitations, and cramps. But it was also the moment at which the membrane burst. As I stepped dripping from the shower cubicle, I discovered that I had passed through a plastic-curtained door into a new world. So certain was I that this was not restricted to the timeless love-capsule we had made of the apartment, that I drew on my clothes and went out into the street. I did not stop to think why I did this. It was an instinct of delight, as when through an early window a child sees snow in the back yard and hurries out to discover a white world.

It was still night on Sunset Boulevard, but the quick dawn was near. Few cars; mainly police patrols returning to the station on San Vincente. A shivering hooker in shorts, tank top, high heels walked the curb in front of the deserted Pussycat Theater. Seeing how I skipped up the sidewalk she watched me go by with a smile on her face. I crossed to the north side, where I met a man in pajamas and bathrobe and slippers walking his dog. The dog, a black Scottish terrier, sniffed at my legs. "Best time of the day," said the man. "You sound cheerful." I was singing "White Christmas," somewhat tunelessly, and without regard to the fact

259

that Christmas was long gone by. "Milhous seems to have adopted you," said the dog's owner. "You should be honored, he's real picky." A block farther on, by Cyrano's, two drunk gays were returning from a late party, singing the blues. "God bless you," they called to me, "God bless everybody." As the coming day flushed on the horizon, the boy-city began to stir. Through the unlit windows of restaurants, staff on early shift moved among unlaid tables. Solemn and unsure as seniors at a prom the shops lined up north and south of the car lanes, overdressed through anxiety. Nobody can hurt you, I told them. You can only hurt yourselves.

A dozen or so early breakfasters sat in Ben Franks. Several pairs of eyes looked up as I entered, and continued to watch me curiously. I ordered coffee and rye toast. There were good feelings here, the night fellowship that forms between those who wake while the town sleeps. Also they were all nervy as fawns. Why should they not be? Where the skin of the world had split and curled back, like a tomato in boiling water, the flesh beneath was helpless, tender. You have no enemy but yourselves, I told them. Nobody else can get you between the legs, where it hurts. Also where it sings. After my sleep-starved nights it might have been that I was hallucinating. No, I told them, mine is the reality, yours the dream. And because they believed me, for my baby face and my antique grace, when I began again to sing they joined me, one by one, humming at first, from table and banquette and bar, until the whole of Ben Franks on Sunset and Alta Loma was crooning "White Christmas" over their hash browns and their pancakes and their crispy bacon. When we were done they grinned and looked sheepishly at each other, and the waitress wrote out my check and said, "You wouldn't feel like singing if you was at the end of your shift, I can tell you." I said I had just got up. "Enjoy yourself while you can," she said. Forever, I said. For this is how I am made to live.

What can I say of this certainty? It is not a lesson learned, but a world regained. I wondered that I had never seen it before. Living is not only easy, it is inevitable.

An analogy: you buy a transistor radio, and every morning you listen to the radio news. You learn which way to angle it to

260

receive the signal most clearly. Sometimes there is interference, but you are well satisfied with it. Then you go on a trip to a different part of the country, and you take your radio with you. Here the reception is not blocked by hills and tall buildings. You switch on your radio to hear the news, and the newscaster speaks as distinctly as if he sat beside you; no distortion, no drift, no crackle, no hiss. For the first time you learn of the existence of distortion and drift and crackle and hiss, because for the first time you are hearing true reception. You say to yourself: so this is how my radio was built to work.

Thus I said about myself: so this is how I was made to live.

Again in analogy, I might say that all my life I had been falling, as if from a high-altitude airplane. In my terror I had thrashed and grabbed at the air to arrest my fall, but to no effect. Now I knew that I was meant to be falling, and that all things needful were falling with me. The path of least resistance was the true path.

I know now that this is the seventh level. To live as I am meant to live requires wholeness, and unwitholdingness, and power. So long as sexual energy, which is to say life energy, flows freely through me, I possess these qualities. Perhaps if mankind as a breed had been less corrupted by centuries of struggle and pain, the convulsive therapy of the levels would not be necessary to lead us back into the garden world of Eden; for surely Eden is an early image of sexual wholeness, where man and woman are one flesh, and are naked and unashamed. Later in the myth the fall, and cherubim with flaming swords stand at the east gate of the garden; which for me is the image of diffusion, the fragmentation of a whole person into isolated parts. It happens in every life, somewhere in babyhood or early childhood. But there is a path back to grace. Sex, which made us whole once, can make us whole again.

I returned to the apartment to find Aurora awake and waiting for me. "Hurry," she said, "hurry." I undressed and lay with her. While I had been out she had grown cold. I fed her my warmth, piped it between her slender thighs. "Ah," she said, as her little breasts kissed my skin. I was still bemused by what had happened to me in the shower, and did not think to resist her desires

261

until it was too late. Her thin limbs suckled me like creepers, her hips raided me. My ardent penis, pent up for days, jangled to orgasm like a fire engine on an emergency call. When she felt the hot juice jet within her she cried out loud, not for her climax but for mine.

In this way I lost my first brief glimpse of the promised land; for when I awoke from the trance of orgasm it was gone. Aurora was clinging to me and weeping without sound. Her tears pressed wet on my shoulder. "You'd gone away from me," she said. "I had to bring you back."

Postscript

22

The events I have been describing took place some years ago. The journey on which I then embarked has not since ceased, and I believe never will; but my account of the levels must be brought to some sort of conclusion. There is a fitting final scene, which occurred not many days after my return from Los Angeles, and before I had left the Rosenthals' house on Abinger Road for the last time. Like all true endings, it is also a beginning.

The telephone call came in the early afternoon, when I was alone in the house. It was Donald, calling from the West London Hospital on Hammersmith Broadway, to tell me that Jeannie had gone into labor.

I ran down the Bath Road to Turnham Green underground station. A train came quickly, and clattered me down the District Line through Stamford Brook and Ravenscourt Park to Hammersmith. I tried to picture Jeannie, whom I had not seen since before my trip to Rome for the World Food Conference, but the picture would not come.

The hospital building was drab Victorian, like a school; high-ceilinged and comfortless. Following the signs, I climbed the wide sweep of stairs and pushed through opaque swing doors into the maternity ward. Sticky rubber mats dragged on the soles of my shoes. At the end of the short many-doored corridor sat a sister drinking a cup of tea. On a wall beside her hung a black-board bearing names and numbers, none of the names familiar to me. I realized that I did not know Donald's second name, which would now be Jeannie's name also. I described Donald to the sister. "Oh yes, oh yes, that would be Mr. Davis. Room Five." So now she is called Jeannie Davis, I thought. It sounded like a different person.

I slipped noiselessly into the darkened room, and none of the group within turned around. The window was screened by a green window shade, which diffused into the small square space a quiet echo of daylight. From a machine drawn up by the bed came a continuous bubbling sound. I stood beside a cylinder of oxygen mounted on wheels. Donald sat in a green gown by the bed's head, his ginger hair disheveled, as if he had recently got out of bed. Jeannie lay supported on many pillows, her face twisted to one side. She was panting rapidly and repeating through her teeth: "Mary had a little lamb, its fleece was white as snow, and everywhere that Mary went the lamb was sure to go." One hand gripped Donald. The fingers of the other hand tapped on the bed rail in time with her rhyme. A stout black midwife was reading the foetal heart variations on the monitor tracing. A young Indian nurse made small clattery noises in a sink.

The contractions passed. Jeannie closed her eyes and laid her head back on the pillows. When she opened them again she saw me.

"Hello, William," she said.

"Hello, Jeannie."

She was exhausted and high and the same and different. Her pale hair spread straggly on the pillow as it had done night after night at my side. To me she looked as tenderly pretty here in her hospital bed as when I had first fallen in love with her, so long ago.

266

"Thank you for coming," she said.

"I thought you wouldn't want it."

"None of that . . ." She tensed her face, released it again, at a passing pain. "None of that's important any more."

"I know."

Donald turned his troubled face to me and repeated Jeannie's words: "Thank you for coming." I was grateful to him for that, for the care he took, within his greater care, to allow me my place.

"I can hardly believe there's anyone in there," I said.

"Maybe there isn't," said Jeannie with a weak smile.

The Indian nurse brought me a green gown, and helped me fasten the laces behind my neck. I asked the midwife how long it would be before the birth. "She's six centimeters dilated," said the midwife. "Oh yes, a few hours yet."

I offered to fetch tea or coffee from the hospital canteen. Jeannie wanted nothing, but Donald gratefully accepted: "A roll, a pork pie, anything." He had not eaten all day. As I left the room Jeannie gasped and clutched at him, and the contractions began again.

In the canteen line I tried Louise's name game with Jeannie's new name. I wrote the letters on a paper napkin: JEANNIE PERRY, DONALD DAVIS. It came out Love, Adore. I put the napkin in my pocket to show to Donald later. On a second napkin I tried JEANNIE ELLIOTT, DONALD DAVIS, which came out Love, Marry; but this napkin I threw away.

On my return I had to wait outside as the midwife was conducting an examination. Donald came out into the corridor to eat his pie and drink his coffee, which he did without losing his anxious and abstracted air. "Would you rather I kept out of the way?" I asked him. "No, no," he said, grasping my arm as if afraid that I would leave there and then, "you must stay, you're part of it."

Back in the labor room he sat beside Jeannie holding a little sponge, which he kept trying to press to her lips to refresh her. Jeannie looked at me from time to time, and once reached out a hand, which I took and squeezed. "Friends?" she said. "Friends," I replied.

She pulled the oxygen mask to her face as the pains returned. "Do your breathing, Jeannie," said Donald, "keep up the breathing." He began to breath for her, rocking forward on his chair with each exhalation.

It was dark outside the green blind when at last the obstetrician broke the waters. The midwife, expecting delivery shortly, removed the covering sheet and raised Jeannie's knees. An overhead surgical spotlight brightly illuminated the area between her legs. I sat quiet on a chair by the wall at the foot of the bed, and when the midwife went to the sink to wash her hands I was afforded an unrestricted view.

For a few moments the clinical environment deceived me, caused me not to make the simple connection. Wires trailed from the abdominal swelling. A rubber sheet was spread below the raised and parted thighs. The monitoring machinery ticked and hummed in scientific modulation. The midwife's hands went *slip-slip-slip* in the hygienic basin. But all at once, with a tumbling lurch of recognition, I saw what it was at which I gazed in awe and admiration: not the outer passage to a dilated cervix, not a vulva, not a vagina, but a *cunt*.

Never in five years of marriage had I been able to look so freely on the object of my desires. Despite the imminent birth, Jeannie's cunt was pretty and snug. She had not been shaved. The rose-pink lips were curling outward, as if she were sexually aroused. I do not know for how long I looked, certainly the midwife seemed to be washing her hands with extraordinary thoroughness, but it was long enough for me to see here in the bright dot of light not only my wife's sweet heart, but every cunt I had ever known, and every pornographic picture that I had ever laid beside me on a pillow, or propped before me on a chair, that I might command the flaunted crotch to milk from out my cock the ticklish sperm.

Silently I revered it, this door to the mystery, this outward sign of inward grace, praying: *Cunt magnificent, my space of bliss, my treasure trove of zero.* Into such a tunnel from which I had fallen had I not so many nights crept back, pressing my way to a remembered bed where not my toes, nor my nose, nor my smooth-sucked thumbs could poke out into any cold beyond the blankets. *Pretty mouth that has no tongue, dumb smiler, lips within lips to give kisses within kisses. Sleeve of blood, sleeve of water, sleeve of life.*

"Push!" cried the midwife. "Push like you're on the toilet!" Her pink and black hands pinched against the perineum. "Not in your throat, dear. In your bottom." "Push, Jeannie," said Donald. "Oh, push, push."

Jeannie's face was contorted and mauve. Crushed screams seeped out of her mouth. "Harder now, dear. He's coming. He's coming."

Before my incredulous eyes the lips were parting. Jeannie gave a cry and a jerk and the head of the baby burst out, like a little burglar, its face squashed flat. There it stayed. Then as if to survey the world into which it had broken it slowly swiveled its head around. I stared at the misshapen greasy scalp and the tiny mucus-clogged ear. It wailed, very softly; perhaps only I heard it. Hello, I said silently to the new person; and I began to cry. Jeannie pushed again, and the little creature tumbled into the midwife's hands, blue as a bruise and streaked with blood. The midwife laid the baby on Jeannie's stomach like an egg in a nest. I came close. Jeannie was too drained even to lift her hands. She lay with her head to one side, her eyes closed, her face blotchy with broken blood vessels. The baby twitched like a sleeping puppy. The midwife uncovered Jeannie's breasts, her beautiful breasts, and laid the baby's purple face to one nipple. The miniature mouth parted, nudged, began to suck. I heard Donald ask, "Is it a boy or a girl?" Tenderly the midwife raised the baby's leg, and through my own warm tears I saw a tiny, perfect, dawn-pink dew-fresh cunt. *Oh my dear one,* I said, *my precious, my angel. My daughter, my lover, my mother.* And I cried and cried.